THE SUMMER ISLAND FESTIVAL

ALSO BY RACHEL BURTON

The Tearoom on the Bay

THE SUMMER ISLAND FESTIVAL

Rachel Burton

An Aria Book

This edition first published in the United Kingdom in 2021 by Aria,
an imprint of Head of Zeus Ltd

A CIP catalogue record for this book is available from the
British Library.

ISBN eBook: 9781800241145
Paperback: 9781800246065

Cover design © Lisa Brewster

Typeset by Siliconchips Services Ltd UK

Aria
c/o Head of Zeus
First Floor East
5–8 Hardwick Street
London EC1R 4RG

www.ariafiction.com

To Dad, with love

'If you are Gamble Gold of the gay green woods,
And travelled far beyond the sea,
You are my mother's own sister's son;
What nearer cousins then can we be?'

(from Child Ballad no. 132 – The Bold Pedlar and
Robin Hood)

Prologue

June 2018

Willow sat in the back of the limousine staring at the bouquet of wildflowers in her lap. These simple flowers had been one of the few things she'd insisted on as the planning for today had got more and more out of hand – flowers that reminded her who she used to be. She'd also insisted on just having one bridesmaid, her best friend Kate who she'd known almost as long as she'd known Charlie, since they were all at university together. Kate would be waiting for her at the church, an oasis of calm on this crazy day. A day that Willow had lost control of months ago.

'Are you all right, love?' her father asked from the seat next to her as the limousine pulled up outside the church. He ran his index finger around the collar of his shirt, looking hot and uncomfortable. Don Warwick was a much-acclaimed session musician, touring the world playing guitar for big-name stars – he was flying out to America after the wedding to play a handful of dates along the west coast. The last time he'd worn a suit, he'd claimed earlier this morning, was on his own wedding day.

'I'm just nervous I guess,' Willow replied quietly, but what she was feeling wasn't nerves. It was fear.

On paper Willow's life was perfect – a First from Cambridge University, an internship in one of the big banks in the City shortly followed by a permanent job offer – she'd been there nearly eight years now. She and Charlie had a beautiful flat in central London and today was her wedding day, perfect in every way – even the sun had come out for the afternoon. Willow had achieved everything she'd ever wanted and had come a long way from her Bohemian upbringing on the Island she used to call home.

So where was this unsettled feeling coming from? A feeling that had been growing for weeks. It wasn't just about Charlie's parents taking over the planning of the wedding – after all she should be grateful to them for that as work had been far too busy for her to do much of the planning herself. This was to do with Charlie. He had changed her life in ways she could never have imagined, introduced her to a world that she would never otherwise have been able to be a part of and for that she was grateful. Wasn't she? Of course she was, but there seemed to be so many rules to fit into that world, so many ways she'd had to change herself – what she wore, how she spoke, what she drank, the way she held herself. Did she really want to be a part of that world for the rest of her life?

'Willow,' Don said gently, pulling her out of the thoughts spiralling in her head. 'We should get going. There's a whole church full of people waiting for you.'

She nodded, shaking away her thoughts as the driver

opened the door for her to step out of the car. This was just pre-wedding jitters. Everybody got them.

Don offered her his arm. 'You look beautiful, love,' he said as she tucked her hand into the crook of his elbow. 'I'm so proud of you.'

Kate was waiting for them outside the church just as she'd promised, and she greeted Willow with a gentle hug. Kate had been in a strange mood all day so it was nice to see her smile. Willow wanted to ask her what was wrong, but she thought she knew. Once Willow and Charlie were married, Kate would be the only single one in their group. It shouldn't matter in this day and age but somehow it seemed to matter to Kate, and Willow wondered why.

'Are you ready?' Kate said.

Willow peered into the church, allowing her eyes to grow accustomed to the gloom. She saw the huge crowd of people that were waiting for her, most of whom she didn't even know, and at the other end of the aisle she saw Charlie, standing with his brother, laughing at some joke or other. As she watched him that feeling of unease or fear washed over her again as she remembered the little digs and jibes Charlie had made about her over the years, as though he was telling her she'd never really fit in – the way he didn't like her to drink too much, the way he'd spoken to Skye that afternoon all those years ago...

'I can't do it,' Willow said.

'What?' Kate replied, her face changing to something that looked like anger.

'Love?' Don asked, his brow furrowing.

Willow started to walk away from the church then, her heels clicking on the paving stones as she strode back towards the limousine – the limousine she hadn't wanted in the first place. She turned to look over her shoulder.

'I can't do it,' she repeated. 'You'll have to tell Charlie.' Just before Kate turned away to go into the church Willow saw the look on her face, her mouth a hard line, her eyes like steel.

The driver was leaning against the bonnet of the car smoking a cigarette.

'We need to leave,' she said, panic rising in her throat. 'Now!'

The driver stubbed out his cigarette and Willow felt her father's hand on her shoulder.

'Just take us back to the hotel, mate,' Don said. Then he turned to Willow. 'I'll phone your mum and get her to meet us there.'

Later when Willow thought about the moment she decided to walk away, she hadn't been able to work out what she'd wanted instead, or where she had wanted to go. All she had known was that she couldn't go through with the wedding. It was a gut reaction, instinctual, as though all those Neanderthal fight-or-flight impulses had kicked in at once. She'd wanted to be anywhere other than a village church in Surrey on a sunny Saturday afternoon.

When her mother had met them back at the hotel, she asked Willow what she wanted to do but Willow had no idea. She couldn't go back to the Great Portland Street flat she shared with Charlie because she couldn't face him if he was already there and, tempted as she was to go to America with her dad, her passport was back at the flat. In the end Willow had hitched up the ridiculously over-the-top skirts of her wedding dress and stepped into her mother's

Jeep to go back to the Isle of Wight – a journey she hadn't made since she had moved to London with Charlie over eight years ago. A journey she had never imagined making again, especially whilst wearing five thousand pounds' worth of surprisingly heavy wedding dress.

I

Willow

Four days later…

Willow sat on the shop counter looking out of the window at the beach beyond, at the sun motes glinting off the sea and the white cliffs in the distance. Her phone had been beeping incessantly for days, sending her a stream of endless texts, WhatsApp messages and Facebook requests all of which she'd been trying to ignore. She couldn't reply because she didn't have the answers.

She didn't know why she'd run away from the church. She didn't know why she hadn't been able to go through with the wedding.

Pushing her phone aside she picked up her father's old mandolin, her fingers tracing the strings, and wondered if she could still remember how to play it. The sensation of the instrument in her hands again made her shiver – music was as much a part of her past as the beach, the cliffs and the sea. Ending up back here after all these years was confusing, as though she didn't know which version of herself to be anymore.

The bell above the door of the shop jangled, jarring the silence. She must have forgotten to lock the door when she shut the shop.

'We're closed,' she called, without looking around.

'Still trying to figure out how to play that thing?' asked a voice that Willow hadn't heard in a very long time. She could almost hear that crooked smile in his words. She'd seen the posters plastered all over the place – the Island's prodigal return from America to play the Seaview Folk Festival. She'd known he was coming back but she'd been hoping to have a little bit more time to pull herself together before she actually saw him.

'It's been a long time Willow,' the owner of the voice said. He spoke more softly this time and it sounded as though he was standing closer, even though Willow hadn't heard his footsteps draw nearer. His voice was unmistakable, even with the American lilt he'd picked up over the years. 'Turn around and let me see you.'

She did as he asked, needing to see him even though she knew exactly what he looked like these days. Everybody had heard of him now.

He was wearing scruffy jeans and boots, an un-ironed shirt and a grey herringbone waistcoat, his hair carefully sculpted into a quiff. He was barely recognisable from the boy who left twelve years before, but his face still held the ghost of who he used to be – a dimple on the left side of his mouth, a crooked smile that could melt hearts, eyes as green as the grass on the clifftops.

Of all the times he had to walk back into her life.

'How are you, Willow?' he asked without taking his eyes off her. 'How are you after all these years?'

The last time she had seen Lucien Hawke he still went by the name of Luc Harrison and they had both been eighteen. They'd left the Island on the same week and, as far as Willow knew, Luc had never returned.

Until now.

He had tried to contact her in the aftermath of what happened on that unseasonably warm September night when everything unravelled, writing her letters addressed to her department at university, letters that she had never replied to. She'd ripped them up and put them in the bin at the Student Union so she wouldn't be tempted to piece them back together again late at night when the loneliness became overwhelming.

'It's been twelve years,' he went on, his lips curving into a smile – lips Willow had loved so much once. 'I've missed you.'

'Why are you here, Luc?' she asked, finally finding her voice.

'I'm here because of the festival,' he began, seeming surprised she was asking.

'I know that,' Willow replied, her voice sharp and unwelcoming. 'What are you doing here in this shop right now?'

He hesitated and Willow noticed his eyes flick away from her for a moment. 'I was looking for Cathy,' he said.

'Mum's not here.'

'Can you tell her I was looking for her?' he asked. 'I tried calling but her phone was off.'

Cathy Cole's phone was always off. Willow had no idea why she had one at all.

'What do you want her for?' she said, turning to face him again.

'I just wanted to…' Luc hesitated again, cleared his throat. 'I wanted to…'

'I'll tell her you were here,' Willow replied willing him to leave.

But instead he started to wander around the shop, his fingers stroking the guitars that hung on the walls.

'It hasn't changed at all,' he said softly.

'The Island or The Music Shop?' Willow asked.

'Both.' He moved towards the rack of sheet music, carelessly flicking through the musical scores. 'So many memories,' he whispered as he turned to look at her again.

Please leave, she thought.

'Isn't it strange to be home?' he asked quietly, but Willow didn't reply. It was strange to be back in the small village of Seaview on the east coast of the Isle of Wight. It was the place where both she and Luc had grown up and where her mother's small business, simply known as The Music Shop, was located. As she watched Luc all those memories of her childhood, of her parents and of him, came flooding back.

'I heard about what happened on Saturday,' he said. 'I'm so sorry.'

She could feel the blush creeping up her neck at the shame of what she'd done, the reason she was back on the Island, the reason her phone wouldn't stop beeping. Everybody knew that she'd run away from her own wedding, even Luc.

'I…' she began, searching for an explanation. 'I just…'

He stepped closer to her.

'I just needed to be on my own for a while,' she said. 'That's why I'm here, I guess.'

That and the fact that she had nowhere else to go. But Luc didn't need to know everything.

'I'd better go,' Luc said but Willow didn't want him to leave after all. When he stopped at the door and looked over his shoulder at her again, she felt a wave of relief.

'Have you seen Skye?' he asked.

'I'm only going to be here for a few more days,' Willow replied as though that was an excuse. She still cringed inside when she remembered what had happened the last time she'd seen Skye and what Charlie had said.

'You should see her,' he said. 'I think she'd like to see you.'

'Have you seen her?' she asked.

He nodded. 'It was good to catch up,' he said with a smile. 'You never know, you might even enjoy it. It might take your mind off...' he hesitated '...things,' he said, waving a hand vaguely.

Willow felt suddenly and irrationally angry. Who was Luc Harrison to walk in here after all these years telling her what to do? Had he and Skye been talking about her, about the wedding, about what Charlie had said to Skye all those years ago?

But perhaps he was right. At the very least Willow owed Skye a long overdue apology.

They stared at each other for a moment as though neither of them wanted to be the first to say goodbye.

'Think about it at least,' he said eventually as he turned and opened the door. The little bell rang again as he walked away.

★

They had grown up together. Luc's mum and Willow's parents had been in a band called The Laurels and when the band were touring Luc and Willow went too, living in each other's pockets, never meeting any other children while being inexpertly educated by a private tutor who was stoned more often than not. Going to school when they were eleven had been a relief to both of them, an order to the chaos of their messy lives.

The last time Willow had seen Luc Harrison, he'd broken her delicate teenaged heart and she'd left for university early. She'd always regretted not waiting to hear his side of the story, always regretted not saying goodbye properly.

Luc had moved to Nashville with his mother, Krystal Kane, and after a few years Krystal had put out a record of covers of well-known country songs that had flown up the charts on both sides of the Atlantic. But nothing had been heard of Luc, and Willow had been surprised that he hadn't recorded anything, hadn't made a name for himself in Nashville's music scene. He'd always been so talented, even more so than his mother.

Then eighteen months ago he had appeared as if from nowhere, wowing the judges in the early auditions for the US TV talent show *American Stars*. He'd gone on to come second in the final of the show and had been picked up by a major record label. Lucien Hawke, as he called himself now, played to sell-out audiences on a regular basis and his first record went platinum in the States. Seeing Luc again in her mother's music shop – somewhere the two of them had played together as children – had left Willow feeling disorientated.

'Is that you, Willow?' Cathy called as Willow let herself into her old childhood home.

'No, Mum, it's a burglar,' she replied, hearing her mum laugh to herself at the long-standing and awful family joke – one her dad had started years ago, long before he left Cathy and moved to America too.

Don had left the Island the same summer that Willow had gone to university. He'd left with Luc and Krystal, splitting up the band and leaving Cathy on her own. Willow had gone to Cambridge to read Economics and spent most of her first term wondering if she'd done the right thing, wondering if she should have stayed and looked after her mother. She had been angry with both her parents and had jumped to a conclusion about her father and Krystal that had never proved to be true.

Willow closed the door behind her and leant against it. The Island was bringing back memories that she thought were long forgotten. Did she regret leaving without saying goodbye to everyone now? Perhaps if she could find the answer to that, she could work out why she had felt the need to walk away from her own wedding and come back to the one place she'd never thought she'd want to return to.

Her mother was sitting in the living room surrounded by paperwork. Willow looked like her mother, small and fair – sometimes when she looked in the mirror these days, she saw the mum of her childhood looking back at her.

'Is that festival stuff?' Willow asked, nodding towards the papers.

'I'm a bit late starting with things this year,' Cathy replied.

The Isle of Wight had a very famous festival every June. That festival, The Big Festival as Willow and her family had always called it, was coming up soon and before too long the Island would be full of musicians and festival goers, and Cathy's shop would start its annual summer rush.

But every August there was a second, less famous festival on the Island. It was set up by Willow's parents nearly thirty years ago and started out with just a few gigs in local pubs in Seaview. Over the years it had grown and now there was a whole weekend of events culminating in a final concert on the beach on the penultimate Sunday of August.

When Willow was a teenager, she would help her parents with the festival. She hadn't been back for so long that she didn't know what to do anymore, but she still had an overpowering need to sit down with her mother and help even though she knew she wouldn't be here in August. She had to go back to work in two weeks.

'Luc Harrison was in the shop looking for you,' Willow said as she sat down.

'Lucien Hawke you mean,' Cathy replied with a smile.

'I didn't realise he was back on the Island already.'

'He arrived last week.'

'Why didn't you tell me?'

'I didn't want to tell you right before the wedding,' Cathy replied. 'And then once we were back here, I figured the two of you would bump into each other soon enough.' She shrugged. Cathy Cole was always infuriatingly vague. 'He wants to start building a fan base back in the UK,' Cathy went on. 'I got the impression he wasn't keen to go back to the States.'

'Why?'

Cathy shrugged again and returned to her paperwork. 'I didn't ask,' she said. 'I do know that he'll be here all summer.'

Which was exactly what Willow didn't want.

'What was it like seeing him again?' Cathy asked.

'It was a bit weird,' she replied. 'But no weirder than being back here in general.' When Willow had left the Island she'd been in search of a normal life – or what she had perceived to be normal. She'd wanted to distance herself from the folk music scene entirely and particularly the one on the Island – and yet here she was, back in the thick of it again.

'I won't be here very long though,' she went on as though trying to convince herself as much as her mother. 'I'm going back to London in a week or so.'

Cathy put her paperwork to one side and took her glasses off, turning to look at Willow. 'Are you?' she asked.

'I have to go back to work, Mum.'

'So this is just a flying visit? You're not coming home?'

'No, Mum, my home is in London.'

'Your home was with Charlie. You walked out on your wedding for reasons that you still haven't explained, and I know you're ignoring his calls—'

'How do you know?' Willow interrupted.

She waved a hand in the direction of Willow's phone, which was sitting on the table in front of them. 'You're ignoring all your calls and messages,' she said. 'That thing beeps all the time and you just stare at it. I haven't seen you answer a call or type a word into it in days.'

Willow couldn't deny it. She didn't know how to answer the questions that everyone was asking. She had let Charlie know where she was and that she was sorry, that she needed some time. She knew that was completely inadequate but right now, what else could she do? Charlie had left a couple of angry, frustrated messages and who could blame him for that? But it didn't make her want to call him back.

'It seems to me,' Cathy went on, 'that you may not have a home to go back to anymore. It seems to me that it might be time to start again.'

'I'm hoping to stay with a friend for a while,' Willow replied. 'Until I get myself sorted.' This was rubbish of course and Willow was sure that her mother knew it was. She hadn't thought about what she was going to do next, but there was something about the idea of starting again that appealed to Willow.

Was it possible to start again from scratch? Was it possible to admit that the choices you'd made weren't the right ones? Because while Willow had spent almost half her life trying to run away from the Island, she didn't feel as though she fitted in with Charlie's life anymore. She still had that feeling of unease that had overwhelmed her outside the church but she just couldn't put her finger on why.

She hadn't been able to think about anything much since Saturday but as soon as Cathy had driven her back into Seaview again, as soon as she'd smelled the sea and heard the waves, she'd been overwhelmed with the sensation that the Island was calling her back and she'd be lying if she said that the idea of spending the summer here didn't appeal. She'd always had fond memories of Seaview in the summer, memories of salt on her skin and ice cream on the beach, memories that a primal part of her wanted to relive.

But not if Luc Harrison, or whatever he called himself these days, was going to be here too. She didn't know if she could cope with that.

'Are you going to see Skye while you're here?' Cathy asked the same question Luc had.

'I hadn't thought about it,' Willow replied. She hadn't thought about anything except the sound of the sea and the mandolins in Cathy's shop. She hadn't thought about those things very hard either because she didn't want to admit the pull they were having on her after just a few days. 'I probably won't have time. She probably won't even know I'm here.'

'Everyone knows you're here, Willow,' Cathy said. 'I wouldn't be surprised if the other side of the Island has heard all about it by now.'

'Do you want some help with the festival while I'm here?' Willow asked in an attempt to change the subject.

'No, Willow, I'm fine,' Cathy replied. 'I've been involved in festivals for most of my life. Besides, it seems to me you've got quite a lot of thinking to do.'

2

Luc

As Luc walked away from The Music Shop and away from Willow, he felt the familiar tightening in his chest, the shortening of his breath. He wanted to turn back, to start the conversation with Willow again but he carried on walking towards the beach instead, knowing he needed to be alone.

He sat in the sand dunes looking out to sea, taking deep breaths in an attempt to slow down his heart rate. He let sand run through his fingers and allowed the smell of the sea and the gentle sound of the waves to calm him as it had done when he was younger.

Why are you here, Luc?

Willow's question echoed in his mind and he didn't really have an answer. To play the festival of course, but he didn't need to be here until August for that. He could have stayed in Nashville for a while longer but he'd been hoping that the familiarity of the Island would help him recover from whatever it was that had been happening to him over the last few months – the exhaustion, the panic, the writer's block – but nothing had changed. He'd been expecting the sand and the sea to work a miracle. He'd thought that as soon as his feet touched the beaches of the island he grew up on, everything would be all right again.

It was strange to be back. Everything felt so familiar yet so different, as though he was wandering about in a dream. Instead of inspiring him, the tangy smell of sea air and the wind blowing in from the Solent reminded him of Willow and of the day he left – the day he'd screwed everything up.

His phone rang and he pulled it out of his pocket looking at the number that flashed up on the screen – his agent calling from LA. Luc's thumb hovered over the screen as he tried to decide whether to take the call or not and he felt his chest tighten again. He killed the call as the panic attack threatened to engulf him and he concentrated on his breath again. He didn't want to talk to his agent. He hadn't got any news and he had made no progress on anything. He closed his eyes but all he could see was Willow.

When his phone rang again, he answered. He couldn't ignore Willow's dad.

'Don,' he said. 'Hi.'

'Have you seen her?' Don asked. 'How does she seem to you?'

Don had told Luc about Willow getting married. Whenever Luc and Don's paths crossed, as they did from time to time when Willow's father was in America, Luc had always asked how she was, what she was doing. When Don had told him he was going to London for the wedding Luc had smiled, but it had felt like a kick in the guts – as though it was finally over. He didn't know what he'd been expecting – for Willow to wait around for over a decade for him to come back?

It had been Don who had called Luc on Saturday to tell him what had happened, that Willow hadn't gone through with the wedding, that she was coming back to the Island. Luc's heart had leapt when he'd heard that, even though he knew he had to keep his heart and his feelings under tight control.

'I saw her today,' Luc said. 'She's helping Cathy in The Music Shop.'

'How does she seem?' Don asked.

'It's hard to say. It's been so long since I last saw her and she didn't exactly seem pleased to see me.'

'But she was OK?' Luc could hear the frustration in Don's voice. Willow's father wanted to be here with his daughter, but he couldn't cancel the tour.

'She looked exhausted,' Luc replied. 'And sad, but I guess that's inevitable. Look, shouldn't you be talking to Cathy about this?'

'Oh you know what Cathy's like: she just tells me everything is fine when it isn't.'

'I can go back,' Luc said. 'I can try to talk to her again if you like.'

'That would be great.' Don paused then, and Luc heard him take a breath. 'Have you told her?' he asked.

'Told her what?'

'About Annelise.'

'God no,' Luc said quietly. 'No, I don't want to tell anyone yet. I can't risk it getting out – it's not fair on Annelise.'

'OK,' Don replied but he didn't sound as though it was OK.

'Besides, Willow has enough on her plate.'

Don didn't say anything.

'Does Cathy know?' Luc asked. 'About Annelise?'

'No, I haven't told anyone. But you are going to have to tell them eventually.'

'Eventually,' Luc replied.

He promised again that he'd look out for Willow until Don could get back. It wasn't a hard promise to make – after twelve years they were back on the Island at the same time. He wouldn't be able to keep away, even though he knew he should.

Luc had never wanted to leave the Island, but Krystal was going and he'd felt he had no choice but to go with her. Leaving for America had been a long time in the planning for Luc's mother, but in the end they had left in a hurry and Luc had never really understood why. Something had happened, some kind of argument between his mum and Cathy. Don had flown out to Nashville with them, but he hadn't stayed for long. He had his own life to live, his own music to make.

Why are you here, Luc?

The memory of Willow's question made his chest tighten again and he concentrated on his breath, determined not to give this rising sense of panic any freedom. He countered it with a question of his own.

Why are you here, Willow?

It had taken him three days to pluck up the courage to go and see her. Even this afternoon he'd walked past The Music Shop several times before he'd finally gone inside. He had watched the shadow of Willow's back through the window as she sat on the countertop. His heart had been in his throat as he'd pushed the door open, relieved that she'd left it unlocked, not sure she'd have let him in otherwise.

When she had turned around to look at him, she'd almost taken his breath away. Luc had wanted to touch her, to hold her, to take her hand and run down the beach with her just as they had done when they were kids. He hadn't expected all those feelings to come flooding back.

Like the Island itself, Willow had looked the same but different – she'd seemed harder somehow, tougher than the girl he used to know. But she was different now – she'd left her past and the Island behind to trade futures in one of the big investment banks in London.

As soon as he'd seen her, all the questions that Luc had been planning to ask her – questions about why she was here and why she had walked away from her wedding, questions about what had happened twelve years ago – died on his tongue and he'd pretended he was looking for Cathy.

When Willow was in front of him, he hadn't known what to say.

He'd had to walk away from her because he couldn't let all these unexpected feelings take over. It wasn't fair on anyone. He'd felt the panic rising inside him, just as he had done twelve summers ago. The panic that had followed him, no matter how far he'd run. It was the panic that had ruined everything in the end.

Coming back to the Island had felt like the right thing to do, but now that he was here it didn't feel the way he thought it would. He'd known Cathy still lived here but he hadn't expected to see anyone else – he'd been hoping to go under the radar for a little while at least. Bumping into Skye had been his first surprise, followed by greetings from people he'd forgotten existed. Everyone said "hello" as though they'd seen him yesterday, as though he hadn't sold over half a million records, as though they hadn't seen him on TV. And to everyone on the Island Lucien Hawke was still just Luc Harrison.

Which was exactly what he wanted. He needed a break from Lucien Hawke.

Why are you here, Luc?

Luc hadn't answered the question and now, as he sat on the beach his breathing finally returning to normal, the question continued to echo in his head.

Why was he here?

Luc had needed a change of scene. He'd been exhausted in Nashville, tired of all the public appearances, the gigs, the pressure after *American Stars* and the album coming out, and he hadn't been able to write. The record company wanted another album but he had nothing left to give.

Not that he was going to be telling anyone that story. As far as anyone knew, Lucien Hawke was back on the Island to play the festival. Not the big famous one that rolled into Newport in a couple of weeks, the other festival on the Island, the one hardly anyone knew about. The one Willow's parents had set up.

As far as anyone knew, that's the only reason Luc was back.

But there was something else, something Luc was barely admitting to himself. He was here to find something. He wasn't sure what it was or where he needed to look, but Luc was here to find the part of himself that he'd left behind, the part of himself that felt as though it had been missing for longer than he could remember. He had no idea if it was here or not – he didn't even know where to start looking – but he needed to come to terms with his own past.

Luc had never known who his father was and for years it had never bothered him; he'd barely thought about it.

But since his life changed completely and he ended up on *American Stars* he couldn't think about anything else.

3

August 1981

'Come on, Catherine, hurry up or Dad will have to leave without you,' her mother called up the stairs as Cathy applied another coat of mascara and teased her hair one last time. She put on a slick of pearly pink lip gloss and took one last look at herself in the mirror.

This will have to do, she thought as her stomach filled with nervous butterflies again and she turned away from her mirror.

'Hurry up!' her mother repeated as Cathy ran down the stairs into the hall.

'How do I look?' she asked.

Her mother smiled. 'Beautiful,' she said. Cathy knew that her mum hated her hair so backcombed and wished that she wouldn't wear so much eyeliner but she also knew how important today was to Cathy – she'd been waiting for this moment for years.

'I'll see you tonight,' Cathy called as she ran out of the

front door to her father's car. 'Late tonight,' she added with relish.

Cathy's father, Brian Cole, had been involved with the Reading Rock Festival since its incarnation in the 1970s and Cathy had grown up amongst his tales of rock legends and biker gangs. She loved music and was accomplished on both guitar and violin and Brian had promised her that the summer she turned sixteen she could come to the festival with him for one day – a day of her choosing – and that she could come backstage and meet some of the bands. Cathy had chosen the Sunday because her favourite band, King Silver, were playing second from last, just before The Kinks.

'Excited?' Brian asked as they headed west out of the London suburb that they lived in.

Cathy nodded. 'And nervous,' she replied. 'Don't show me up, Dad, will you?'

Brian chuckled to himself. 'Just don't wander off anywhere though,' he said gently. 'I need to know where you are all the time.'

By day Brian Cole worked in the City, but by night he played guitar in a folk-rock band at a club in West London. That was how he'd come to be involved in the Reading Festival in the first place. The owner of the club had come up with the idea back in the late Fifties and the very first incarnation of the festival took place at the Richmond Athletic Ground twenty years ago. Brian had run the front-stage security right from the start and saw the festival move from Richmond to Windsor to Kempton and various other locations before securing its current site on reclaimed landfill in Berkshire.

Cathy knew that her father was nervous about taking her, understandably so considering the stories he regaled her with every year, but she also knew how important music was in his life, had been since he was a child living in the East End of London. She knew how proud he was of her musical abilities and how much he encouraged her.

Besides, she'd paid her dues over the years, counting out all those wristbands.

One of Brian Cole's biggest security problems, one that had bugged him more than anything his day job could throw at him, was how to make sure everyone who came into the festival had actually paid for a ticket. In the early days the fences had been easy to jump over and people handed their tickets back to friends on the other side so they could get in too. Everything was unregulated and uncontrolled.

In 1972 Cathy's little brother, Connor, had been born. Cathy could remember visiting her mother and Connor in the hospital and she could remember the plastic tag around his wrist with his name and date of birth on it. She hadn't had one of those when she'd been born seven years earlier apparently, and she could remember her dad being fascinated by the wrist band.

'We should have these for the festival,' he'd said to his wife.

Cathy's mum had smiled back indulgently. 'Even on the day after your first son is born all you can think about is that festival,' she'd said.

Cathy hadn't thought any more about the wristbands, but a few years later when she was ten, she watched her father take delivery of thousands of wristbands, all of which were destined for the wrists of festival goers. For the next several summers Cathy had helped Brian count the wristbands – which eventually got festival branding on them – into piles of a hundred, packaging them up for the next stage of their journey. She had dreamed of the day when she too would be able to go to the festival.

That day had finally come, and Cathy swallowed her nerves as she settled back into the car seat. Everybody knew how excited she was about today, how excited she'd been about it for years, but she had a secret that she was holding to herself like a delicate package. She wanted what those musicians had; she wanted the fame and fortune and the ability to make music for the rest of her life. She wanted to meet someone today who would help her get that ball rolling. She wanted to be the next Janis Joplin, the next Chrissie Hynde, and she was willing to do whatever it took to get there.

By the time King Silver came on stage Cathy had already had the best day of her life. When they'd arrived she'd been given a lanyard with her Backstage Pass attached to it and been introduced to a couple of other girls her age whose fathers had worked with Brian on the festival for years. Within an hour they were the firmest of friends and were wandering at will between the stages and the various tents. Brian had told them to keep their passes hidden under their jackets as there were plenty of fans who would try to steal them, and it had become quite a game to walk up to backstage security who would promptly turn them away until they showed their passes at the last minute. Security didn't find it as funny as they did.

Cathy had spent the day veering between feeling very young and extremely sophisticated. She'd spotted so many famous people and had tried to act cool about it while inside she felt like a small child at Christmas. She'd eaten strange food, listened to music she'd never heard before and drunk lukewarm beer out of a plastic cup. Everyone else, from the roadies to the drum technicians, from security to the band managers seemed so at home here, and there were moments when she felt out of place, just a stupid kid from a suburb of West London. She had tried and, she suspected, failed to act nonchalant when Ray Davies smiled at her. And she'd tried not to cry when her dad told her off for bitching about someone's dress, because you never knew who was listening.

By the time King Silver took to the main stage, to a cheer so loud it vibrated the very ground beneath them, Cathy was in complete sensory overload. But this was the moment she had been waiting for.

Watching her favourite band from the side of the stage was surreal. For the rest of her life she would struggle to watch any band from the front of the stage again. She was so close to them that she could hear them talking to each other in between tracks. So close that she could see when the lead guitarist broke a string, so close that when King Silver's frontman, Storm Tyler, played his mandolin she could hear the reverb of the strings underneath his fingers. She could see the crowd undulating as they all jumped up and down in unison. During the acoustic numbers she had tears in her eyes, which she desperately tried to blink away. She didn't want everyone thinking she was an inexperienced kid.

She felt her father squeeze her shoulder. 'Don't worry, kiddo,' he said. 'Storm has that effect on us all.'

King Silver were a band right on the brink of becoming stratospherically famous. They'd met ten years earlier at university and had gone from strength to strength, citing their various eclectic influences as anyone from Led Zeppelin to Pentangle. Lots of girls Cathy knew were obsessed with them and it certainly didn't hinder their fame that Storm Tyler was very easy on the eye. Brian had teased Cathy about her crush on Storm, telling her that he would let him know. She hadn't really believed that her father knew Storm at all until the band came off stage and the singer came over to shake Brian's hand.

'Neil,' Brian said. 'Fantastic gig, mate, you're just getting better and better.'

Cathy stared at her father. Who was Neil?

'Storm in front of the fans please, Brian.' Storm laughed as he looked over at Cathy and she noticed the light catch the gold of one of his teeth.

Neil? Cathy thought. *That's not very rock 'n' roll. No wonder he changed it.*

She realised that her father was introducing Storm Tyler to her.

'Cathy's a very accomplished musician herself,' Brian said.

'What do you play, Cathy?' Storm asked. His green eyes were staring directly into hers and Cathy clammed up completely, her mouth dry. So much for playing it cool and talking to people who could help her pave the way into the music business.

'Guitar and violin,' she managed eventually.

Storm looked at her for a moment, his eyes moving up and down as though he was appraising her. She couldn't work out if it made her feel good or uncomfortable.

'You should try the mandolin,' he said. 'If you can play guitar and violin then the mandolin will come easily to you.'

Cathy didn't say anything as Storm bid her father goodbye and walked off to join his bandmates with his mandolin tucked under his arm.

4

Willow

The morning after Luc Harrison walked back into her life, Willow was in The Music Shop restringing a mandolin for one of her mother's customers – a job that Cathy had given her while she stayed at home to go through the festival paperwork.

She was surprised by how quickly she worked, surprised that she still knew how to do this after all these years. At the same time she was reluctant, not wanting to go back to being the person she used to be. She didn't want to be here at all but where else could she go?

For the first forty-eight hours that Willow had been back on the Island, she hadn't set foot outside of her mother's house, embarrassed and ashamed about what she'd done. Instead she sat on the sofa in her pyjamas eating Heinz tomato soup and ignoring her beeping phone.

'If you're not going to talk to me about what happened,' Cathy had said on the third day, 'you can help me out in the shop. I'm sure you still know what to do.'

Willow had worked in the shop on Saturdays when she was a teenager and little had changed. It wasn't a case of whether or not she could do it, but whether or not she wanted to.

'It's up to you,' Cathy had said when she protested. 'You can talk or you can work, but you can't sit around here doing nothing all day – it's not good for a person.'

She'd known her mother was right, so she'd chosen the lesser of the two evils – working in the shop.

The Music Shop had always been Cathy's pride and joy and Willow knew how much her mother must trust her to leave her in charge. She had forgotten this place, this shop she had spent so much time in when she was younger, and the recording studio next door where so many bands had come and gone over the years, where some world-acclaimed albums had been recorded. She'd forgotten the peaceful ambience, the plate glass window near the counter that looked out over the sea, the rows of guitars and ukuleles, the racks of sheet music and brightly coloured guitar picks. She had forgotten the smell of the guitars and mandolins that her mother made by hand.

Musicians came from all over the world to commission one of Cathy Cole's handmade instruments, and people said that nobody could tune a mandolin like her. Don used to joke she must have made mandolins in a previous lifetime.

Customers trickled in and out all morning, greeting Willow as though she'd never been gone. Nobody asked any awkward questions and nobody made her feel anything other than at home. She could easily have allowed herself to slip back into this life, but she'd worked too hard at getting away to let that happen.

The shop wasn't busy enough to distract her overthinking mind and nobody was in the recording studio today. She picked up her father's mandolin again and allowed her fingers to begin to pluck out a few chords. She immediately felt the tension in her shoulders and jaw release as a fleeting sense of contentment washed over her. But as soon as she put the mandolin aside again the embarrassment and shame of walking away from her wedding returned.

Her phone was full of messages from her friends asking her about it, asking her what had happened and where she was. She still hadn't replied. What could she say when she didn't know what had happened herself?

Not one of those messages had asked Willow how she was feeling. Nobody had asked her if she was all right. Not even Kate.

She hadn't heard from Kate at all.

Willow wasn't used to being alone and had forgotten the quiet, slow pace of the Island. She was used to spending long days working in the City, with barely a moment of silence, barely a moment to think. The solitude of her mother's shop was almost overwhelming and at lunchtime she shut up The Music Shop and walked down the street to where Skye's shop was based.

She'd been thinking about Skye since Luc and Cathy both mentioned her, wondering if it was worth going to see her, wondering if it was worth digging up the past. In the end that strange feeling of loneliness drove her to it. The more she thought about the friends she'd left behind in London, the ones eager for salacious gossip and the ones she hadn't heard from at all, the more she thought about the friendship she'd had with Skye – the friendship she walked away from because of Charlie, because she'd been embarrassed about where she came from and who she'd been before she met him.

There was only really one main street in Seaview and it was an easy place to find your way around. That's why the Seaview Folk Festival had always been so successful: all the pubs in which the musicians played were so close together that you could see every act if you timed it right.

It was a street full of shops and hotels, of coloured awnings and ice-cream carts. Seaview felt as though time had forgotten it sometimes – a chocolate box town by the sea, the sort of place you'd read about in children's stories from the 1950s.

Willow passed the old sweet shop, surprised to see Mrs Cartwright behind the counter still – she must be ninety these days – and resisted the temptation to go in for a bag of lemon pips. She was determined not to get lost in nostalgia while she was here. She wanted to focus on moving forward, not back, and she was beginning to wonder if the only reason she'd been drawn back to the Island was to make amends in some way.

Was that the reason she walked away from Charlie on their wedding day? Because she couldn't move forward until she'd made amends with her past?

On the other side of Cartwright's sweet shop there was a gap between the buildings and a small side street with direct access to the sea. Willow stopped in her tracks and peered down towards the beach where she could see the corner of the beach huts and the coloured parasols stuck into the sand. It was still early in the season and the beach was relatively quiet. She was tempted to forget about Skye and walk through the gap and down to the beach, tempted to dig her toes into the sand, dip them in the sea.

This small passageway between the shops was the way she used to come down to the beach with Luc and Skye when they were teenagers, the way they walked back at night stumbling a little after drinking too much of the cider that Skye's dad brewed in his shed. They'd hung out in the old beach hut a lot that summer. Skye's dad had let it fall into rack and ruin so he'd no longer let it out to holidaymakers. Skye had managed to convince him to let them use it and they kept a kettle and an old radio and Luc's stash of weed there.

The passageway was also the way Luc had walked her home from the beach on the last night they were ever together and she could almost taste the fermented apple on her tongue, the sensation of seawater washing over her skin.

For a moment the memories hovered thickly in the air around Willow and she turned away before they trapped her. She walked on determinedly towards Skye's shop.

Skye owned a tattoo studio, which might seem an odd thing to do in a small place like Seaview but, according to Cathy, she had built up quite a reputation since moving back to the Island, having tattooed some of the legends of folk and rock music. When Willow was growing up, everyone she knew had tattoos. Don was covered in them and she even had one herself. Charlie hated it of course and had made her promise to have it removed once they were married, but what Charlie thought probably didn't matter anymore. Willow and Skye had got matching tattoos done just before they both left for university. It had been one of the last days they had spent together on the Island.

She stood outside Skye's shop for a moment remembering. The two girls had parted on good terms, full of big intentions to stay in touch through university. But once Willow was at Cambridge and Skye was at art college their emails and phone calls had become increasingly sporadic until the point they barely heard from each other at all. Willow suspected the fault lay with her. As the months had passed and she'd read the emails from Skye's exciting, bohemian London life, she felt as though she were drifting away, as though she and Skye had nothing in common anymore. They'd never discussed it because Skye's parents had moved to Bournemouth not long after Skye left for art college so the two girls didn't even see much of each other during the summer vacations from university when Willow came back to the Island for a few weeks.

Now Willow wondered if Skye had been another reminder of the life she used to have, the life she had been trying to distance herself from even before she met Charlie.

She had missed Skye though and had tried to rekindle the friendship. Eight years ago, when Willow and Charlie had moved to London they had met up with Skye for lunch in a pub. It had been such a delight to see Skye again that Willow had slipped back into being the person she used to be and Charlie hadn't liked it. He'd been so rude and Willow hadn't done anything to stop him. Would Skye be able to forgive her for that afternoon? Willow knew she had to find out, because she still missed Skye as much as she ever had.

She pushed the door to the tattoo studio open and heard the bell tinkle – it made exactly the same sound as the bell in The Music Shop, and the same sound that the bell in this tattoo studio used to make when it was under previous ownership.

Skye and Willow had been tattooed by an artist called Darren who had a dubious and mysterious past. Skye had confided in Willow on the day they'd had their tattoos done that, after her degree, this was what she wanted to do – create living pieces of art on people's skin. Despite everything it was wonderful to see her living her dream.

There used to be a red and black sign reading 'TATTOO CRAZY' in gothic script above the door of the shop. Now the sign was hand-painted and read 'Clouds in the Skye'. Willow stepped inside.

The last time she'd been here the shop had been dark and smelled of disinfectant and incense, and thrash metal had been playing on the stereo. Now it was light and airy, the walls were painted white and there were fresh flowers on the reception desk. Paintings by local artists, including Skye herself, hung on the walls and Willow could smell the calming fragrance of lavender and rose essential oils.

A big cream sofa covered in brightly coloured cushions sat next to the reception desk and it all seemed so welcoming that Willow felt as though she could curl up there and sleep all afternoon.

She called out a greeting.

'Just a minute,' Skye's voice called back. It sent a shiver down Willow's spine to hear her again in the place where they had spent their last full day together.

Willow turned to look at the paintings on the walls, an eclectic mix. There were seascapes in watercolours and oil and some more modern abstract paintings in charcoals, pastels and acrylics – mostly by artists whose names she didn't recognise. Back when Skye's mum owned the local art gallery, they'd known all the local artists. Willow didn't know what happened on the Island anymore.

'Willow,' Skye said as she came out into the reception. Willow turned around to look at her but before she could take her in, she saw Luc following Skye from the room at the back of the shop, ducking his head slightly as he came through the doorway.

She had come here to make amends, but she couldn't do that in front of Luc because it would mean admitting to Luc what had happened between Charlie and Skye in the pub that day. And being with both Skye and Luc would mean talking about the past, a past that she had been avoiding thinking about for over a decade.

'I'm sorry,' she said as she headed back towards the door. 'I can see now isn't a good time.'

'Willow, come back,' she heard Luc call from behind her.

'Maybe later,' she replied, not sure if she would be able to pluck up the courage to come again. She heard the bell on the door jangle behind her as she walked away.

The last time the three of them had been together was etched on her brain and she could still remember it as though it was yesterday. It was a hot September afternoon in the middle of a week of unseasonably warm weather right at the end of their last summer on the Island. It had felt like the end of everything. Everyone was leaving that summer.

They had spent the day together in Skye's dad's old beach hut, drinking the last of the stolen cider, smoking the last of Luc's weed. They had known that afternoon was the end of everything but none of them had been able to articulate how they felt. The unspoken words had hung heavily in the air of the beach hut along with the smoke. Skye had left early for a family dinner, her grandparents had come over from Bournemouth to wish her well at art college, and Luc and Willow had been left alone.

Willow took a deep breath of sea air. The memories of that last day on the Island, coupled with the embarrassment she still felt about the last time she'd seen Skye, had made her run. She didn't know if she could make amends with her past after all.

'Don't do this,' Skye called as she caught up with her. 'I know what you're thinking.'

'Remembering,' Willow replied, turning around to look at Skye, the two of them facing each other for the first time in eight years. At first glance Skye looked the same, the smattering of freckles across her dark skin, her hair piled up on top of her head and secured with a scarf, her brown eyes heavily made-up – but there were lines around those eyes now and a weariness that seemed older than her thirty years.

'Are you still angry with me?' Willow asked.

'Of course not,' Skye replied. 'I was never angry with you that day.'

She had been angry with Charlie, with the way he'd treated her. Willow knew that and she'd done nothing to stop him. She hadn't stood up for her childhood friend.

'Thank you,' Willow replied. It's all she could say.

'I heard,' Skye said quietly. 'About the wedding. I'm so sorry.'

Willow looked away. 'You have nothing to be sorry about,' she said.

'Come back to the shop,' Skye said. 'We can talk there.'

'I don't want to talk,' Willow replied, looking back at Skye.

'OK.'

'I can't. Not with Luc there.'

Skye nodded, understanding. 'Luc's thinking of getting another tattoo,' she said, making light conversation.

Willow hesitated for a moment. She shouldn't leave The Music Shop closed for too long, but she didn't want to go back just yet after all.

'How about a cup of tea?' Skye asked. 'No deep and meaningful conversations, just tea.'

Willow nodded and started to follow Skye back to the tattoo studio.

'It's good to see you again, Willow.'

5

Luc

Luc watched Skye leave the shop, chasing after Willow, and he wondered why Willow had left as soon as she'd seen him. Could she still not look at him? He wanted to explain what had happened that day, what had prevented him from turning up to meet her. It had been the last day they could be together before he'd left for America and he had ruined it.

He'd thought about that day so many times over the intervening years but had never been able to remember any of the detail. He could remember how nervous he had been about seeing Willow, but excited too. He'd wanted to talk to her about what had happened between them the night before, when he'd told her that he loved her. He knew what it must have looked like when he hadn't turned up the next day, when they'd had to say goodbye awkwardly in front of their parents later that night. He'd tried to explain everything in the letters he'd written to her at Cambridge, but she'd never replied. Perhaps she'd never received them.

All he could really remember about that afternoon, and the days that followed, was the sensation of his anxiety spiralling out of control. It had been the first panic attack he'd ever had and it had stopped him spending that last day with Willow, prevented him from telling her how he planned to come back for her as soon as he could. Such childish plans really, imagining that they would somehow survive a long-distance relationship when they'd only just admitted how they felt.

It had been almost inevitable that their friendship would never make it through.

Skye had always felt like an anchor to Luc, someone he could rely on, and he knew that Willow had felt the same. The three of them had met on their first day of secondary school and had been inseparable for the next seven years. Skye's parents hadn't been part of the folk music scene and her mum had always put meals on the table at normal times and her dad had worked in an office. It had felt like stability to Luc when he was growing up, and he had craved that.

Perhaps that was what he was hoping to find on the Island again now?

Luc had come to see Skye this morning to distract himself. Willow had been the first thing he'd thought of when he woke up but he had forced himself to stay away from her – despite his promise to Don. Seeing Willow again when all the feelings he had about her felt so fresh and so raw would be a mistake. He couldn't afford to make that mistake; it wouldn't be fair on Willow. It wouldn't be fair on Annelise.

He'd decided to go to see Skye instead, to talk about a tattoo that he'd been thinking of getting, to keep his mind off Willow. There was so much he wanted to say to Willow, so much he should have said twelve years ago, but as soon as he'd seen her again, as soon as she'd looked at him with that hardness she'd developed, he couldn't do it.

Why should today be any different?

His phone rang and Luc saw his agent's number appear on the screen again. He still didn't have anything to say so he stuffed the phone back into his pocket unanswered as the bell above the tattoo studio door jangled and Willow and Skye came back in.

Even though he'd been trying to avoid Willow he was relieved that Skye had managed to convince her to come back. He walked into the little kitchen at the back of the shop to put the kettle on. He'd missed the ritual of making tea while he'd been touring in America, staying in hotels that never had kettles.

'How long have you been back?' Willow asked Skye as the two of them followed him into the kitchen and sat down at the small Formica table.

'I came back after I finished my tattoo apprenticeship in London,' Skye replied. 'I missed the Island.'

Luc put the teapot on the table and Willow finally looked at him. Her expression was unreadable.

'Really?' Willow sounded as surprised as Luc had been when he found out that Skye had come back. They'd spent most of their teenage years talking about all the things they were going to do when they finally got off the godforsaken Island. It had been particularly important to Skye, but they had all wanted to find somewhere else that suited them, somewhere better to fit in.

Skye smiled. 'I know, I know,' she said. 'I always said I'd

never come back but it turned out I missed the place. Didn't you?'

Willow shook her head. 'I've never missed the Island,' she said. But there's something in the way she said it that made Luc think that she wasn't telling the truth. 'I found everything I wanted in London.'

'But you came back anyway,' he interrupted. He didn't mean to say anything. He'd thought he would leave quietly once he'd made the tea but he wanted to know why she was really back. It was more than just the wedding – he knew that – and she might feel more comfortable talking with Skye here too.

'I'll pour the tea,' Willow said, ignoring him and reaching for the teapot. 'And you can tell me all about how you came to buy the tattoo shop.'

Luc propped himself against the counter, still debating whether to leave or not.

'As soon as I got back I came here to see Darren,' Skye explained. 'I wanted to work for him, see my own clients and build a business of my own but it turned out he was selling up and moving back to the mainland.'

'Wasn't he from the north somewhere?' Willow asked.

'Manchester,' Skye said. 'I thought that was the end of it and I didn't really know what else to do. I should have called first, before I left my job in London. But Mum persuaded me that I should try to buy the place off him.'

'Well it looks fantastic,' Willow replied. 'Much better than it did when Darren had it.'

'And none of that awful music,' Luc said quietly. If there was one thing that bonded them all together back in the day it was their mutual hatred of Darren's taste in music.

'Enough about me though,' Skye said. 'What about you?' Skye directed the question at Willow. 'Why are you back on the Island after all these years?'

'As if you don't already know.'

'OK fair enough,' Skye said, holding up her hands, palms forward. 'I think probably all of Seaview and half of Ryde know that you walked out on your wedding. But how are you? Are you OK?'

Luc noticed something that looked like relief pass over Willow's face and then she smiled. It wasn't much but for a moment it almost felt like old times, sitting around drinking tea and confiding in each other.

'I don't know how I am,' Willow said eventually. 'I thought I had everything I wanted but...' She trailed off as though she'd run out of words. As though she had no way of explaining what she was doing here.

Luc knew how that felt better than anyone.

'All I ever wanted was to get off this Island,' Willow said.

'We all did,' Luc replied but still Willow didn't look at him.

'I wanted to get away from folk music. I wanted to get a normal job and get married and have babies.' Luc ignored the pinch of envy and guilt he felt when he thought about Willow having a family with someone who wasn't him. 'I got my degree, I got my dream job, I worked hard and earned good money. I met Charlie at Cambridge and he trained as a lawyer. We bought a flat in the centre of London and we got engaged. We spent two years planning a wedding and then...' She shrugged. 'I thought it was everything I ever wanted,' she repeated, and Luc noticed the past tense, as though that life wasn't what she wanted anymore.

'I never really believed you when you said you wanted all those things anyway,' Skye said after a while, looking at Willow over the top of her mug. 'All that stuff about money and comfort and a normal life. It never rang true. And then when I saw you…' She stopped for a moment, shrugged. 'I'm just surprised you kept up the pretence this long,' she said. It sounded to Luc as though they had seen each other over the intervening years. What had happened?

Willow looked up then, staring at Skye. 'What's that supposed to mean?' she asked. Luc gripped the countertop harder, hoping they wouldn't have an argument. He'd always hated it when they argued.

Skye put her mug down. 'I didn't mean anything by it, Willow,' she said gently, reaching over to take Willow's hand. 'I'm sorry, it's just I always thought deep down you would come back to the Island one day, even if that meant walking away from that life you built. This is where we belong.'

'I don't know,' Willow replied.

'Don't you think it's strange how you came back at the same time as Luc?' Skye asked. 'It's like serendipity.'

Skye had always believed in things like serendipity, that everything in life was mapped out and happened for a reason. Luc, on the other hand, believed that life was a series of random events that you had to make the absolute best of.

But Willow hadn't explained anything; she hadn't said why she was back, why she wasn't on her honeymoon. Maybe she didn't know.

Luc was thinking about leaving, when his phone rang again and when he saw her name on the screen he answered automatically.

Annelise.

'Hello, sweetheart,' he said as he answered, kicking himself as soon as the words tumbled out of his mouth. He hesitated for a moment, looking over at Skye and Willow who were staring at him. He wished he hadn't answered after all. 'Can I call you back in ten minutes?' he asked.

'My agent,' he explained as he hung up. He could see by the way they looked at each other that they didn't believe him.

'I should go,' Willow said, draining her tea.

'You'll come again won't you?' Skye asked as Willow stood up. 'We should talk.' She paused, her eyes flicking to Luc and then back to Willow. 'Just the two of us,' she said.

Willow nodded.

'I'm here all the time,' she went on. 'I live upstairs.'

Luc watched Willow get ready to leave.

'Willow, wait,' he said as he followed her out into the shop.

Willow turned around and, for a moment, she looked eighteen again until that hardness washed over her face as though she was putting on a mask.

Was the mask to do with the Island or something she was so used to wearing in London that she didn't know how to take it off?

He leant against the doorframe and hooked his thumbs into the pockets of his jeans to stop himself from touching her.

'Have you spoken to your mum about the festival?' he asked.

'I offered to help but Mum turned me down,' she replied. 'And I haven't congratulated you on your headline slot. Nice going, Lucien Hawke!'

47

She grinned and it surprised Luc that she seemed genuinely excited for him. For a moment he thought that maybe he could do this after all. But then he watched her face fall. 'I won't be here by then though,' she said.

He felt himself blush and he looked down so she couldn't see colour in his face. He scuffed the toe of his boot against the floor.

'I didn't really want to headline and I'm not sure it will help anyway,' he said.

'Help in what way?'

'Did Cathy not say anything?'

'She said that she'd let herself get in a muddle,' Willow replied. 'But she does that every year. Like I said I offered to help—'

'She hasn't got council permission,' Luc interrupted.

'What?'

'There's been changes at the council. She usually gets the licences and permissions for the festival automatically every year but this year there's a problem. I don't really know why, I haven't seen the letter but you should ask to read it.'

'I can't believe it. Mum's been running that festival for years. The council can't stop us.'

'Well they can,' Luc replied. 'And if we don't do something about it there isn't going to be a festival this year.'

Willow looked at him for a moment as though she was going to say something else, but then she nodded and walked away.

Luc ignored the sensation of disappointment in his stomach.

6

The three girls arrived at the Astoria on Tottenham Court Road as soon as the doors opened. After handing their tickets over to be torn in half, they stepped inside and didn't even stop at the bar before walking into the auditorium, determined to get to the very front of the stage for King Silver's final show of the year.

'I've heard it's really easy to get backstage here,' Jenny said. 'There's hardly any security.'

Cathy smiled but didn't say anything. She had her own plans to get backstage tonight and she didn't really care if her two friends joined her or not.

She had just finished her first term at the Royal Academy of Music. Living and studying in central London had been everything she'd imagined it to be, but her favourite part of it was the live music. Whether that be classical concerts at the Royal Albert Hall or gigs like tonight, Cathy loved every moment and every spare penny she could get her hands on went towards concert tickets. She finally felt as though she had found her calling, as though she was on a path that was taking her to the place she wanted to be most – on the stage itself.

She didn't pay a lot of attention to the support act, a singer-songwriter called Don Warwick who had been hailed in the *NME* recently as "the new Nick Drake".

'He looks more Kris Kristofferson than Nick Drake if you ask me,' Cathy's friend Pip said into her ear during the support set. Pip was also at the Academy – an accomplished pianist.

Cathy laughed and looked again at the young man on stage. 'Cute though,' she said, as she stood near enough to notice the ice blue of his eyes and the softness of his lips. Don was playing acoustic guitar tonight, although Cathy had heard he was also something special on the mandolin.

But Cathy wasn't here to see Don Warwick, she was here to see Storm Tyler. She'd seen King Silver live three further times since that memorable Reading Festival two and a half years ago, but she had never got to meet Storm again. Tonight, she was determined to change that. Ever since she'd spoken to him Cathy had been sure that Storm played a part in her future and she was determined to begin that future now.

When King Silver finally came on stage forty minutes late, they were greeted by a rapturous roar from a crowd that had been becoming restless as they waited. As the opening bars to "Chord of Plenty" rang out through the venue's PA system Cathy allowed herself to absorb the atmosphere and imagined what it would be like to be on the stage instead of in front of it.

The viscous aroma of sweat and beer and cigarette smoke

invaded Cathy's nostrils and she wondered if you could smell that from the stage too. As she turned to look behind her she saw a sea of fans jumping in time to the music and everyone in the seats above standing up and dancing. A group of bare-chested men in leather jackets were climbing on each other's shoulders to form a human pyramid.

'Look at them,' Jenny shouted as she nudged Cathy and looked in the direction of the men. 'They're creating a phallus shape to challenge the father figure of the lead singer.'

Cathy stared at Jenny for a moment before collapsing into giggles. Jenny was studying psychology at University College and had taken her recent Freudian module a little too seriously.

Halfway through the show the rest of the band took a breather and Storm Tyler took a seat on a high stool to begin his short acoustic set.

'Hello,' he said to the crowd in general, although Cathy was sure he was looking straight at her. As the crowd erupted into another huge cheer Storm grinned and Cathy could see the glint of his gold tooth. 'Some of you might know this one,' Storm continued when the noise had died down.

Cathy recognised the opening chords as Storm plucked them out on his mandolin. It was an old Ballad Book classic called "Gamble Gold", but the version that Cathy had heard was upbeat and jaunty and was completely different to the way Storm had arranged it. As Storm played his mandolin, his voice lilted through the verses, making the whole thing feel much sadder, much more haunting. Cathy could feel the energy change as the audience stood in rapt silence.

She knew, as she stood there with the music washing over her, that tonight was going to be special.

Tonight could change the whole trajectory of her life if she allowed it to.

In the end getting backstage wasn't as difficult as Cathy had thought it would be. It had been a bit of a waiting game and Pip and Jenny, getting bored, had gone off to a nearby pub. Not long after they left a security guy came to find Cathy.

'Brian Cole's daughter?' he asked.

Cathy nodded. She'd asked her dad to tell Storm, if he saw him, that she was coming to see the band tonight and that she'd love a signed T-shirt. She hadn't known if her dad had got through or not but clearly he had.

'Storm says any daughter of Brian's is a friend of ours,' the security guy said, winking at her in a way that made her feel uncomfortable. Cathy stopped for a moment. What was she doing? She didn't know any of these people. Was she being an idiot? Her dad wasn't here to keep an eye on her this time. She suddenly felt like a little girl again, the confidence and bravado leaking out of her and leaving her feeling deflated.

'Put this on,' he said handing her a lanyard with a backstage pass on. She took a deep breath, trying to find that bravado again before it was too late. She put the lanyard around her neck and stood up a little straighter, tossing her hair.

She was led through what felt like a maze of corridors to a white door that had a handwritten sign on it that read "King Silver". The security guy knocked on the door and Cathy could feel his eyes travelling up and down her body as they waited. She didn't want to be here anymore. She almost turned and ran.

But then the door opened and Storm was standing in front of her. He smiled and Cathy felt safe again.

Storm looked over Cathy's shoulder to where the security guy was still lurking around and his face changed.

'I can take it from here, Nigel,' he said sternly. Cathy heard Nigel's tongue click in his mouth in an impatient, annoyed way before he walked away.

'Come in, come in,' Storm said. 'There's only me here I'm afraid; the rest of the lads have already left. Can I get you a beer?'

Cathy shook her head. 'No, thank you,' she said. She felt strangely out of place in this room that smelled of sweat and beer and men. She looked around her at the discarded beer bottles, the cigarette stubs squashed into plates of sandwiches, a pair of Levi's slung over the back of a chair, an open pack of guitar strings. Everything seemed to be covered in the remnants of a white powder that Cathy was pretty sure must be cocaine.

'I just wanted to say hello,' she said, trying not to sound nervous, trying to remember that this could be the night that changed her life. 'And to tell you that I started playing the mandolin, like you suggested.'

'You did, you did,' Storm said, gesturing for Cathy to sit down. 'Brian told me. He also told me you're very good at it and that you got into the Royal Academy.'

Cathy blushed and looked away. Getting into the Academy seemed somewhat incongruous in comparison to Storm's life on the road, the beer and drugs and plates of old sandwiches.

The women he must meet, she thought and felt very young again.

'The Royal Academy is all well and good,' Storm said. 'But where do you see it leading you? What do you want out of life, Cathy Cole?' He looked straight at her, his green eyes sparkling and Cathy felt as though he could see directly into her soul.

'I want to know what it feels like to be on stage,' she said. 'Not the sort of stages we have at the Academy, but a stage like tonight, a stage like the Reading Festival. I want to know what that sea of people looks like from the stage. I want to know what it feels like to know that they're jumping to the rhythms that I wrote.'

She stopped suddenly, feeling childish and silly again, unable to look Storm in the eye. She heard the deep rumble of his laugh and thought that he was laughing at her.

'That's wonderful, Cathy,' he said and when she looked at him again his green eyes glinted at her. 'That's wonderful. And take it from me, it feels amazing to know that all those people are jumping to the tunes that I wrote.'

'I've started writing some songs of my own,' she said quietly.

'Then I should hear them sometime,' he replied. 'Maybe next time I see your father.'

'Really?' Cathy couldn't believe that he meant it. 'You still see my father?'

Storm nodded. 'He was a good friend to me and the band in the early days. I try not to forget the people who supported us before we were famous. Try to remember that, Cathy, because they're your real friends.'

Cathy watched Storm's face change from smiling to

something else. A furrow appeared between his eyebrows and he looked as though all the happiness had been drained from him. Before she could think of anything to say there was a loud knock on the door.

'Come in,' Storm called, his face changing once again, the smile back.

A woman poked her head around the door. 'That journalist is here, Storm,' she said.

'Of course,' Storm replied standing up and offering his hand to Cathy. As he stood, she noticed he was unsteady on his feet, not quite as sober as he appeared.

'It's been wonderful to see you again, Cathy,' he said as he held her hand. 'Really it has.'

When Storm Tyler looked her up and down, even though he was eleven years older than her, she didn't feel uncomfortable, she felt on top of the world.

'Storm,' she said as she started to walk away. 'Is your real name Neil?'

'Did you father tell you that?'

'No,' Cathy said shaking he head. 'It was just something I heard.' She didn't tell him that she remembered her father calling Storm by his real name at the Reading Festival. She didn't tell him that she'd been thinking about it ever since.

'Then I can neither confirm nor deny the rumour,' Storm said, grinning at Cathy. She saw the glint of the gold in his tooth as she walked away.

7

Willow

'Why didn't you tell me the festival was in trouble?' Willow asked as she walked through the door of her mother's house later that afternoon.

Cathy was in the living room again. Willow moved a big pile of paper to one side so she could sit down on the sofa as Cathy put down her pen and looked away.

'I didn't want to bother you,' she said. 'Did Luc tell you?'

'Yes,' Willow replied quietly. She tried not to think about Luc leaning against the doorframe of Skye's shop or the way her heart had felt too big for her ribcage when he'd smiled at her. She tried not to think about whoever it was that called him – the person who definitely wasn't his agent. The last thing she needed was for all those old feelings about Luc Harrison to come flooding back now. It had only been a few days since she walked out on her wedding; she couldn't let herself feel anything for anyone. She couldn't let herself get hurt again.

But when she thought about his lips curling into a smile, something unfamiliar fizzed inside her.

'I told him not to say anything to you,' Cathy said. 'What can you do to help?'

'Anything you want me to do.' Willow didn't know why, but she felt strongly that the festival needed to go ahead, even though she wouldn't be here to see it.

'Willow, you haven't been home for the festival since you graduated from university. It's changed a lot since then and the council get stricter every year with the permissions.'

'Luc said that was the problem,' Willow replied, ignoring the jibe about her never coming home. She couldn't argue it after all. She hadn't been to the festival for over eight years. 'That one of the licences or permissions hasn't been granted.'

'There's a new councillor this year called Roger Beck. He's an officious little so-and-so.' Cathy looked at her. 'Do you remember him? His sister was in your year at school.'

Willow did remember Roger Beck. He was a couple of years older than her and he'd always been a bit of a bully. He'd also always hated the festival and nobody had ever really known why. Everyone else in Ryde and Seaview loved it and looked forward to it all summer. Everyone else was always really supportive, but Roger Beck had never liked anyone to have any fun. If Luc, Skye or Willow were ever doing anything they shouldn't be doing, like skipping school or smoking, Roger had always made it his business to find out and tell the head teacher. He clearly hadn't changed a bit.

'Who made Roger Beck a councillor?' Willow asked. 'Who on earth voted him in?'

'Nobody's admitting to it,' Cathy replied. 'But somebody must have done and now he's trying to withhold my alcohol licence and get us to keep the noise down after 7pm.'

'After seven? It doesn't even get going until after seven!'

'I know,' Cathy said sadly and Willow felt that over-whelming need to help again. She couldn't bear the thought of the festival not happening, couldn't bear the thought of the sadness it would bring to her mother.

'Look, Mum, I know I've not been here for years but I'm here now so what can I do?'

'Oh, Willow, you've got your own life to get back to.'

Willow took a breath. 'I'm not sure I have,' she said quietly, verbalising the creeping realisation that had been coming over her since she saw Skye and Luc earlier.

'What do you mean?'

'I don't know if I have a life to go back to.'

'What happened, Willow?' Cathy asked, putting her paperwork to one side. 'Why did you walk out of your wedding on Saturday? What's going on?'

Something had happened to stop Willow from going through with the wedding. Something had made her get into her mother's Jeep, still in her wedding dress, and come back to the Island. But she wasn't sure if she was ready to talk about what that something was.

'Mum, we've got this festival to sort out,' she said, trying to change the subject, trying to escape the feeling of claustrophobia that returned every time she thought about her wedding day or about her life in London. The festival was something to focus on, a constant in her life that had always been there, even if she hadn't always been on the Island for it. It had to go ahead.

'We can do that later,' Cathy replied. 'Nothing is more important than my little girl – you know that.'

Willow felt tears burning the backs of her eyes and Cathy

drew her into a hug. 'Your dad's coming back soon so he can help with the bloody festival for once,' she said. Don came back every summer for the festival even though he and Cathy weren't together anymore. 'Now tell me what happened. I'm worried about you.'

'I don't really know,' Willow replied. 'You remember when I was a teenager and I used to feel as though I didn't fit in?'

'Yes. But your dad and I never really understood why you felt that. You, Skye and Luc were thick as thieves right up until that week you left.'

'I never felt creative enough,' Willow replied making air quotes around the word "creative". Willow had grown up in a family of musicians and surrounded by artists and other creative types. Luc had become one of the best guitarists on the Island and had been playing live since he was fifteen and Skye had been offered an unconditional place at art college when they saw her portfolio. Her parents had taught Willow to play guitar and mandolin, but she had never felt as though she had much talent for either. 'Everyone had so much talent and we were always surrounded by musicians and artists when I was growing up and I wasn't part of that – I was good at maths.'

'Every artist needs a good accountant,' Cathy said with a smile.

Willow leant back against the sofa. 'I don't really know what I'm trying to tell you,' she said. 'But over the last few months I've just had that same sense of not fitting in that I used to have when I lived here, as though I don't really fit into Charlie's life anymore and I'm not the person he wants me to be.'

'Surely Charlie just wants you to be yourself,' Cathy said. 'Surely he can't expect you to change who you are for him?'

'He's helped me change for the better,' Willow said, not sure if she was trying to convince her mother or herself. 'But recently I've felt as though I'm a constant disappointment to him.'

'And that's why you couldn't marry him?'

Willow paused for a moment, remembering her wedding day, remembering standing at the door of the church with her father.

'All I know is that I looked into that church on Saturday and saw all those people waiting for me with their phones ready to take a picture as I stepped into the church and I felt as though I couldn't breathe. I felt trapped and claustrophobic, as if the life I'd tried to create for myself had become too tight suddenly.'

'And so you walked away,' Cathy said.

'I couldn't go through with it; I couldn't tie myself to a life I wasn't sure about.'

Cathy turned around to look at her daughter, tucking her legs underneath her. 'Why did you leave the Island in the first place?' she asked.

'To go to university.'

'I know that, Willow, but why did you leave early? And why were you always so reluctant to come home in the holidays?' Cathy paused. 'I know I should have asked this years ago,' she went on, 'but why have you not been home for nearly eight years?'

'Why didn't you ask years ago?' Willow asked.

'I think that perhaps I didn't want to hear the answer.'

Willow didn't say anything for a moment as she thought

about that summer twelve years ago and in particular that night that she and Luc had been alone. The night before he went to America. She turned away from her mother, feeling the heat rising in her cheeks and an unexpected worm of desire unfurling in her stomach. For months afterwards she had thought about that night obsessively, trying to work out what she had done wrong. And for years she had done her best to pretend it had never happened, to pretend that Charlie was the only man she had ever slept with.

Willow had been in total denial about how she had felt that summer. Luc was leaving, her parents were separating, The Laurels were splitting up for the final time. Deep down Willow had been devastated and had had to deal with more change than her eighteen-year-old self could cope with. She'd smiled and laughed and pretended that everything was fine and she'd coped by drinking too much cider and skinny-dipping in the sea, jumping off the groynes – something she'd always been told not to do.

'Be careful, Willow,' Luc would say but she just told him that she was fine even though he knew she wasn't.

Neither of them had been fine.

After Skye had left to see her grandparents that night, Willow and Luc had finished off the cider together, still not speaking about the next day, still trying not to acknowledge that Luc was leaving. It had been almost dark but still warm when they decided to go swimming one last time before the summer ended. When she'd jumped off the groyne that night Luc had caught her.

'You shouldn't do that, Willow,' he'd said softly, his hands around her waist as he'd pulled her towards him. 'I don't want anything bad to happen to you.'

And then he had been kissing her, his lips on hers, his tongue in her mouth. He'd tasted of salt and fermented apples and she'd kissed him back, not wanting that moment to end. She'd felt him harden against her belly and he'd pulled away, his green eyes holding her gaze, and an unspoken agreement passed between them as he'd pulled her up on to his hips and she'd wrapped her legs around his waist. There had been something about knowing that everyone was leaving, about knowing that nothing would ever be the same again, that made them both reckless. It had been the first time for both of them and it had come out of nowhere.

Except it hadn't really. They'd both known the way they'd felt about each other for a long time.

Afterwards they'd lain on the beach together, Luc's jacket covering them, fingers still exploring, not quite ready to let each other go.

'I love you, Willow,' Luc had said.

She hadn't been expecting him to say that. She hadn't been expecting him to voice the words she'd been feeling for years.

'I love you too,' she'd said.

'I won't be in America forever. I promise.'

He'd walked her home, holding her hand and she'd felt his sadness as strongly as her own.

'We've still got tomorrow,' he'd said when they got to Willow's house. 'I'll meet you at the beach hut after breakfast.'

She'd nodded and kissed him goodnight.

But he hadn't turned up at the beach hut the next day. She'd waited for him all morning. She hadn't seen him again until it was time for him to leave. She'd been too angry with him to do more than accept his chaste kiss and his promise of calling her as soon as he got to America and she'd been too upset about her father leaving to think about anything at all.

She had loved Luc since she was eleven years old and she had thought that everything would be all right. She'd still been young and naïve enough to think that they could somehow maintain a relationship and the Atlantic Ocean in between them wouldn't be an obstacle.

She had left for Cambridge early, gone before Luc had touched down in Tennessee, long before he could call her. Cathy had seemed glad of the excuse to drive Willow to Cambridge, to get away from the Island for a few days.

Willow had always known deep down that it was more than just what had happened on that last day that had made her cut off contact with Luc, that there was a deeper reason as to why she never gave him the benefit of the doubt or a chance to explain. That summer when Luc left, when her father left, had shattered the life that she had taken for granted and it had stopped her wanting to be part of that life anymore. It was only now that she realised how angry she had been with her father too and how much damage that anger had done over the years by her not acknowledging it.

'I was so angry that summer before I went to university,' Willow said to her mother now. 'I was so angry with Dad for leaving, at Krystal for taking him away—'

'That's not quite what happened,' Cathy interrupted.

'Why did he go then?' Willow asked. Cathy had always sworn that Don didn't leave because of Luc's mum but Willow had always had her doubts about that, no matter how much her parents denied it. She couldn't think of any other reason why he would have gone then, at the same time as Krystal and Luc.

'It was complicated,' Cathy said quietly and Willow sighed. Her mother had never wanted to talk about the past, however much Willow questioned her. She'd always been fascinated by her mother's life before she was born but Cathy had never really wanted to answer her endless questions.

'I felt as though Dad was abandoning me,' Willow confessed. 'Dad and Luc.' She paused. 'Skye was leaving too and her parents were moving to Bournemouth and the Island just didn't feel like home anymore.'

'Your father never abandoned you,' Cathy said.

'I know. I know that now.'

When Willow looked back on that summer, she knew that she hadn't been abandoned. Everyone was leaving to pursue their own dreams, to spread their wings and live their lives. Somewhere beneath all the anger and self-pity, Willow had been doing the same when she went to Cambridge. When she'd left the Island she'd been looking for her own tribe, somewhere she fitted in, with other people who were good at maths and weren't obsessed with guitar strings and chord structures.

'I left early because I didn't want to stay here without Dad and Luc,' Willow said. 'And I've always assumed that the reason you were happy to take me to Cambridge was because you didn't want to be here then, either.'

Cathy didn't reply. She didn't need to.

Willow had hoped that everything would happen instantaneously, the moment she arrived at Cambridge. She'd thought doors would open and new friends would appear. But the truth was that she'd spent most of her first year feeling homesick for somewhere she didn't even want to be, missing Luc, regretting not saying goodbye to him properly or waiting for him to call, and worrying about her mum all alone. She'd drunk too much and kissed too many strangers and hadn't worked as hard as she should have done. It hadn't been until the end of her first year when Charlie had asked her to go to the May Ball with him that she'd started to feel as though she could move on, as though she could find a new way of being.

'I'm sorry I haven't been back to the Island for such a long time,' she said. 'But you know how much Charlie hated it here.'

Cathy laughed gently. 'He really did, didn't he? Do you remember that time the tide came in and he got trapped at the far end of the beach?'

'He had to be rescued.' Willow smiled. Charlie hadn't understood Willow's life on the Island, the quietness of it, her mother's handmade mandolins. It was the polar opposite of the world in which he'd grown up, with his expensive education and his barrister father. 'He only likes beaches if the sand is white and the sea as warm as a bathtub.' Willow tried not to think about how she should be on honeymoon in the Maldives right now.

Willow had fallen into Charlie's way of living and between them they'd earned money and accumulated all the trappings of success – the life that Charlie had planned, the life that they had both said they wanted. And instead of going to the Island to visit Cathy over the years, Charlie had paid for Cathy to visit them, for premium hotels, front-row theatre tickets and teas at the Ritz.

'I don't mind that you didn't visit,' Cathy said. 'I'm not going to pretend that I was very comfortable with all those theatre trips and fancy hotels, but I thought you were happy and that's all that mattered to me. But now I can see that you're not happy and I wonder if you ever were.'

'I thought I had everything I ever wanted,' Willow replied echoing the words she had said to Skye.

'Everything you wanted or everything Charlie wanted?' Cathy asked.

How had Willow never seen this before? How had she never realised that in her quest to find a life away from the Island she had let Charlie take control of everything?

But if her life in London didn't fit and life on the Island didn't fit, then what was she supposed to do?

'You never talked about what happened between you and Luc at the end of that last summer,' Cathy said, asking about those months she had never wanted to talk about. 'You don't have to tell me, but I think I've got a good idea of what went on. The point is, have you let go of all that and moved on?'

'Of course I have,' Willow replied with more conviction than she felt. 'It was years ago.'

'Have you really dealt with it though?' Cathy persisted. 'Or have you just buried it down to get on with your life with Charlie? Because if you have I wouldn't be surprised if it all reared its ugly head again right before you were about to get married.'

'There was nothing to deal with,' Willow said dismissively but she knew her mother was right. If there was really nothing left to deal with why did her stomach flip over every time Luc Harrison smiled at her?

'Did you watch *American Stars*?' Cathy asked.

'Some of it,' Willow replied not wanting to admit that she had watched every episode in secret on her laptop when Charlie wasn't there, not wanting to admit that her thoughts had been turning to Luc a lot recently, more so than they had done for years.

'What did you think?'

'I thought he deserved to win.'

Over the last year Luc had been everywhere she turned. It had been the strangest feeling to hear people at work talking about this musician called Lucien Hawke and knowing that he was the boy she had grown up with. Willow had never told anybody about Luc after she left the Island and, when one of her colleagues worked out that they were the same age and grew up in the same place, she had just dismissed him as somebody she'd known at school, somebody who wasn't really in her group of friends. She'd ignored the gnawing feeling of guilt she'd felt whenever she'd said it. Luc had meant everything to her once and, try as she might, he ended up being impossible to forget.

'What did Charlie think?' Cathy asked.

'About what?'

'About your childhood friend on the TV show.'

'He didn't watch it,' Willow said quietly. 'I've never told Charlie about Luc.'

'You've never told him?'

'No.'

'Why?'

'Because Luc was my past and Charlie is my future.' She paused. 'Was my future.'

'The past comes to catch up with us all in the end, Willow.'

'That's very cryptic. What do you mean?'

'Do you still love Charlie?' Cathy asked.

The fact that Willow paused was answer enough. She certainly thought she loved him, but somehow that hadn't been enough in the end. It had seemed enough when she'd accepted his proposal on that Cornish beach, it had seemed enough when his mother had taken over the wedding planning and had told Willow that the church had a waiting list of well over a year. Willow hadn't really wanted that church, Charlie's mother had, but Willow had wanted everyone to be happy, so she'd agreed. She thought she loved Charlie enough for it not to matter.

'I don't know,' Willow replied, even though she was fairly sure she did know because all she could think about was Luc Harrison leaning against the doorframe of Skye's shop with his thumbs tucked into his pockets, that lazy smile playing on his lips. 'I thought I did, but how can I when I couldn't bring myself to marry him? When I've embarrassed myself and him in front of all his family and friends.' The feelings of anger and shame roiled in Willow's stomach again.

'Perhaps because someone else still has a piece of your heart,' Cathy replied. She had a strange faraway look in her eye and for a moment Willow didn't think she was talking about Charlie and her anymore. But who else could she be talking about?

'Mum—' she began.

'So what are you going to do?' Cathy interrupted as though she'd suddenly come back down to earth. 'Are you going back to London next week as planned?'

'I don't have a lot of choice,' Willow replied. 'I need to go back to work.'

'You don't want to take some leave?'

She could take some leave; she'd got enough owing to her. But she'd worked so hard to get where she was and she was reluctant to let that go, to seem weak in the face of adversity. Working in the City required extra fortitude, especially for women. But at the same time she didn't know if she could go back, if she could face what was waiting for her, and all because of an instinctual impulse that struck outside a church in Surrey last Saturday morning.

But maybe her mother needed her help. Cathy seemed to have a lot going on, problems with the festival for starters, not to mention that the next few weeks were the busiest of the year for The Music Shop. If Willow had to take leave for reasons other than purely selfish ones then perhaps work, and Charlie, would understand?

'Do you need my help?' she asked.

'Well,' Cathy said slowly. 'If you decided to stay for a while you could carry on helping me out in the shop while I sort all this out.' She waved her hand at the paperwork in front of her. 'The Big Festival starts next week and the shop is going to get really busy.'

'I found out this morning that I can still string a mandolin almost as well as you,' Willow replied.

'Of course you can,' Cathy said, and Willow felt a sudden sense of belonging – something she hadn't felt in years.

Coming back to the Island hadn't been anything like she'd expected – she'd thought she would hate being back and be desperate to leave, desperate to go back to her life in London. But far from being the claustrophobic small town that she remembered, so far Seaview had helped her to breathe and to be. Its big skies and beautiful beaches had made her realise that it was her life in London that felt too small, too tight.

Everything about being back had surprised her, from Skye's warm welcome to the way all her mother's friends had treated her as though she'd never been gone. Instead of remembering all the things she'd hated about the Island, her memories had come full circle to the good things – the music, the friendliness, the sound of the waves.

And Luc.

She hadn't expected to see Luc again.

'So are you going to stay?' Cathy asked interrupting her thoughts.

'I'm going to think about it,' Willow replied.

Willow's parents first started The Seaview Folk Festival in 1990. She and Luc were two at the time so it had been a part of her life for as long as she could remember. It began as a few friends coming together to play at the end of the festival season and rapidly grew into something so much more. Within a year the famous open mic night at The Three Doves pub had begun and, by the time Willow was four, the last night of the festival had moved to the beach and a portion of the profits were given to local charities.

It had always stayed relatively small for legal reasons. After the early days of the original Isle of Wight festival had wreaked havoc on the Island, in 1971 Parliament added a section to the Isle of Wight County Council Act stating that no open-air gatherings of more than 5,000 people would be allowed on the Island without a special permit and it was 2001 before the more famous Isle of Wight Festival started up again. Cathy and Don had always kept the numbers small; that way they were always guaranteed the necessary licences.

Until this year anyway.

Don had first come up with the idea of the festival just after Willow had been born. Both Cathy and Krystal were stuck on the Island with new babies while Don was on the road with whatever band needed a touring guitarist. They were both bored and missing touring, so Don had the bright idea that they should try to set something up locally. Nobody ever anticipated what a huge success the folk festival would come to be.

Coming back during the planning stages of the festival, Willow felt as though she had stepped out of an ordered life, a life filled with routine and discipline, and stepped into the chaos that was life on the Island. She tried not to think about Luc's crooked smile and his green eyes and instead she concentrated on scrolling through her phone, reading the messages Charlie had left, noticing that he hadn't been in touch for the last three days.

She knew she wouldn't be ready to go back to London in a week's time, but if she stayed on the Island there was so much uncertainty. She'd have to see Skye again and she'd have to talk to her about that afternoon in the pub. She owed Skye an apology for that at least. Luc would be here all summer as well and it would be impossible to avoid him as he was so involved with the festival. Could she spend a summer with him and not talk about what happened when he left?

And on top of everything else there was this mess with the festival. She wanted to find Roger Beck and tell him exactly what she thought of him. While that wouldn't help her mother's cause, it would help her get rid of some of her own frustration.

The festival had always made Cathy so happy and Willow had to make sure that it went ahead. She had no idea how, but she'd have to work it out because she knew that cancelling the festival would break her mother's heart.

Willow thought about that faraway look in her mother's eye when she'd spoken about someone else having a piece of her heart. Cathy was ostensibly talking about her still having feelings for Luc, but was there more to it? Did someone still have a piece of her mother's heart? Someone who wasn't her father?

Sometimes Willow wished that she had spoken to her mother more about what happened when she and Don had separated, but she'd been so wrapped up in herself and her feelings for Luc that summer, so wrapped up in dreading him leaving, dreading never seeing him again, that she hadn't noticed anything else.

And now she had to make a decision – whether to stay on the Island and help her mum make sure the festival went ahead or go back to London, back to the job she loved and had worked so hard for, back to her house and her mortgage.

Back to Charlie.

Logically there was no decision to make here – she couldn't afford to take the summer off. She had some savings but they wouldn't cover the huge mortgage that she and Charlie had on their central London apartment and she had every intention of paying her way, whatever might happen to her relationship. She had to go back to work.

Didn't she?

She couldn't let herself get sucked into the music and the gentle, slow pace of life. She couldn't let herself be lulled by the lap of the waves on the shore and the screech of the seagulls over the cliffs. She had to remember why she left in the first place. They were all different people now; they had all moved on. Skye's life might be here but Willow's was in

London. And Luc's life was clearly in America if that phone call was anything to go by.

Before she made any decision though she had to speak to Charlie.

When she finally called him the next morning his mobile rang out. It didn't go to voicemail and the ringtone sounded strange, as though he was abroad. But where would he have gone? He didn't answer the landline in their flat either and Willow hung up before the answer machine kicked in. She didn't want to listen to the sound of her own voice on the outgoing message. Her voice from a previous time, a happy time, the night they'd moved into that flat.

'We haven't seen him,' Charlie's secretary told Willow when she tried to call him at his office. 'Nobody has heard from him since before the...' She stopped abruptly.

'The wedding,' Willow finished for her. Charlie's secretary mumbled in agreement and hurried to get off the phone as though she was embarrassed to talk to Willow, as though her inability to get married was contagious.

She could call Charlie's parents but she didn't relish the thought of having to listen to them as they told her about all the shame she'd brought on the family and the money she'd wasted.

So she took the coward's way out and sent him an email.

8

Luc

Luc walked away from Seaview to the far end of the beach and thought about all the gigs he used to play with his mum and Cathy when he was a kid, the pubs he'd played in over his last couple of summers on the Island, the night he'd won the open mic competition at the Three Doves when he was only sixteen.

What had happened to that Luc? Where had he gone?

His phone rang and his agent's number flashed up on the screen again. He couldn't ignore the call again. He had to admit that he had nothing, not even the opening bars of a song.

'Hi,' he said, thinking about answering that call in Skye's kitchen, kicking himself for saying the word "sweetheart". He'd noticed how their eyebrows had shot up, how Willow had tried to leave as quickly as possible afterwards and how awkward it had felt when he'd spoken to her about the festival licences. He shouldn't have lied about Annelise but there were some things he couldn't talk about, some things that had to remain a secret.

'Luc,' his agent's voice bounced off a satellite somewhere, loud in his ear. 'What have you got for me?'

Luc took a breath. 'Nothing,' he admitted. 'I've got nothing.'

'We haven't spoken for three weeks and you've got nothing?'

'Nothing's changed,' Luc said quietly as he stood up and started to walk back along the beach. 'I still can't write anything. I'm still getting panic attacks. Christ knows how I'm going to get on a stage in two months' time.'

'You need help, Luc. I'm an agent, not a shrink. I think this is beyond my remit, but you need to do something. If you don't come back in September with enough material to fill an album, you're in breach of contract.'

'Can't you get me an extension?' Luc asked. 'Isn't that what I pay you for?'

'I can try, but it would mean telling the record company the truth. How comfortable are you with that?'

Not comfortable at all.

'Give me a couple of weeks,' Luc said. 'Can you do that?'

'I can do that,' his agent replied ending the call. Luc carried on walking, not really knowing where he was going.

The panic attacks had started the day he'd left for America. He'd spent the summer after his A levels in a kind of limbo trying to work out what to do with his life. He'd known Willow and Skye were leaving the Island, off to university, and he had resigned himself to stay, to work on his music, to get a job in one of the pubs and to be here when Willow came home for the holidays. He had thought everything would stay the same and he was comfortable with that – he'd never liked change or instability. He knew his mother had been planning to go to America for a long time, of course, but he'd never really thought about going with her until she'd told him she'd sorted out his visas as well.

'I'm not the only one who'll have a lot more opportunities over there,' she'd said.

Luc had been eighteen, he could have done anything he wanted but he could see only two choices in front of him – leaving with Krystal or staying on his own, knowing Willow would be away for weeks at a time. Neither choice had felt like the right one.

He'd been on the beach when he had his first panic attack. It had been early in the morning, too early to meet Willow at the beach hut as he'd promised, but he'd been too excited about seeing her, about the fact that she loved him too, to sleep. He'd got up and gone for a walk, writing songs in his head as he strolled along the shore, dreaming of the life that he and Willow could make together once she'd got her degree.

Out of nowhere he felt as though someone had tightened a vice around his chest. He'd thought he was dying. There hadn't been anyone else around, nobody to call on for help as he'd felt the breath being squeezed from his body and his heart feeling as though it was going to explode. His arms had hurt and his ribs had hurt and he could hear himself gasping for breath. He'd doubled over, his hands on his knees, and he'd closed his eyes but all he'd been able to see were red dots, which had frightened him even more.

He'd wanted to feel safe, to hide away. There had been fishing boats on the beach that morning and he had crawled into one of them and curled up into a ball. He had still been lying there hugging his knees to his chest like a small child when Don found him. Don had known exactly what was wrong and had sat in the boat with Luc, telling him everything was OK, that he wasn't going to die, until his breathing had slowed down and his vision had cleared and the pain in his arms had disappeared.

'It's a panic attack,' Don had said. 'It used to happen to me years ago before I went on stage. It's why I stopped playing solo.'

'You played solo?' Luc hadn't known that.

He'd smiled. 'Yeah, not for long though. I got a lot less anxious when I was in a group, that's why I formed The Laurels.'

Luc had nodded slowly; he'd understood. But he hadn't understood why it was happening to him right then. It made sense to feel like this before going on stage, although Luc never had, but why would it happen standing alone on a quiet beach on a day when he'd felt so happy?

'What happened earlier today or yesterday?' Don had asked. 'Anything out of the ordinary?'

He'd shaken his head. He could hardly have told Willow's father about the previous night.

'I'm just scared about…' he'd begun, but he'd had to stop talking as the tight feeling around his heart had returned at the thought of going to America, of not seeing Willow for months or even years.

'About America?' Don had asked and Luc had nodded.

'Well you know I'm going to be coming with you,' Don

had continued. 'I'm not going to stay in Nashville for long but I am going to go with your mum, help her settle in. You don't have to worry, Luc; everything will be OK.'

But it hadn't been OK. It had taken hours for Don to calm him down and by the time he'd got to the beach hut it was locked up, Willow had long gone. He hadn't been able to find her until she came to say goodbye that evening and by then it was too late. He'd always wondered what would have happened if he had been brave enough to tell her the truth about that day. Instead he'd let her think that he didn't care, that he'd slept with her and then discarded her the next day.

And he'd never forgiven himself for that.

When Luc put his phone back into his pocket, his agent's voice still echoing in his ears, he realised he was on the same stretch of beach that he had been on when he had that first panic attack. The fishing boats weren't there anymore and there was a new café on the promenade, but this was the place where it had all begun. Those panic attacks had plagued him for years and he'd only ever told a handful of people about them.

This was where it had begun. Perhaps this was where it needed to end.

9

February 1984

'You've done what?' Brian Cole shouted at his daughter as she sat on the sofa in the living room of her parents' house.

'I've left the Academy,' Cathy repeated as calmly as she could. 'I've quit my degree course.'

'But why?' Cathy's father was pale, his tone clipped. 'Why on earth would you give up on your dreams like that?'

'I have other dreams now,' Cathy said. 'Besides, I won't be here.'

'Won't be here,' Brian repeated, standing up. 'What nonsense. Where will you be?'

'On tour with Storm Tyler,' Cathy said, her voice soft.

'Storm Tyler!' Brian shouted. 'Over my dead body you will. You'll sit there, and you won't move and if you're not going to finish your degree then you'll get a job.'

As her father walked out of the room, slamming the door in his wake, Cathy thought of all sorts of things she could shout back at him. Like how was she supposed to get a job if she wasn't allowed to move off the sofa? But she'd promised herself that she wouldn't do that, she'd promised herself that if she was going to live her dream then she was going to do it like an adult. She was nearly nineteen now and she could do anything she wanted.

Everything had happened so quickly from that day in December when she had met Storm again in his dressing room at the Astoria. He had got in touch with her at the Academy the week afterwards and taken her out for dinner at a small, dark Moroccan restaurant in Soho. Cathy had never really been into the labyrinth of streets behind Leicester Square at night before and had felt a mix of fascination and embarrassment as she walked past the neon signs that advertised the strip clubs. She'd noticed Storm smiling to himself as he walked next to her and she'd felt naïve and hopeless.

'I want to hear you play,' he'd said, cutting to the chase as they ate their couscous. Cathy had never eaten anything like it before and wasn't sure she was enjoying the different spices and the apricots and sultanas that were mixed in. She'd thought it was probably an acquired taste. She wasn't sure she enjoyed eating while sitting on a cushion on the floor either, or the unmistakable smell of marijuana that drifted from the room at the back of the restaurant. She knew that if she wanted to inhabit the world Storm lived in, she had a lot to learn.

'You do?' she'd replied surprised, fork frozen halfway to her mouth.

'Of course I do,' he'd said, grinning at her. 'There's something about you, Cathy Cole, and I want to help you find what you're looking for, because I don't believe for a moment that you're going to find it at The Royal Academy.' He'd said those last words with a hint of a sneer as though he had no time for the formalities of music training, as though true art came from the soul – and Cathy agreed with him. Only a few months into her course and she was bored already; bored of the violin, bored of the piano, bored of the theory and the tediously dry lectures. All she wanted was to be on a stage, playing her music, feeling the rhythm.

Storm hadn't said anything else about it, hadn't told her when he wanted to hear her play or where – instead, as they ate, he'd told her about his life on the road, the music he was writing and the solo album he was planning.

'King Silver are important to me, but I think it's time I did something new to get the creative juices flowing, you know?'

Cathy had nodded but she didn't know. How could she know?

But what she did know was that she was ready for something else, something more exciting than anything the Academy could offer her. She had a feeling she was sitting on a cushion opposite her destiny and she had made sure she'd come prepared. Since she had last seen Storm the previous autumn, Cathy had been working hard – not on her college work, much to the consternation of her tutors, but on her own songs. If Storm wanted to hear her play, at least she had something to play for him now.

'You're not really enjoying that are you?' Storm had asked, nodding at the plate of couscous Cathy had hardy touched. She'd looked away blushing with embarrassment.

'Not really.'

'Shall we go and get some chips?'

They'd eaten hot chips soaked in vinegar out of paper bags as they'd walked through the freezing cold streets of London at night, as drunken revellers fell into them and men in business suits hurried past.

'How can I contact you?' Storm had asked as Cathy crumpled up her chip wrappers.

'We have a payphone,' Cathy had replied thinking about the bedsit she shared with Pip. 'But it's down the hall and anyone can answer it.'

'Not ideal. What are you doing next Thursday?'

'Nothing I guess,' Cathy had said with a shrug. She was desperately trying to sound nonchalant while fate took control of her destiny.

'Play for me then. I'll get a message to you.'

He'd flagged down a black cab for her then, much to her disappointment, signalling the evening to be over. As she'd got in he bent to kiss her cheek.

'Until Thursday,' he'd said.

Cathy had spent almost the whole week practising the two songs she knew were her strongest – one was a Ballad Book song and the other was one she'd written herself. She'd skipped lectures and tutorials to stay at home and practise, only going into the Academy to check her pigeonhole for the longed-for note from Storm. By the time it had arrived on Wednesday morning she'd all but given up, assuming Storm had changed his mind and was preparing herself to go back to her course with a sufficient excuse to explain her absence that week. She'd felt sick with relief when the note finally came.

Storm had an apartment in an unassuming building near Green Park station. He'd buzzed Cathy up when she'd arrived and had told her to come to the top floor. The lift was an art deco design from the 1920s with a wrought-iron gate that made a precarious ascent. Cathy had clutched the case of her mandolin and hoped she'd practised enough.

Storm's flat was a melting pot of styles, painted white with modern art covering the walls and cushions and throws that looked as though they came from Africa and the Middle East scattered about. The flat had smelled of spices and something else that Cathy hadn't been able to put her finger on. He'd made her herbal tea and told her to take her time, but she had needed to get it over with. Storm had a small room at the back of the apartment where he practised – his acoustic guitars and mandolins lined the walls and every surface was littered with empty coffee cups, beer bottles and screwed-up balls of paper.

'Sorry about the mess,' he'd said, his green eyes glinting. 'This is where I've been writing and I didn't really think about anybody else being here. We can use the living room if you prefer.'

'Here's fine,' Cathy had replied, sitting down on a stool and beginning to tune her mandolin.

She'd played both pieces back to back with barely a pause in between. She hadn't looked at Storm while she played but she'd felt his eyes on her, watching her every move. When she'd finished she finally looked at him.

'That second piece,' he'd said. 'Where's that from?'

'I wrote it,' she'd replied quietly.

'I like it,' he'd said thoughtfully, scratching the stubble on his chin and still not taking his eyes off her. 'And I like you. Do you have more material?'

She'd nodded and Storm had continued to look quietly at her. She'd felt as though he was undressing her somehow, trying to see what lay underneath.

'Let's have a beer,' he'd said eventually.

One beer had led to several, to a Chinese takeaway followed by a spliff. When he'd kissed her Cathy had known that she wouldn't be going home that night and when he'd inevitably taken her to bed she hadn't told him that it was her first time.

'You're my muse, Cathy Cole,' he'd whispered later that night. 'You have been for a long time.'

The next morning Storm had told her about the solo tour he was doing in the summer and he'd asked her to come with him. This was the big break Cathy had been waiting for since that day at the Reading Festival over two years before and there was nothing her father could do to stop her.

10

It was early when Willow opened up The Music Shop on Saturday morning and, despite it being nearly midsummer, the sun was still low in the sky. She'd woken just before dawn to the sounds of seagulls squawking from the beach behind the house and hadn't been able to get back to sleep for thinking about Charlie, wondering where he was and who he was with. Just a week ago she'd been unable to sleep because it had been her wedding day.

She turned on the lights and unlocked the display cabinets and walked to the back of the shop to unlock the door to Cathy's workshop where the safe with the day's petty cash was. Willow had always loved her mother's workshop. It smelled of wood and glue and potential. This was where Cathy did the work she was so extraordinary at, the work Willow couldn't possibly emulate – Willow might be able to string a guitar or mandolin but this was where her mother made them by hand. She looked at the beautifully curved pieces of wood that lay on the countertop and wondered whose hands they would end up in and what music they would help to create.

She set up the cash register, anticipating a busy day ahead. The Big Festival started in less than a week and that usually meant a lot of business for The Music Shop. She leant against the shop counter and looked out of the big plate glass window towards the sea. The shop doorbell jangled behind her.

'We're not open yet,' she said without turning around. But she already knew who it was.

'Hello, Willow,' he said, and her stomach flipped over.

How could Luc Harrison still do this to her after all these years? A week ago she had been getting ready to marry Charlie and now she couldn't get Luc out of her head. She shouldn't be thinking about Luc, or the person who phoned him, the person who he'd called "sweetheart". She should be thinking about Charlie who hadn't replied to her email.

She turned around and Luc handed her a takeaway coffee.

'What are you doing here so early?' she asked, taking the cup from him.

'I couldn't sleep,' Luc replied. 'Would you like a chocolate croissant?'

She didn't usually eat carbs – part of the strict regime created for her by the personal trainer that Charlie paid for, but there was nothing usual about her life right now, so she took one anyway, biting into it with relish and savouring the warm chocolatey flavour. It had been a long time since she allowed herself anything like this. She'd been concentrating on fitting into her wedding dress.

'Did you talk to your mum about the festival?' Luc asked.

'That's why I'm here looking after the shop,' she said. 'So Mum can work out the best course of action with the council.'

Standing in the shop with Luc reminded Willow so much of her past and of all the things that she had pushed aside to make way for her life with Charlie. She could remember the day Cathy first opened The Music Shop. She'd been ten years old and the party had gone on all day and half of the night, spilling out onto the beach. She'd played the mandolin with her dad and danced with Luc as the moon came up. The memory was as clear as if it had happened yesterday. Willow had never seen her mum as happy as she had been that day.

It had been Don's idea that Cathy turn her skill with musical instruments into a business and at first all they were looking for was a workshop space to rent so that Cathy didn't have to make guitars on the kitchen table. But when they found the shop unit that looked out over the sea and when they discovered that the rent was affordable, The Music Shop became a reality and it had become something of a celebrity in its own right.

'You know who's behind all these difficulties with the council permissions, don't you?' Willow asked bringing herself back to the present.

Luc's mouth was full of croissant so he couldn't reply. He just raised his eyebrows in question.

'Roger bloody Beck,' she said. 'Do you remember him?'

She watched him swallow. 'That little...' He stopped, taking a gulp of coffee. 'He's still making a nuisance of himself then.'

'He's a councillor now and taking out the full weight of his endless disapproval on the festival licences.'

'Who voted for him?'

'I asked the same question but Mum says everyone is denying it.'

'Someone must have!' Luc smiled, and it lit up the whole room. Willow watched Luc licking the crumbs of his croissant off his fingers and her stomach fizzed again. She looked away.

'How long are you staying?' he asked.

'Not long,' she replied. 'I have to go back to work next week.' But as soon as she said the words, she knew she wouldn't be. The thought of going back to London made her feel uncomfortable in a way she didn't want to think about too much and she turned to look out of the window towards the sea.

'So you're not staying for the festival?'

'It's strange being back,' Willow said, ignoring his question. 'You must feel that too.'

'It is, but I did come here for a reason,' he replied. 'Why did you come back?'

'I didn't have anywhere else to go,' she admitted, meeting his eyes as she turned towards him.

'Serendipity, like Skye said.' Luc leaned over the shop counter towards her. He was so close she could smell his aftershave. The electricity between them was as strong as it ever had been and as Luc's gaze dropped to her lips she felt her breath catch in her throat. When the shop bell jangled they both nearly jumped out of their skins.

'Disturbing something?' asked the new arrival.

'Dad!' Willow exclaimed, walking around the counter to greet him as he enveloped her in a huge bear hug. 'What are you doing here? You're not due back until next week!'

'I came back early,' Don replied. 'I needed to see my little girl. How are you, Willow? I've been so worried.'

'I'm OK, Dad,' Willow said quietly, stepping away from her father. 'You didn't need to rush back; you didn't need to cancel gigs for me.' She paused. 'But I'll admit that it's so good to see you.' She hadn't seen her father enough over the years and she was overwhelmed with regret.

'I flew over on Rocco Beezon's private jet,' Don said with a grin.

'Rocco's here?' Willow asked.

Rocco Beezon was a friend of Willow's dad. He was also the lead singer of a rather famous band from Seattle. He was one of those people who look like they haven't had a wash in a while but was actually a multi-millionaire.

'He's headlining The Big Festival on Friday,' Don replied.

Don walked over to where Luc was standing and slapped him on the back.

'Good to see you, mate,' he said leaning against the shop counter. 'How are you?'

Luc shrugged and Willow saw a look pass between the two men that she couldn't work out, as though Don knew something about Luc that nobody else did.

'Must be nice for you two to catch up after all this time,' Don said.

'She's the same but different,' Luc responded, looking at Willow.

'It's weird,' Willow said. 'Everything's weird.' Luc smiled and she felt her breath catch again. She dipped her head and looked away. She hadn't felt awkward with Luc this morning, not like she had the first time he was here, or in Skye's shop. But now her father had arrived and she didn't want him to get the wrong idea – it had only been a week since her disaster of a wedding.

'Where are you staying, Dad?' she asked. 'At the house?'

'No, I'm staying with Rocco. He's renting a place in the same apartment block as you, Luc.'

'It'll be good to catch up with him,' Luc said, without much enthusiasm. 'I stayed with him earlier in the year,' he explained to Willow. 'When I was recording in LA.'

Luc's life must be so different these days but he still felt so familiar. She'd seen him three times now and he hadn't really told her anything about his life; he hadn't even mentioned *American Stars*. But why would he? They weren't friends anymore, not really. Luc Harrison was in her past. The chemistry she was feeling was nothing but old memories.

'Anyway,' Don said. 'I'm jet-lagged and need a sleep but your mum said I could pick up a ukulele that she's made for Rocco.'

'Did she say where it was?' Willow asked.

'Still in the workshop,' Don replied. 'It's the only one there. I can get it—'

'No,' Willow interrupted. 'I'll go.' She was glad of the excuse to step away into her mum's workshop – the excuse to have a moment alone, away from Luc.

The workshop was messy but Willow spotted the ukulele straight away. It needed stringing and she started to hunt around for an open packet so as not to break into one of the new packs in the shop. There were plenty of guitar strings scattered about, but the steel would break the delicate bridge of the ukulele. She started to open drawers, hunting for the nylon strings she needed.

She knew she was using the ukulele strings as an avoidance

tactic – she could easily take this ukulele out to her dad as it was and Rocco could find his own damn strings. Rocco Beezon had that same sense of entitlement that so many of her parents' friends did – it was one of the reasons she'd wanted to get away from musicians in the first place. They always seemed to think that what they wanted should come first. But she kept looking for the ukulele strings anyway to avoid being near Luc. Not that being in a separate room stopped her from thinking about him.

The nylon strings were in the last drawer she looked in, but as she pulled them out, something else fell out with them – a black plastic rectangular box – something Willow hadn't seen in about twenty years. She put the strings to one side as she opened the box. Inside, as she'd suspected, was a DAT – a digital audio tape, something that a lot of recording artists had used during the Eighties and Nineties. Her parents' band used to record to DAT and Willow remembered listening to early versions of their songs on tapes just like this.

But what was it doing here? Willow knew that her mother kept all The Laurels' old recordings meticulously archived in the attic back at her house. It was one of the few things she was truly organised about and she wouldn't have left one of the tapes here amongst this jumble of ukulele strings.

She examined the tape and found an inscription, written in pencil on the inlay card – NF/GG/Aug 1999. Willow knew that this had nothing to do with The Laurels – Cathy had never labelled their recordings like that. She felt goose bumps on her arms as she wondered what she'd found and why it had been hanging around for the last nineteen years.

It could just be junk of course – but there was something about it that made her think otherwise.

11

Luc

Despite her father being right next to him, Luc couldn't take his eyes off Willow until she disappeared into her mum's workshop. He had to stop thinking about her. He had to stop seeking her out. Willow was his past. He had to think about his future now.

'How does she seem, do you think?' Don asked when Willow was out of earshot.

'It's hard to tell,' Luc replied. 'Like I said on the phone I haven't seen her for so long but…' He paused.

'But what?'

'There's something she's not talking about,' Luc went on. 'I don't think she's telling anyone why she walked away from her wedding.'

'Maybe she doesn't know,' Don said.

'Maybe.'

'And how about you?' Don asked. 'How are you doing?'

'I'm fine.' But he felt so far from fine right now.

Don looked at him for a moment as though weighing something up. 'You're writing again?' he asked.

Luc nodded and turned away so that Willow's dad couldn't see the lie in his face.

'Are you here all summer?' Luc asked, changing the subject.

'I'm here for as long as Willow needs me.'

'She says she's going back to London next week, back to work.'

'I don't think that's a very good idea,' Don replied. 'It would be nice if she stayed a bit longer don't you think?'

'I guess,' Luc replied, refusing to think about how much he wanted Willow to stay.

He could see that Don knew he was lying about writing again. He and Luc had talked about the anxiety and the writer's block when they had both been staying at Rocco's place in LA earlier in the year, just before everything had got so bad that Luc had stopped working completely.

By the time he had arrived in LA he had already known that he needed to come back to the Island, but he hadn't imagined for a moment that Willow and Skye would be here too. He wanted to tell Willow everything but he didn't know where to start. He didn't know if he should tell her anything at all now that these old feelings were floating back to the surface.

Before he had time to think too much about it, Willow came back with the ukulele.

'Sorry it took so long,' she said. 'It needed stringing.'

Don smiled, taking it from her. 'I could have done that.'

Willow shrugged. 'It's done now,' she said.

'Well I'll see you two later,' Don went on, stifling a yawn. 'I need to go to bed.'

'That's not very rock 'n' roll, Dad.'

'I'm an old man now, my love,' Don said as he left. 'I need my beauty sleep.'

Once her father had left the shop Willow put something down on the counter in front of her. 'I took a long time because I found this,' she said quietly sliding the object towards Luc. He picked up the DAT and turned it over in his hands. He hadn't seen one of these for years – most musicians stopped recording to DAT over a decade ago.

'The Laurels used to record on these didn't they?' he said looking at her. 'I wonder what's on it?'

'How would we even play it to find out? Does anyone still have DAT players?' She seemed odd, almost shifty as though she didn't want anyone else to see the tape. 'Even the studio uses Pro Tools these days.'

'Tom Newell has bought Pro Tools?' Luc asked, surprised that he'd stepped into the digital age. Tom Newell had arrived on the Island nearly twenty years ago and had taken over the small recording studio that was attached to The Music Shop. Don and Cathy had built it originally just to record for The Laurels but musicians visiting the Island over the summer often wanted to record while they were there so they had been happy to hand the day-to-day management over to Tom when he asked about it. Over the years many famous records had been made there, as Tom was happy to tell anyone who had the misfortune of getting into a long and boring conversation with him.

'I guess Tom might still have a DAT player though,' Luc said as he turned the tape over in his hands and noticed the pencil inscription on the inside of the case. This recording, whatever it was, had been hanging around for a long time, but what did NF/GG mean?

A sensation that felt like a memory but not quite as strong washed over him as he looked at the tape. It felt as though he was trying to grab hold of something, but it slithered out of his fingers. He was suddenly very aware that this tape was significant somehow. He put it back on the counter and Willow immediately picked it up and put it in the back pocket of her jeans.

'It's probably just an old recording of Mum's,' she said. 'And if it is then we shouldn't listen without checking with her first.'

Luc wanted to step closer to her, lean across the counter towards her, his eyes on her lips as they had been when Don walked in.

He needed to get away from her, to do something, anything, to take his mind off her, off the past, off the fact he couldn't seem to write music anymore. He looked at her again and their eyes locked. He couldn't help himself as he kissed her on the cheek.

'It is lovely to see you again, Willow,' he said. 'I hope you decide to stay for longer than just another week.'

The bell jangled behind him as he left, and he could still feel the sensation of her skin on his lips.

12

June 1984

Cathy spent the next few months practising her songs and writing new ones. By early summer she had nearly an hour's worth of material that she was confident with and Storm asked her if she was ready to play in front of an audience.

She had seen Storm once a week since the night she had spent at his apartment. He would take her out to dinner and then they would go back to his flat and get stoned and play music together before falling into bed in the early hours of the morning. Cathy had never felt more beautiful, more independent, more grown up in her life.

Brian had stopped paying her half of the rent on the bedsit when Cathy dropped out of the Academy and, when she told Storm about this, a part of her had hoped that he would ask her to move in with him. But instead he had offered to pay the rent for her instead. There was something about this that made Cathy a little uncomfortable, the first time she had ever felt uncomfortable with Storm since the day she met him, but she was in no position to argue. When the first rent cheque arrived she found out once and for all that Storm's real name was Neil as she'd suspected.

'I'm ready,' she told Storm when he asked her if she thought she'd like to play for an audience. She didn't feel ready but she knew she couldn't just keep playing the same songs over and over again in her bedsit or Storm's apartment. She had to get out there and feel the fear.

It was just a small pub on a street parallel to the one Storm lived on, but it was crowded with folk fans, most of whom were star-struck to find Storm Tyler there and disappointed to discover that he wasn't playing. Despite that, Cathy's set was well received and, afterwards, she felt a sense of accomplishment that she had never felt when she was at the Academy.

Storm caught her arm as she came off stage, the crowd still cheering as she left.

'Play with me,' he said, his green eyes glinting.

'On stage?' Cathy asked stupidly. She couldn't believe she was about to play on stage with Storm Tyler.

'Of course on stage.' Storm grinned. 'Where else?'

They played "Gamble Gold" as an encore, to an appreciative crowd. It was a song they'd played together many times late at night at Storm's apartment and the song that Cathy felt had sealed her fate when she had first heard Storm perform it at the Astoria nearly a year before.

Had it really been less than a year? Life could change on the turn of a coin.

'You are ready, aren't you?' Storm had whispered to her as he trailed kisses down her collarbone, his fingers entwined in her long blonde hair, in the small room at the back of the pub as they packed their mandolins away. Cathy's stomach fizzed, not just at his touch but at the thought of touring with him, opening for him in just a few weeks' time.

'Lucky bitch,' Pip said the next day when Cathy told her about it. Cathy had been disappointed Pip hadn't turned up at the pub to see her play the night before. She wondered if Pip were jealous and if this somehow marked an end to their friendship. The thought of it made her feel sad. She wondered how many other people she would end up leaving behind.

A few days before the start of Storm's solo tour Cathy met up with her mother in the café at Liberty's.

'It's not too late you know,' her mother said.

'Too late for what?' Cathy replied.

'To stop all of this. To cancel this tour with Storm, to go back to university or to come home with me. It's not too late.'

'I'm not cancelling the tour,' Cathy said stubbornly, sticking her chin out.

'You know your father will never speak to you again if you go.'

'That's not my problem,' Cathy said. 'Or my choice,' she added quietly.

'Oh we always have a choice,' her mother replied.

For a few moments they sat in silence, drinking their tea, listening to the murmur of conversations around them and the gentle clink of teaspoons against china.

'Do you agree with Dad?' Cathy asked eventually in a small voice.

Her mother shook her head. 'No,' she replied. 'I think he's being stubborn. I think we must let our children go out and make their own mistakes, so if you ever need me, Catherine, I will be there. All you have to do is call, OK?'

Cathy nodded and shortly after made her excuses and left. As she stepped back out onto Regent Street, she blinked back the tears in her eyes.

13

Willow

The first thing Willow thought about when she woke up the next morning was the tape. She hadn't been able to stop thinking about it since she'd found it, but at least it had stopped her thinking about Luc's eyes, or his smile, or the sensation of his lips against her cheek. She should be thinking about Charlie, about her future and his place in it – if she even had the right to decide that anymore. She shouldn't be thinking about tapes or Luc or that spark that still seemed to be there between them.

Willow had seen the way Luc had examined the DAT the day before and she couldn't work out if he knew something about it or not. But she did know she had to find a way of listening to it without telling her mother. It might just be an old recording of The Laurels, but she knew that if she told her mum that she'd found it, Cathy would dismiss the tape and it would disappear forever.

The only answer was to talk to Tom Newell, to listen to his endless anecdotes and to find out if he had an old DAT player. But she didn't have time for that today. First she had to see how far her mother had got with the planning permissions and then she had to have lunch with Skye.

She wasn't much looking forward to either.

Skye had come into The Music Shop not long after Luc had left the previous day.

'I haven't got long,' she'd said. 'Saturday is my busiest day, but Luc says you're going back to London next week and I wanted to catch up with you before you went.'

Willow had nodded, ignoring that uncomfortable feeling that she got every time she thought about going back to work.

'Well, can you come over for lunch tomorrow?'

'I'll have to check with Mum.'

'Please, Willow.' And Willow had felt as though she didn't have a choice.

Skye had made soup, which she served with home-made bread and salad. She reminded Willow so much of Cherry, Skye's mum, not just in the way she looked and the food she served, but her every gesture, the way she stood. Looking at Skye now made Willow feel nostalgic, as though she wanted to go to Bournemouth and find Cherry and hug her in exchange for all the hugs she had given her in the past.

'Do you live here alone?' she asked, pushing the memories away.

'Mostly, although Bob visits when he can.'

'Bob?' Willow asked.

Skye grinned the unmistakable grin of a woman in love. 'He's my boyfriend,' she said. 'He still works in London and lives in Southampton but we're hoping he'll be able to move here soon.'

Willow nodded, not knowing what else to say to avoid the conversation she knew she had to have. Her mouth felt dry.

'Skye, that last time I saw you,' she began. 'In the pub…'

'Don't worry about it, Willow,' Skye said waving her soup spoon in the air. 'It was a long time ago.'

'I need to apologise.'

'You don't need to apologise for what Charlie said,' Skye replied. 'It's him who should be apologising, but I'm guessing I probably won't see him again.' She smiled and Willow knew that things were going to be all right.

She had been so excited to see Skye that lunchtime. She'd only been in London a few months and she'd known that Skye was there, working as an apprentice in a tattoo studio in Camden. They had arranged to meet in a nearby pub.

'We'll eat sandwiches and drink cider,' Skye had said. 'If we try to imagine the sound of the sea it'll be just like old times.'

Willow had been disappointed when Charlie's tennis match had been cancelled and he'd decided to join them for lunch.

'It'll be nice to meet one of your old friends,' he'd said. By that time Charlie and Willow never went back to the Island. They'd stopped going when Charlie got stranded by the tide and had to be rescued.

Lunch hadn't gone as planned and all hopes of drinking cider and reminiscing about life on the Island had been scuppered by Charlie's presence. Willow had been very aware of the two different parts of her life that were meeting around the pub table that afternoon and she'd been careful not to talk too much about Luc, or what had happened just before he left for America. It wasn't hard not to talk about old times as Charlie kept up an almost constant monologue about his job, their flat, their life in London and how well Willow had done "considering her background". Willow had wanted to kick him. Had he any idea how rude he was being?

After an hour Skye had made her excuses and left.

'Maybe we'll do it again sometime, Willow,' she'd said.

'I don't think so,' Charlie had replied. He'd been smiling when he said it and for a moment Willow had thought she'd misheard.

'How could you be so rude?' she'd said as Skye had walked away. Charlie had shrugged and Willow had chased after Skye, catching up with her in the street outside and almost begging her to try again sometime. But Skye had shaken her head, telling Willow that they'd both changed too much. As she walked towards the tube station she turned around.

"It's not you, Willow," she'd said. "It's the company you keep."

Charlie and Willow had argued about it when they'd got home – of course they had – but Willow knew that the life she had with Charlie was the life she had chosen, the life that she wanted too.

'People change, sweetheart,' Charlie had said. 'And they move on. It's not very nice but it is just part of life.'

She'd gone to bed after that telling herself that Charlie was right. Skye wasn't part of her life anymore.

'I don't need to apologise for Charlie,' Willow said now. 'But I do need to apologise for not standing up to him, for not telling him he was wrong.'

Skye nodded. 'I just figured that you'd changed, that you'd got off the Island and away from music like you wanted and found your people somewhere else. But I kept thinking about that afternoon over the years and...' She trailed off.

'And what?' Willow asked, trying not to sound defensive.

'What I said was pretty harsh too, and I'm sorry for that. But I've always wondered if that life really was what you wanted or if it was what Charlie had convinced you that you wanted.'

Willow didn't say anything for a moment, it was a question her mother had posed as well and honestly, she didn't know the answer to it anymore.

'Is that what you meant the other day when you said you never believed me about wanting that life in London?' she asked eventually.

'I guess,' Skye replied thoughtfully. 'There was just something about that afternoon that never rang true for me.' She shrugged and tore off a piece of bread. 'But I'm not going to pretend I'm sorry you didn't marry him.'

Willow laughed then, surprised at how easy this felt. She'd thought it was going to be hard; she'd built this apology in her head up into something it didn't need to be. Was that what she was doing with Luc as well?

'Charlie came along at the right time,' she said. 'I met him at the end of my first year at Cambridge. Most of that first year was awful. I lurched constantly between wanting to come home and never wanting to set foot on the Island again. I was so angry with my dad for leaving and with Krystal for taking him away and with Mum for not forcing him to stay. I didn't know what was going on, but Charlie changed everything. Meeting him gave my life meaning again and I was able to start over.'

'And yet you couldn't marry him?' There was no judgement in her question.

'I never told Charlie about Luc,' Willow said slowly. 'I put Luc in a box in my head and I tried not to open it. But then he went and almost won *American Stars* and everyone I knew was talking about him. When they found out he was from the Isle of Wight I had to admit to vaguely knowing him.'

'Vaguely?' Skye repeated, raising her eyebrows.

'I know.'

'Is this why you couldn't go through with the wedding?' Skye asked. 'Because you'd lied to your fiancé? And because maybe seeing Luc all over the TV again made you remember him – sprung him out of the little box in your head?'

'Maybe,' she replied. 'Although none of that was going through my head when I decided not to go through with it. It was a very instinctive decision. Although...' She paused.

'Although what?'

'I feel as though I'm missing something.'

'Something about you and Charlie?'

Willow nodded, that uneasy feeling returning, making goose bumps appear on her arms. What was she missing? What was it about Charlie's behaviour recently that had made her run away?

'I never told you this,' Willow said, changing the subject, 'but Luc and I slept together the night before he left. He told me he loved me and...' She paused. She couldn't believe it still hurt after all these years.

'And you never told Charlie about him?' Skye asked, her eyebrows raised.

'No,' Willow admitted. 'But that wasn't what I was going to say.'

'I kind of figured the two of you must have slept together at some point that summer,' Skye said. 'I spent half the time feeling like a spare part watching you make eyes at each other.'

'Firstly,' Willow said. 'We were not that bad! And secondly...' She paused again.

'Secondly what?' Skye asked gently.

'We were meant to meet up the next morning at the beach hut. We'd planned to spend his last day on the Island together but he never turned up and I couldn't get hold of him. I didn't see him until he was leaving for Southampton airport that night and we had to say this awful, awkward goodbye in front of my parents and his mum.'

'Why did you never tell me any of this?'

Willow sighed. 'Because I was embarrassed and ashamed. I thought everything he'd said had been a line and I'd fallen for it. It was easier just to keep quiet and leave for university as soon as possible.'

'Well that answers a few questions,' Skye said, tapping her finger on the table. 'But I doubt anything he said to you that summer was a line, just to get you into bed.'

'What other explanation is there?'

'I don't know, I guess you'll have to ask him.' Skye paused. 'Why have you never asked him before?' she asked. 'Why did you never give Luc a chance to explain where he was that day?'

'Because it wasn't just about Luc,' Willow replied quietly. 'It's taken me years to realise this but when both he and Dad left together, I felt as though they were both abandoning me.

I always pretended I was OK about Mum and Dad splitting up and Dad leaving but…' She trailed off, unable to find the words for what she was beginning to realise.

'But you weren't OK,' Skye said.

Willow shook her head. 'I felt so angry and resentful and I think by not acknowledging that to myself or anyone else it allowed me to ignore my past, to pretend it hadn't happened.' She looked away from Skye for a moment. 'And that left a big open space in my life for Charlie to swoop in.'

Skye was quiet for a moment. 'I had no idea you felt like that,' she said after a while.

'Why should you? I didn't really realise myself.'

'I can't say anything about your relationship with your dad – I never knew him that well,' Skye went on. 'And perhaps it doesn't matter anymore but I'm fairly sure Luc meant everything he said to you that summer. He was crazy about you; he always had been.'

'Really?'

'Really, and if the way he was looking at you the other day was anything to go by I'd say he still is.'

Willow surprised herself with the bubble of laughter that burst out of her. 'Don't be ridiculous,' she said. 'Even if you're right about when we were kids, it's been twelve years and he's moved on. You heard him on the phone the other day.'

'Ah,' Skye replied with a smile. 'The mysterious "sweetheart".'

'Yes. There's no way that was his agent. Didn't you think it was odd?'

'What's really odd is that Luc told me he wasn't seeing anyone,' Skye said.

'You asked him?'

'Yeah, when he first arrived, before you came back,' Skye went on. 'He told me his life in America was complicated, that he needed some time out, which is why he came back to the Island. I assumed it was girlfriend trouble but he told me that a girlfriend would just complicate everything even more.'

Willow tried to ignore the sinking feeling in her stomach – as if she was ever going to be Luc Harrison's girlfriend anyway.

'Maybe it was his agent,' she mused.

'Or a groupie!' Skye replied, her eyes sparkling.

'Do you think he has groupies?' Willow asked. 'What a weird thought.'

'Who knows? You know better than I do what wankers musicians can be!' Skye broke into laughter and Willow couldn't help but join in.

Later as she was leaving, Skye said, 'Maybe you should talk to Luc about the day he left.'

'Maybe,' Willow replied reluctantly.

'Perhaps it's time you allowed him to explain.'

Willow nodded, knowing Skye was right. She had always known that something had happened that morning that had stopped him coming to the beach hut. He'd hinted at it in the letters he'd written but he hadn't told her what it was so she'd assumed at the time it was a lie. But Luc had never been that sort of person.

'It's so good to see you again,' Skye said, wrapping Willow in a huge hug. 'I wish you were staying for the whole summer.'

Willow stepped away and looked down Seaview High

Street towards the sea. The gulls circled overhead, waiting for a tourist to drop a chip. She had felt so comfortable with Skye today and she could feel the familiarity of the Island, the familiarity of her childhood, wrapping itself around her. Every day that she stayed the Island felt more like home. Every day that she stayed she felt the mandolins in her mother's shop calling out to her to play them. She didn't want to go back to London, but the thought of everything she would be giving up if she didn't, made her stomach churn.

'I'll see you before I go,' she said.

'That would be great,' Skye replied. 'Today has felt just like old times.'

And when she smiled, Willow knew exactly what she had to do.

'Michael, it's Willow,' she said as her boss at the bank answered her call on Monday morning.

'Hello, Willow,' Michael replied. 'I was wondering if you'd call. Marcy told us what happened.'

Marcy was the only person from Willow's work who had come to her wedding, the only person Willow had invited. Willow had been compartmentalising her life for so long that she didn't even realise she did it anymore and she had compartmentalised her work so much that she hadn't wanted anyone to come to her wedding, to see her in a non-work setting. She'd only invited Marcy because she'd pestered Willow so much.

'How are you?' Michael asked.

'I don't know,' Willow replied. It seemed to be the only answer she had for anybody anymore, but there was one thing she did know – she couldn't go back to work in a week's time. 'I was wondering—'

'If you could take some time off?' Michael interrupted. The relief Willow felt at not having to say the words herself was immense.

'Yes,' she replied. 'Is it possible?'

'You've accrued quite a lot of holiday,' Michael said. 'So you could use that initially. After that we do have a paid leave policy that is at the company's discretion and we could sort something out with HR.'

'Oh I'll only need another week or two,' Willow said hurriedly. She had worked so hard for that job and she knew that taking time off would be seen as a weakness. Nobody who dealt in futures could be seen to have an Achilles' heel.

'How are you really feeling, Willow?' Michael asked.

'I honestly don't know,' she said. 'As though my head is full of cotton wool and I can't think.' She looked at the instruments and books and music paraphernalia in her mum's shop as she spoke. 'As though London is a very, very long way away.' As soon as she said it she felt as though she'd said too much, as though she'd killed her career in one sentence. But Michael surprised her.

'You must take as much time off as you need,' he said. 'Burnout is a serious problem in our industry – you know that – and the company is trying to take a more compassionate stance on it where we can.' He paused. 'We can't risk getting sued.'

Burnout. Is that what was wrong with her?

'I don't know…'

'Take the rest of the summer, Willow,' Michael said gently. 'I'd rather see you back here fit and well and ready to take on the world in September than to have you come back now and need to watch your every move in case you make a mistake because your mind's not on the job.'

Willow didn't say anything for a moment as she tried to weigh up the feeling of anxiety at the possibility of losing her job, of not having the money to pay her half of the mortgage, with the feeling of relief that she wouldn't have to go back next week. She hadn't realised how much she didn't want to until she had been standing outside Skye's tattoo studio the afternoon before.

'There's at least a month's salary owing to you in holiday pay alone,' Michael was saying. 'I'll get HR to contact you to sort out the details. I don't need to know what's going on in your life, Willow, and whatever you tell HR will be in confidence, but I do need to know that my staff are capable of doing the job.'

'Thank you,' Willow replied. It sounded hollow and weak.

'And if you don't want to come back in September—'

'I'll be back in September,' she interrupted.

'Well, we'll see,' Michael said before hanging up the phone.

Willow looked around The Music Shop again. This was her life, for now at least.

Charlie finally called about half an hour later. There was an echo on the line and he sounded far away.

'Where are you?' she asked. 'You sound different.'

'I'm surprised you care,' he replied.

'Of course I care, Charlie – I know it doesn't seem like it but I do.'

'Have you any idea how much money my parents spent

on that wedding?' he went on. 'Have you any idea how embarrassed and humiliated they were after all their hard work?'

'I never asked for any of it,' Willow heard herself say as though she was listening to herself from far away. 'I never wanted that big fancy country wedding that they insisted on. I never understood why we had to go along with everything your mother wanted.'

He didn't say anything for such a long time that Willow thought he'd hung up. She wouldn't blame him; she didn't know where that outburst came from. But it was true. It hadn't been the wedding Willow wanted – she didn't want to get married in a church – she'd never been to church in her life. She didn't want a string quartet; she didn't want the big white dress that she'd practically had to starve herself to get into. She didn't want any of it. And yet she had gone along with it all, smiling and nodding and never saying anything, because she'd been trying so hard to avoid getting married on the Island, getting married amongst memories of the past.

She had been trying so hard not to think about Luc and his new-found fame that she hadn't had time to wonder if she might be marrying the wrong man.

'Do you have the first clue of the shame you've brought on me and my family?' Charlie said eventually. He sounded pompous and overblown. 'Why did you do it? You owe me an explanation at least. You could have told me if it wasn't the wedding you wanted, we could have had something smaller.' His voice was quieter, steadier now. 'Why did you do it?' he repeated.

'Because I don't love you.' The words were out of

Willow's mouth before she realised she was even thinking them. But as soon as she said it, she knew it was true. She hadn't loved Charlie for a while. She couldn't remember when she stopped.

'You don't love me!' he exclaimed, and Willow could imagine the incredulous look on his face. Charlie couldn't possibly imagine anybody not loving him – he was the sort of person everyone loved. But perhaps other people didn't know him as well as Willow did, perhaps they hadn't seen the parts of him that weren't loveable. He started to say something else but the line had become muffled and Willow couldn't make out his words.

'Charlie, where are you?' she asked. 'I can hardly hear you.'

'I'm in the Maldives,' he replied as the line cleared.

'You've gone on honeymoon on your own?'

'Not on my own no,' he said quietly. 'I got the tickets changed. I took Kate.'

'You've taken Kate on our honeymoon?' Willow repeated. Kate, her maid of honour and her only bridesmaid. Willow cringed as she remembered the look on Kate's face when she told her father she couldn't go through with it, that she wanted to go back to the hotel. Kate would have been the person who broke the news to Charlie.

Kate. The only person who hadn't messaged her since the wedding.

'I've not taken Kate on honeymoon,' Charlie said quietly. 'I've gone on holiday with a friend so as not to waste even more money. You made it very clear that you didn't want to come.' He paused and neither of them said anything for a moment.

'What do you want to do, Willow?' he asked.

The door of the shop opened and the bell jangled. Willow made another mental note to take that bell down before it drove her mad, and to start locking the door when the shop wasn't open. She turned around to see Luc, clutching two coffees and a bag of pastries again.

'I don't know what I want, Charlie,' she said, holding her hand up to Luc and turning away from him. 'But now isn't the best time to talk.'

She heard Charlie sigh in frustration. 'When are you coming home?' he asked.

'Not yet,' she replied.

'What about your job?' Charlie's voice rose again. 'What about our flat? You can't just walk away from your life, Willow.'

But I can, she thought. *If I want to.*

'I have to go, Charlie,' she said quietly, blinking back the tears that were burning the backs of her eyes.

'But we need—'

'I need some time to think,' she interrupted, suddenly sick to death of Charlie and his family telling her what she did and didn't need. 'Let me know when you're back in London and we'll talk.'

14

Luc

Luc could see that Willow was trying not to cry as she ended the call and turned to him. He handed her the coffee he'd bought.

'Thanks,' she said quietly as she took the drink.

'Everything OK?' he asked casually.

'Not really – that was Charlie. My almost husband.'

'Ah.'

'He's gone on honeymoon.'

'By himself?'

'No. With my maid of honour.'

'Ouch,' he said.

'He says it's just as friends, that he didn't want the holiday to go to waste but...'

'But you don't believe him?'

'I have no reason to not believe him,' she replied carefully, as though she didn't want to lay any blame on this man she'd almost married. 'I have no reason to not trust him.'

'Not many men would take a woman on a romantic

holiday and stay just friends,' Luc said quietly. 'Not that I want to generalise. How long have they known each other?'

'We've both known her since university.'

There was nothing Luc could say to make her feel better. He didn't know these people and telling Willow that he really didn't think very highly of this almost husband of hers wasn't going to help anyone, so he handed her the bag of pastries instead.

'Any closer to working out what made you a runaway bride?' he asked but he immediately regretted it as he watched her close down on him. If she wanted to talk about it at all, Luc wasn't the person she was going to talk about it with. He had to accept that. He would be doing them both a favour if he just kept away.

'What are you doing here again?' she asked, dodging his question.

'I just thought it would be nice to see you,' he replied.

Willow looked at him for a moment and he wondered what she was going to say. Then she smiled and it felt like the greatest reward he could ever have.

'It's nice to see you too,' she said.

They drank their coffees and talked about the Island, how it was still exactly the same as it had been when they were kids. How familiar it felt.

'Did you ask your mum about the tape?' Luc asked, but he knew she wouldn't have done because he was pretty sure she thought that tape was as significant as he did.

'I don't think it's a recording of The Laurels,' she said quietly 'There were some initials and a date written on the back. You saw that too I think.'

Luc nodded and Willow reached under the shop counter to get the tape so they could look at it again.

'The only way to find out is to listen to it,' Luc said. 'I think we should ask Tom Newell.'

'I guess so,' Willow replied reluctantly.

'Yeah,' Luc laughed. 'I know he's a bore but who else is going to have a DAT player these days?'

'It's not that.'

'Then what is it?'

'This is going to sound ridiculous,' she said. 'But I'm just not sure if I want anyone else to know about it, let alone listen to it.'

'You think it's something special, don't you?' Luc asked.

'Imagine if it is,' she replied. 'And it fell into the wrong hands.'

He'd been thinking the same thing: that this tape Willow had found was something unique that had been hidden for years, whether intentionally or not. He wasn't sure what she meant about "the wrong hands" but he did understand the feeling of proprietorship she had over the tape because he felt it too.

'Let me have a think,' he said. 'I'll work something out. In the meantime, keep the tape safe.'

'Luc,' Willow said quietly. 'I had lunch with Skye yesterday.'

'She said she was going to invite you.'

'I told her about the night before you left,' Willow went on and he looked away from her. He didn't want to think about it. He didn't want to talk about that night.

When he looked back at her again she was picking

nervously at her empty coffee cup and all the light that had been in her eyes was gone.

'Luc, I meant what I said that night,' she said. 'And I'm fairly sure you did too. I've never understood what happened, but coming back here has made me realise what a difficult time that summer was for both of us and...' She trailed off as though she'd run out of words.

Tell her, the voice in Luc's head said. *Tell her what really happened*. He looked up and his eyes met hers.

'What happened,' he began. 'That summer—'

'We were both in a bad place that summer,' Willow interrupted. 'We both know that. My parents were splitting up, you were leaving, Skye and I were off to university.' She paused. 'I didn't handle it all very well.'

'You were eighteen,' Luc said.

'We were both eighteen.'

He took a breath, knowing that there was so much more to it than that. So much more that he needed to tell her.

'I'm sorry, Willow,' he said instead. It sounded woefully inadequate, but she smiled up at him and his heart felt as though it would burst.

'It's OK,' she said.

'Thank you,' he said quietly, his mouth dry.

She walked up to him and he wrapped his arms around her, burying his face in her hair. She smelled of coconuts and Parma violets and he wanted to stay there breathing her in forever. When he'd walked into this shop five days ago and had seen Willow for the first time in so many years he'd figured he was the last person on the planet that she'd ever want to see again.

But as he stood here now with her in his arms it felt like

the most natural thing in the world even though he knew he shouldn't be here with her. He thought briefly of Annelise and let his arms fall, stepping away from Willow.

'I need to tell you something,' he said.

'OK,' she replied leaning against the counter.

'That morning before we all left for America, I was coming to meet you but...' He paused, his chest tightening. *Not now*, he said to himself. *Not in front of her*. He dug his fingernails into the palms of his hands. 'That morning I had a panic attack.'

He'd said it. The words were out in the open.

'I never knew you had panic attacks,' she replied. She looked so concerned he could barely stand it.

'That was the first one,' he admitted. 'It came from nowhere and I thought I was dying.'

'What caused it?' she asked.

'I didn't really know at the time but looking back I guess there was so much going on that summer like you said, so many changes.'

'Do you still get them?'

'Occasionally,' he said. 'But I know how to manage them now.' That wasn't really true though and he found himself unable to meet her eyes. There was so much she didn't know, so much he was hiding from everyone and he remembered sitting on the beach the other day thinking about how he needed to end all this, the secrecy, the lies. He needed to be honest with people about how he felt, about his writer's block, about Annelise.

But he couldn't. Not yet.

'I should leave you to it,' he said, standing up again. 'Let you get on with opening the shop.'

'Are you OK?' she asked. The concern in her face was too much. He didn't deserve it right now.

He grinned, but he wasn't sure how genuine it looked.

'Of course I am,' he said. 'How's your mum going with those planning permissions?'

'She's working on it. She's appealing the council's decision next week.' She paused. 'The irony is that Charlie is a planning lawyer and could actually help us, but obviously I'm not his favourite person right now.'

'You and Charlie—' Luc began, not really sure what he was going to ask.

'I think it's over,' she interrupted. 'But I have no idea how to unravel the last twelve years of my life, how to start again. I just needed to run away and now I don't know what to do.'

'I know that feeling,' he said quietly, immediately regretting it when he saw the look she gave him, the question in her eyes.

Instead he took a step towards her, bending to kiss her on the cheek just as he had done on Saturday.

'You know, Willow,' he said, 'not a day has gone past when I haven't regretted the way we had to say goodbye.'

15

Cathy took a deep breath before stepping out of the wings and following Don Warwick out on to the stage. She clutched her mandolin tightly as the audience applauded and she sat on the stool that the more famous Krystal Kane usually occupied. Cathy was finally getting her chance.

When Storm had introduced her to Don Warwick on the first day of the tour, she recognised him immediately as the support act that had opened for King Silver at the Astoria the previous autumn. She was surprised to see him and his bandmate Krystal – who were both a few years older than Cathy – playing together as The Laurels. She'd always assumed Don was a solo act and she'd also assumed that Don and Krystal were a couple. But she'd been wrong about that, just as she'd been wrong about assuming she'd be Storm's support. It had quickly become obvious that Cathy was merely along for the ride, and for Storm's evening entertainment should he wish her to be.

She shared a tour bus with Don and Krystal. She never got

to play, except on the bus and occasionally at a soundcheck. She shared a room with Krystal unless Storm asked for her, in which case she spent the night with him. After a couple of weeks on the road Cathy was bored, regretting giving up so much to just be Storm Tyler's bit of fun when none of the other groupies who hung around outside his dressing room grabbed his interest. She remembered the night she had hung around waiting for him at the Astoria. Was that the reason Storm thought she wouldn't mind being treated like this? Did he see her as nothing more than another of his groupies?

The only thing that stopped her giving up and going home was that she couldn't stand the thought of her father being right. She couldn't stand to see the smug look on his face when she walked back into her parents' house with her tail between her legs, or to listen to him tell her about how he had known Storm for years and knew what he was like, how he had warned her this would happen.

Besides, she was on the road with proper musicians. If nothing else she was learning, storing it all up for next time. She knew her big break would come if she just stayed determined, if she just played the long game.

Her break came, in the end, sooner than she'd expected. During the third week of the tour when they were due to play a venue in Exeter, Krystal came down with food poisoning.

'Why don't you come on stage with me tonight?' Don asked.

'Me?' Cathy said. A feeling somewhere between excitement and terror coursed through her body.

'Yes you.' Don laughed. 'You know all the songs, you're just as good as Krystal on the mandolin and you sing well.'

'I'm not ready,' Cathy replied. She didn't know why she was making excuses when the one thing she had been waiting for was being offered to her.

'Cathy, we all know that you came on this tour thinking you'd be supporting Storm,' Don said kindly. 'And to be honest I'd like to see you do this, to show Storm that you're more than just his plaything.'

Cathy blushed at that and looked away. She couldn't deny that she was embarrassed about what had happened and had wondered what Don and Krystal must think of her. But Don seemed genuinely annoyed on her behalf and at the same time thought she was a good enough musician to share the stage with. That had to count for something.

'Go on,' Don encouraged. 'Don't make me go out there alone.'

Cathy still wavered. She wondered what Storm would say.

'We can open with "Gamble Gold" if you like.' Don grinned.

'But that's Storm's encore!' Cathy said.

'Sod it, we're having it tonight.'

And so out on the stage later that night Don introduced Cathy to the audience and then looked at her and winked before counting them in. As they played the opening chords to a song that Cathy had come to know so well, a sense of enormous wellbeing washed over her. She was finally where she belonged.

Later, after the gig, Storm caught up with her in the dressing room she was sharing with Don.

'You stole my song,' Storm said. Cathy couldn't quite make out his tone.

'It's a Child Ballad man,' Don replied. 'Anyone can play it. And Cathy plays it even better than you.'

There was a pause as Storm's green eyes, glazed slightly from an ingestion of substances stronger than alcohol, flicked between Cathy and Don. She didn't know how he would react and realised she was holding her breath.

And then Storm started laughing – a deep throaty chuckle, his mouth open so Cathy could see the glint of his gold tooth.

'She does as well,' he said walking over to her and crouching in front of her. He took her head in his hands, his rough calloused fingers at the base of her neck and kissed her, his tongue finding hers. He tasted of stale whisky and cigarettes. He smelled of some other woman's perfume.

Cathy had promised herself that she wouldn't go to Storm's bed that night if he asked. She had told herself she was sick of the way he treated her and that, if Don saw her as a musician of equal calibre to him, then Don and Krystal were the people she should be asking for advice.

But when Storm was there, touching her, kissing her, she couldn't resist him. Cathy had worked out now what her father had known all along – that Storm was trouble. But still she couldn't resist him. Nothing could get him out of her system, even knowing that he was bad for her, that he wasn't the man who was going to help her get what she wanted.

As Storm trailed kisses along Cathy's neck, she caught a glimpse of Don looking at her sadly before leaving the room.

16

Willow

Willow began to fall into a gentle routine as her initial two weeks on the Island turned into three. She tried not to think much further into the future than the next day and she still got that strange anxious feeling every time her mind wandered to London or to her job. She had googled the word "burnout" more times than she cared to admit but she still couldn't work out if that was what she was suffering from. She had no idea what she was going to do, but she did know that her mum needed her to help with the festival and she would stay in Seaview until that was done.

'How do you feel about being back?' her mother asked. 'Do you feel like you're settling in?'

'Yes,' Willow replied, surprising herself with her answer, surprising herself with how quickly Island life had consumed her despite her resistance. She'd started playing her father's old mandolin regularly, even though she'd told herself that life was behind her now. 'Some mornings when I first wake up it almost feels as though I've never been gone.'

'It's funny how it has that effect on people,' Cathy said. 'Your father's the same. Even though he spends more time in America than here these days, whenever he comes back for the festival he says it feels like he's back home.'

'I didn't say it felt like home,' Willow replied. 'But...' She wasn't sure what it did feel like. She wanted to ask more about her father, about how her parents managed to remain friends after they broke up. Perhaps they might have some advice that would help her, but she didn't know where to start.

'Do you feel like that after you've been away?' she asked instead. 'As though you're coming home?'

'Not in quite the same way,' Cathy said. 'Maybe you have to be born here like you and your dad,' she paused. 'And Luc. I wonder how he feels about being back?'

Willow shrugged.

'Have you spoken to Charlie?' Cathy asked.

'He was supposed to call me after he got back from the Maldives but I haven't heard anything.' It bothered her that she seemed to care so little about what Charlie was doing. She'd been with him for almost a third of her life and yet she had just let him slip out of her mind now that she was back on the Island.

Now that she was able to do what she wanted, eat what she wanted, spend time with who she wanted.

'Don't worry too much about Charlie going on your honeymoon with your friend,' Cathy said, but Willow hadn't really been worrying about that at all. She knew she probably should be, but her mind drifted too easily to Luc, to his mysterious phone call and to the festival. 'Perhaps you should try calling him again though,' Cathy went on.

But as one day merged into another Willow didn't call Charlie. Instead, each morning as she opened up The Music Shop for her mother, Luc would arrive with coffee and they'd chat for a while about nothing in particular before the shop started to get busy. He never asked her about Charlie, or how long she was planning to stay and she never asked what he did all day on the Island after he left the shop, or whether there was anyone waiting for him back in Nashville. Every day he told her how good it was to see her again, every day he kissed her chastely on the cheek and every day this simple routine felt better and better and further away from her life in London.

'Have you seen much of your dad?' Luc asked one morning.

'He comes in every afternoon to correct my mandolin playing,' Willow replied. 'He's a much later riser than you!'

Luc's eyebrows shot up at the mention of the mandolin.

'You're playing again?'

'Not really, just messing about.' She didn't want to admit how much she was enjoying playing with her dad again. It reminded her too much of all the other things she knew she had missed out on when she left the Island, while she was busy creating a different life for herself with Charlie.

Willow knew how close Luc and Don had been over the years and she had always felt a little envious of their relationship. It was one of the reasons why she was so angry when he left for America with Luc and Krystal. Despite what Cathy had always insisted, despite what Don had told her, Willow had always assumed that at some point Don and Krystal had been an item, and in those early days when she was alone at Cambridge she had always thought that her father was looking after Luc when he should have been looking after her.

She knew none of those fears held any truth. But still she had kept her family and her past at arm's length for far too long and she regretted that now.

'If Krystal and Dad weren't having an affair,' she asked Luc quietly, 'why did Dad leave?'

'I have no idea. Something happened that summer – something that you and I didn't know about.'

'I guess we both had a lot on our own plates back then. I guess we just didn't notice.'

But Willow had noticed and she guessed from what Luc had told her about his panic attacks so had he. She had tried, back then, to ask her mum what was going on, to get her to talk about why Don was leaving and what all the whispered conversations were about that stopped whenever she or Luc entered a room, but Cathy had been as reluctant to talk about it as she was to talk about her days on the road before Willow was born.

The Big Festival came and went and it turned out that Luc was more famous than Willow had thought, that he did indeed have the odd groupie or two just as Skye had suspected. As the Island filled up with music fans, she saw him being asked to sign things: a record cover, a guitar, even a girl's bikini on the beach one afternoon although Willow didn't think Luc knew she'd seen that.

When she asked him about it he dismissed it. 'Just a few die-hard British fans of *American Stars*,' he said. 'Most people didn't watch it, hardly anyone knows who I am.' But Willow knew a lot of people who had watched that show, a lot of people who would love to see Lucien Hawke play somewhere much bigger than The Seaview Folk Festival. Why had he chosen her parents' festival? What was he hiding? What was he running away from?

Luc and Willow met Skye's partner, Bob Harris, when he visited the Island for a few days. The four of them had dinner together and it felt comfortable – more comfortable than Willow had ever felt with the couples that she and Charlie knew in London – couples who were always trying to outdo each other somehow. Bob was a marketing consultant and was making plans to start expanding his freelance work so he could eventually move to the Island. A voice in the back of Willow's head thought he was mad to give up his London salary to live on this Island, but that voice wasn't as loud as it used to be.

'How did you meet?' Luc asked.

'I tattooed him,' Skye replied. Bob looked the least likely person in the country to have a tattoo but apparently appearances were deceptive.

'I asked her out in the hope she'd give me a discount on the ink,' he said.

'Did she?' Willow asked.

'Of course not!'

When Luc walked Willow home afterwards and he slung his arm around her shoulders, she didn't step away even though she knew she should. She still hadn't called Charlie and her life in London was beginning to feel as though it had happened to a different person in a different dimension.

She tried not to think about London at all, and she tried not to think about Luc's life in Nashville and the people who would be waiting for him. There were 101 reasons why Willow and Luc could never be together and whatever her treacherous heart might tell her when she was with him, she knew that between them they had thrown away their only chance twelve summers ago.

'Do you still want to listen to that tape?' Luc asked one morning over coffee in The Music Shop.

'Of course!' Willow replied. 'But I've nothing to play it on.' She had a sudden urge to check that the tape was in her bag, just as she had about a thousand times a day since she found it.

'Well,' Luc said. 'I've booked a session with Tom Newell at the studio. I've told him I want to lay down some tracks while I'm here, songs inspired by the Island. I asked him if he had a DAT recorder.'

'Does he?'

Luc nodded. 'He droned on for a while about his state-of-the-art Pro Tools system but I kept insisting that I wanted to record on DAT so he said he'd get the old equipment set up for me.'

Willow chewed her lip. 'Luc,' she said quietly. 'Don't take this the wrong way, but I don't want to give you the tape.'

To her surprise he laughed. 'I know, Willow. I've seen how shifty you are around it and I figured you wouldn't want to give it to me, so I've come up with a plan for that too.'

'You have?' Clearly Willow hadn't hidden her feelings about the tape very well and she felt embarrassed. She'd never paid much attention to gut feelings before, but the one she had about this tape was too strong to ignore. Just like the one she'd had on her wedding day.

'I told Tom I wanted to get you back into music so you'd be coming with me.'

'I don't want Tom there when we listen to it,' Willow said. She sounded paranoid now but Tom liked to "help" out with all the musicians who used the studio. It used to drive Willow's parents mad when they first handed over the reins to him. They hadn't expected him to be so hands on.

'Don't worry about that either. I remember what Tom's like so I told him I wanted to be alone with you.' He winked at Willow and her stomach flipped. She didn't want to feel like this about Luc; it was too complicated.

'Christ, Luc, I've literally just walked out on Charlie – what are people going to think when that rumour starts getting around the Island?'

But Luc just smiled and Willow tried to ignore the fact that the idea of a night alone with Luc Harrison felt more exciting than it should do.

'Why are you so worried about this tape?' he asked.

'I'm not sure. I just have this feeling that it's important.'

He looked as though he was going to say something but then his phone rang. He glanced at the screen and his expression changed completely. He put the phone in his pocket and made his excuses. He didn't kiss Willow's cheek when he left. Whoever was on the other end of that call was important to Luc and was probably the same person who had called him in Skye's kitchen. The person who he called "sweetheart". Suddenly a night alone with Luc Harrison in Tom's recording studio didn't seem like a good idea at all.

★

Luc didn't bring coffee the next morning and Willow assumed that whoever had phoned him the previous day had reminded him that he probably shouldn't be spending so much time with her.

Later that morning she got a text from him telling her to meet him in The Three Doves at 7pm because the recording session was booked for that evening. He reminded her to bring a mandolin to make his cover story look realistic and Willow rolled her eyes at his presumption.

Instead of coffee with Luc, that morning Willow was treated to the smug smile of Roger Beck in the shop.

'Willow,' Roger said, drawing out the last syllable as he walked in, the bell jangling behind him. 'I was hoping to run into you.'

'Seeking someone out at their workplace hardly counts as running into them,' she replied, pretending not to notice the hand he extended towards her as she kept her eyes on the mandolin she was restringing.

He laughed, a strange fake sort of noise and Willow looked up at him. He was wearing a beige jacket with suede patches at the sleeves and thick-framed glasses and he looked exactly like his father used to look. He must only be thirty-three but he seemed so much older.

'Same old sense of humour,' he said as though they were once friends. 'It's good to see you back.' Willow wished people would stop saying that, as though she was back for good.

'What do you want, Roger?' she asked.

'I heard you were back and I just wanted to see how you were.'

'Roger, we both know that you know I'm back because

I submitted the appeal for the festival permissions and I'm pretty sure that half the Island knows I'm back because I left my husband-to-be at the altar on our wedding day. As there is a planning appeal meeting on Monday I really don't think us chatting about the good old days is appropriate, do you?'

His smile faded to something a little more unpleasant at her words. Willow had been hoping to avoid Roger completely until the appeal on Monday. She'd figured he was unlikely to come looking for her or to hang out in musicians' haunts like The Three Doves. Clearly she had been wrong.

'Willow, I think we should be civil about this,' he said. 'We both know that your mother's little festival has had its heyday now. Nobody is interested in folk music anymore and I happen to know that the ticket sales are down year on year.'

Were they? Willow had no idea. Cathy hadn't mentioned anything about it.

'Well, we'll see about that at the planning committee meeting, won't we?' Willow said with as much certainty as she could muster. 'Trust me, Roger, the Island wants this festival. I don't know why you don't.'

'Nobody is interested anymore, Willow. Let it go.'

Willow felt a stab of anger at this. Surely that wasn't true? The folk festival was as much a part of Seaview as the sand and the sea and the clifftops and Cartwright's sweet shop.

'Plenty of people are interested in folk music,' she said. 'Luc Harrison just won *American Stars* and lots of people will pay to see him.'

She watched Roger's face grow paler and his fake smile get tighter when she mentioned Luc's name. What was it about Luc and the folk festival that made Roger so angry?

'He didn't actually win though did he, Willow?' he said unpleasantly.

'Why are you doing this, Roger? Mum's festival has been going for nearly twenty years. People love it and it brings business to everyone in Seaview. It makes people happy so why are you hellbent on destroying it when it's never caused you any harm? We'd all be so sad if we couldn't have a festival this year.'

His lips were so thin now that they had almost disappeared entirely.

'What do you care about the festival?' he asked quietly. 'You haven't been back for years. But now here you are again, you and Luc and Skye, all back together again like you were at school.'

'Roger, what on earth—' Willow said, shocked at his anger now.

'I'll see you at the planning meeting,' he interrupted. 'And you'd better come up with a very good argument for this festival, a better one than Luc Harrison playing at it, if you want the council to approve it. You can trust me on that.'

He turned on his heel and walked out of the door.

17

Luc

The feelings Luc had for Willow weren't as firmly boxed away in the past as he'd hoped they were. He couldn't stop thinking about her. It was driving him mad and it definitely wasn't helping him focus or get over his writer's block. He knew that he'd almost kissed her right before his phone started ringing. Annelise couldn't have timed that call better if she'd tried.

The phone call had brought him back to earth – just as the one he'd accidentally answered in Skye's kitchen had three weeks ago. He was back on the Island for a reason, the same reason he'd done *American Stars* in the first place, the same reason he couldn't allow himself to be distracted or let himself fail. The same reason he had to get his feelings for Willow under control before he ended up hurting her all over again.

He had to concentrate on writing this next record and he had to make sure the festival went ahead. And at the end of the summer he had to go back to Nashville.

He didn't have a choice.

He had to stop thinking about Willow to protect both of them and to protect Annelise, and that was why he'd skipped his usual morning coffee with Willow in an attempt to keep away from her.

But now they were in The Three Doves together, it felt like old times again and Luc didn't know how he could keep away from her.

Which meant he had to tell her the truth, and soon.

He sat opposite Willow at the pub table rather than on the bench next to her. It wasn't much but if it just put a bit of distance between them for the time being then that was for the best. He tried not to notice when his knees brushed against hers as she told him about her visit from Roger Beck.

'I don't understand why he's still so angry,' Willow said. 'He started off perfectly politely – he looks exactly like his dad now – and then he just got really cross. All I did was refuse to shake his hand.'

'Willow.' Luc laughed. 'You should probably at least try to be nice to him for the sake of your mum's festival.'

'It's not like he holds the future of the festival in his hands. He's just put in an objection based on nothing. All Mum and I have to do is convince the council that we're not a nuisance and we'll be fine.' But Luc saw a cloud cross her face that contradicted that statement and he wondered what else had happened to make her worry. 'I'm more interested in why he's still holding a grudge anyway,' she went on.

'Isn't it obvious?' Luc asked.

'Isn't what obvious?'

Luc grinned. 'Roger Beck was head over heels in love

with you at school. Absolutely crazy about you. I thought you knew that. Skye thought it was hilarious.'

'What?' Willow frowned. 'Why did nobody tell me about it?'

'Would you have gone out with him if we had?'

'No, but…' Willow trailed off. 'You think that's what this is all about? Because he had a crush on me at school and I ignored him and now he's finally got a chance for revenge by blocking the permissions for Mum's festival?'

'I don't think it's what it's all about,' Luc said, remembering how many other boys had a crush on Willow when she was at school and how oblivious she had been to it all. 'I don't know if you remember this but Roger's dad was always against the festival too. He thought it brought the wrong element into town, especially back in the day before they started The Big Festival up again.'

'He was?' Willow had never been as interested in the folk festival as Luc had been.

'Yeah, he's just fighting his dad's battle coupled with his unrequited love for you and this is what you get.' Luc laughed spreading his hands.

'Shut up,' Willow said smiling. 'I feel a bit sorry for him.'

'For Roger?'

'Well he doesn't think much of you either. He was very derogatory about *American Stars*.'

'Hardly surprising that he hates me is it, seeing as he was in love with you.'

Willow felt her cheeks colour at this, a memory of lying naked on the beach with Luc flashing into her mind.

'Where did you rush off to yesterday?' Willow asked,

changing the subject. 'Is everything OK? I missed you this morning.'

Luc had been hoping she wouldn't ask that question, hoping she wouldn't really notice that he hadn't brought her a coffee today. But hearing her say that she missed him made his heart sing.

Before he had time to think of an answer he was interrupted.

'Here they are,' a voice shouted across the pub. 'Love's young dream!'

Does he have to be so loud? Luc thought as he drained his pint and stood up to greet Tom. He caught Willow's eye and she gave him a disgruntled look that told Luc in no uncertain terms that she wasn't happy about this picture of reunited love that he'd painted. Luc winked at her and she looked away.

'Tom, can I get you a drink?' he asked, regretting it almost immediately. If he said yes they'd never get away.

'I'm off to see Willow's mum tonight,' Tom said. He always did the sound for the folk festival so that must be what he and Cathy were talking about tonight. He didn't seem to know about the permission for the licences, which was a good thing. 'Another time?' he said.

'Sure.' Luc nodded with no intention of letting there be another time.

'Do you need keys?' Tom asked.

Willow shook her head. 'I've got Mum's keys with me,' she said.

'Right well, I've left the DAT player out like you said, although why you don't want to use Pro Tools—'

'Trust me,' Luc interrupted, tapping Tom on the shoulder

before he could continue with a monologue on the glories of Pro Tools. Cathy had told Luc that it hadn't been that long ago when Tom Newell thought that Pro Tools was the work of the devil.

'Are you ready, Willow?' he asked turning to her and she nodded picking up her dad's mandolin and her handbag. Luc saw her check for the tape for the third time since she'd arrived.

'Well have fun, lovebirds,' Tom called after them as they left, his wheezy laugh following them out of the door.

'I'm going to kill you,' Willow said as the pub door shut behind them. 'What were you thinking telling him you wanted to be alone with me?'

'Well it's not a lie, is it?' Luc replied and when she looked at him and smiled, he had to dig his fingernails into the palms of his hands to stop himself taking her face in his hands and crushing his lips against hers. He walked a little bit ahead of her in an attempt to stop himself thinking about what that would feel like.

'Ready?' he asked as they arrived at The Music Shop. Willow walked around to the back of the shop to open the studio door and Luc followed. His mouth was dry at the thought that in just a few minutes they'd know exactly what was on that tape. Because, just like Willow, Luc was sure it was significant and Willow was the only person he trusted with that tape. Despite everything, right now there wasn't anyone else he'd rather share this with.

Luc opened the door and walked into the familiar surroundings of the studio. Tom might have gone all out on the modern equipment but the studio itself looked exactly the same as it had done years ago when Willow and

Luc used to watch their parents record here. The carpets were as old as time, the walls hadn't seen a lick of paint in years and there was a strange musty smell. Luc noticed a coffee cup sitting on a desk by the door and wondered how long it had been there.

'It smells of musicians,' Willow said with a shudder. 'I haven't ventured in here since I've been back and this is why. It always was a dump and Mum would never let me clean it up.'

Luc remembered how as a teenager Willow had been always tidying up The Music Shop when she worked there at weekends, always moving stuff around to make it more aesthetically pleasing. She'd wanted to do the same in the studio but Cathy had never let her. He led her into the studio now and pulled up a stool as he got the DAT player ready.

'Hand it over,' he said. 'I promise I won't let it leave your sight.'

She passed the tape to him and he noticed her hands were shaking. What was she so nervous about? Luc felt as though they were opening up a whole can of worms and he wasn't sure if it was to do with the tape or the fact that they were alone together here, against his better judgement. For a fleeting moment he thought about giving the tape back to her and walking her home. When he looked at her, she was biting her lip.

'You sure about this?' he asked and she hesitated just for a moment.

'Yes,' she said eventually. 'Play it.'

'Here's the moment we've all been waiting for,' Luc said as he put the tape into the player.

He pressed play and they waited in silence. Luc was

holding his breath and when he didn't hear anything he thought the tape was blank, that there was nothing on it and all of this had been a waste of time.

Then he heard the sound of a man clearing his throat and a voice he didn't immediately recognise echoed out of the speakers. '"Gamble Gold" Take one,' the man's voice said.

What followed was Child Ballad number 132, a song that Steeleye Span made famous in the 1970s. But for Willow and Luc it would always be the song that The Laurels used to close with when they toured with them as children.

One of Luc's earliest memories was being backstage with Willow at one of their parents' gigs. They both had ear-protecting headphones clamped over their heads and were holding each other's hands. The Laurels had played their version of "Gamble Gold", a ballad that told the story of how Robin Hood and Little John came across a random pedlar in Sherwood Forest one afternoon. When the pedlar refused to hand over his belongings Robin set on him with a sword. After fighting almost to the death, it turned out that the pedlar was, in fact, Gamble Gold, Robin's cousin, so off they went to have a pint together as if nothing untoward had happened. Luc had always thought it was a ridiculous song but Willow had loved it. He could remember dancing with her backstage as The Laurels played, just as he could remember dancing with her when The Laurels played "Gamble Gold" at the opening of The Music Shop and at a hundred other occasions before and since.

But this wasn't the version of "Gamble Gold" that Luc knew – this wasn't a jaunty singalong tune to finish a gig with. This was a haunting version of the song that sent shivers down his spine. It was stripped down to its bare bones, just one man, his mandolin and a female backing vocalist. By the time the song was over Luc felt completely overwhelmed.

'Bloody hell,' Willow whispered and when he looked at her she was pale as a ghost.

'What's the matter?' he asked.

'That voice,' she said. 'You recognise it right?'

'I do but I can't quite place him.'

'Not the guy,' Willow said. 'The backing vocalist. It's Mum.'

Luc looked surprised. 'Are you sure?'

'Of course I'm sure. She's been singing to me since I was in the womb. I'd know that voice anywhere.'

Luc rewound the tape a little so they could hear it again.

'So it is,' he sa'.' softly. 'Wow.'

Willow too'. a breath. 'So the GG stands for "Gamble Gold" I ᵒ⸳⸳ ₛ,' she said.

Luc smiled. 'Do you remember when The Laurels used to play it?'

'Mum always loved that song,' she replied. 'The lead vocal must be whoever NF is. You said you recognised the voice?'

He was sure he recognised the voice but he needed to listen again. He rewound the tape again, and this time he knew for sure. If it was who Luc thought it was then this tape was even more significant than he had first thought. He stopped the recording halfway through, a surge of adrenaline ripping through him – but this time it wasn't an impending panic attack, it was excitement. He couldn't remember the last time he felt like this. He stood up, fumbling for his phone and stabbing at his music app as he attached it to the studio speaker system.

'Are you OK?' Willow asked.

'Listen,' he said.

After a moment the opening chords to a song they both knew very well started to play. It had been one of their favourites growing up.

'King Silver,' Willow said quietly. '"Chord of Plenty". I haven't listened to this in years.'

'Wait,' Luc said, holding up a finger. He wanted her to hear it too.

And there it was, the voice from the DAT tape. The voice of Storm Tyler, lead singer of King Silver.

'Storm Tyler,' she said. 'I can't believe I didn't recognise it.'

'Jesus,' Luc whispered under his breath. He was right, this was huge.

'So this is a demo of Storm Tyler singing "Gamble Gold" with my mother in August 1999?' Willow double-checked and Luc nodded. 'But didn't Storm disappear sometime in the late Eighties? I thought he was dead.'

'There are a lot of theories about what happened to Storm after he disappeared,' Luc told her. 'There are whole websites dedicated to him and there are a lot of obsessive King Silver fans full of conspiracy theories. It's almost as ridiculous as those "Paul is dead" rumours that ran around after The Beatles released *The White Album*.' Willow looked at him in a wistful kind of way and Luc suspected that she hadn't listened to any of the music that they loved as kids since she'd left the Island and he wanted to know why. Why had she drawn a line under everything she'd ever loved?

'But this is definitely Storm Tyler isn't it?' she asked. 'And it's recorded in 1999.'

'I'm positive it's him and I don't think he's dead. Someone would have produced a death certificate by now. I think he's just lying low. I think the music business destroyed him.' Luc knew how that felt now. He wanted to tell Willow but this was neither the time nor the place.

'But my mother knows where he is,' Willow said. 'Or at the very least she knew where he was in 1999.'

Luc didn't say anything, he just stared at the DAT player.

'My mother and Storm Tyler,' Willow repeated.

'You had no idea that she knew him?' Luc asked.

'None, I just told you – I thought he was dead.'

They sat in silence for a moment and Luc thought about the enormity of this tape they'd found. For a few years in the 1980s King Silver had been one of the hottest bands around. They'd split for a few months in 1984 while Storm embarked upon a solo tour but things hadn't worked out and King Silver got back together the next year, but by 1987 they'd all gone their separate ways and Storm Tyler hadn't been heard of since.

'What does the NF stand for?' Willow asked after a while.

'Neil Flannigan I'm guessing. Storm's real name.'

'Could you imagine what people would say if they knew we had this?'

'I know. You were right, Lil.' The nickname just slipped out. He'd always called her Lil when they were younger, a hangover from when he was small and couldn't pronounce "Willow" properly. He didn't realise that he'd done it until Willow looked at him, her eyes locking on his. Luc looked away first, taking the tape out of the player.

'This is something important,' he said, avoiding her gaze.

'You have to keep it safe and I don't think we should tell anyone about it just yet.'

But she didn't reply and when Luc looked at her again, her brow was furrowed as though she was trying to catch a memory that she couldn't quite get hold of.

18

After Cathy's debut performance with The Laurels, Don decided to make it a regular thing, turning the duo into a trio with Cathy on mandolin and sharing vocals with Krystal. Cathy wasn't sure how happy Krystal was about this arrangement. While the older woman was perfectly nice to Cathy there was an underlying feeling that Cathy was an imposter, someone who was only there through pity. If it hadn't been for Don regularly telling her that she was bringing something special to The Laurels, something that had been missing, Cathy might have run away from the whole thing.

Not that she had anywhere to run to. Despite what her mother had told her about keeping in touch if she needed anything, Cathy was determined not to ask for help, or to beg her mother for her father's forgiveness. Pip had sublet Cathy's room in the flat so she couldn't go back there, not that she could afford the rent until she found a job.

Cathy hadn't spent the night with Storm since the first

time she'd performed with Don, when Krystal had been ill. In fact, other than on stage each night none of the members of The Laurels saw Storm at all. Even his stage performance was becoming erratic. He started turning up late and cutting his sets short. He played shambolically, forgetting the lyrics to his own songs or giving up on a song halfway through and mumbling at the audience about how he didn't like that one much anyway. To Cathy it looked as though he had forgotten his own songs, but nobody said anything so she kept her misgivings to herself.

Each night when he came off stage he would walk past her and Don and Krystal, barely acknowledging them, and disappear to God only knew where. Cathy had gone back to sharing a room with Krystal. Storm had even started getting from venue to venue under his own steam and Cathy wouldn't see him from one evening to the next.

Cathy knew that Storm drank a lot. She couldn't remember the last time she'd seen him without a drink in his hand and every time she saw him, every time he breezed past her without a hint of acknowledgement, he stank of alcohol. She also knew that alcohol wasn't the only drug he indulged in and often remembered the white powder all over the dressing room in the Astoria when she'd visited him there after his gig. She'd overheard Don and Krystal talking about it on more than one occasion and, although she never joined in the gossip – still feeling too inexperienced to have much of an opinion, it was starting to feel as though things were getting progressively worse.

A lot of musicians drank and took drugs – everyone knew that – but this was more than just the usual overindulgence on tour. Storm's performance was suffering and the audiences weren't happy. As the tour progressed Cathy felt a low grumbling, a vaguely discontented energy, emanate from the crowd each evening as rumours of Storm's increasingly erratic behaviour preceded him from one town to the next. The Laurels found themselves playing longer and longer sets to try to distract from Storm's increasingly appalling timekeeping and although they were well received night after night, the crowd weren't there to see The Laurels.

Cathy felt as though they were all burying their heads in the sand. She knew Don had spoken to Storm's manager but it hadn't changed anything and she had a feeling that things were going to take a turn for the worse. The Laurels carried on regardless, playing their support set pretending everything was all right.

Until the night, towards the end of the tour, when Storm didn't show up at all.

At first everyone thought he'd just been delayed, his manager insisted he was on his way. The Laurels extended their set – they'd become quite adept at that over the previous weeks – adding in a few Ballad Book favourites and, much to Cathy's delight, a song that she had written and the trio had been working on together. It was the last song they played and the audience seemed to like it, applauding enthusiastically and some of them asking for more. It was the first time that Cathy had experienced that feeling she had asked Storm about in his dressing room at the Astoria, that feeling of an audience listening to the songs you wrote and enjoying them. She knew she had a long way to go, but it felt like a first step. Don had nudged her as the audience applauded and caught her eye, winking at her, and

Cathy had felt a sense of gentle euphoria wash over her as though she was right at the beginning of something.

The feeling was short-lived. As The Laurels came off stage they were greeted by Storm's manager telling them that Storm had stepped out in front of a taxi and was now in hospital. He had mild concussion and a couple of broken ribs but, in the circumstances, had decided to cancel the rest of the tour.

'Was he drunk?' Don asked, but Storm's manager didn't reply.

'Of course he was bloody drunk,' Krystal muttered as she walked back to the dressing room.

The three of them sat backstage for a while trying to take in what had happened.

'Well The Laurels have had some good exposure,' Don said, trying to find a silver lining. 'Perhaps we could work on that, start playing bigger venues than we were before. After all,' he went on looking at Cathy, 'we're a proper band now.'

'We're going to have to do something,' Krystal replied, but Cathy still got the impression Krystal would be happier if she wasn't there. Perhaps Krystal was right: this tour hadn't been quite what she'd imagined and she was beginning to wonder if going home with her tail between her legs was her only option now.

'I don't know if I can go on being a part of The Laurels,' she said quietly. 'I think I should probably just try to make amends with my father and go back to the Academy.'

'You can always come and stay with me,' Krystal said unexpectedly, so much so that even Don looked at her in surprise, confirming Cathy's suspicions that Krystal hadn't been entirely happy about her becoming a permanent member of the band.

'What?' Krystal went on when she realised that both Don and Cathy were staring at her. 'Cathy's got a lot to learn about being on the road, but she's a talented musician and we'd be mad to lose her. She can stay in the box room in my flat.'

Don sat back in his chair and grinned. 'You've a heart of gold, Krystal Harrison,' he said.

'Harrison?' Cathy asked.

'Kane is just my stage name,' Krystal said. 'But don't you go telling anyone that. And don't go getting ideas that I'm all heart either, Miss Cole. That room is tiny.'

Tiny it might be, but Cathy was beyond grateful for the second chance.

As autumn moved into winter The Laurels found themselves getting more and more gigs in pubs and small venues in and around London. Their name was starting to become known within the folk scene and their performances were often sold out. This was partly due to Don's relentless hard work at getting them exposure and with the money they'd made from gigs, the band had even managed to record a few songs to sell on cassette at concerts. But the gentle rise of The Laurels also came down to the reputation they'd earned as being versatile and reliable during the disaster that was Storm Tyler's solo tour. Word had got around about how strong their support set had been and how they'd carried on playing until the bitter end, even when everyone had known that the tour had fallen apart completely.

As The Laurels got more and more gigs and Cathy found herself busy all the time, she tried not to think about Storm – she believed that everyone came into your life for a reason and, while she may have had high hopes for Storm Tyler that hadn't worked out, if it wasn't for him she would never have met Krystal or Don and she wouldn't be starting out on the career of her dreams.

Nothing was heard from Storm for some time. Nobody seemed to know where he had disappeared to after his run-in with the taxi, or what his plans were. Rumour had it that the other members of King Silver were planning their own comeback without him.

And then, in January, Cathy saw him again. Not in person but on the front cover of the *NME* – staring back at her from the newsstand outside Krystal's apartment. She bought a copy without really thinking about it and devoured the interview when she got back home, before she'd even taken her coat off. Storm was back in the recording studio with King Silver. He was thinner, sober and brimming with more ideas than ever before – or so he said. Cathy wondered if it really was possible to change your life around in just four short months.

She mentally wished him well and tried not to think about him, concentrating on her own career, her own creativity, her relationships with Krystal and Don. She didn't drink, she didn't take drugs – she didn't want to end up like Storm. And she'd come to a gentle peace with herself about her relationship with him. She didn't regret anything she'd done

– she was young and experiences were important – but she was at a point where she thought she could say she'd be happier if she didn't see him again.

Until a few weeks later when he knocked on Krystal's front door.

'I've come to see Cathy,' he said.

And in that moment everything changed.

19

Willow

By Monday afternoon Willow was starting to feel nervous.

'Are you sure you don't want to do this yourself?' she asked.

'You'll be much better at it than me,' Cathy replied. 'As long as you don't mind.'

Cathy had asked Willow to present the case for the festival at the planning committee meeting that evening. She thought that the committee were more likely to listen to her because of her professional experience and background.

'But don't you think that they are more likely to listen to someone who hasn't been away from the Island for years?' Willow said. 'Someone who actually set up the festival in the first place? Perhaps Dad should do it?'

'Oh I don't think so, Willow. Your father and the council have never really got on. I've had to smooth out all sorts of misunderstandings over the years.'

'Is he coming tonight?'

Cathy shook her head, looking nervous and worried. 'It's probably best if he doesn't.'

'And you're sure you don't want to do this?' Willow asked one last time. 'You're sure you want it to be me?'

'Please, Willow.'

'OK, Mum, I'll do it. But I do need to find something to wear.'

They searched through Cathy's closet looking for something suitable and, not for the first time, Willow was grateful that they were the same size.

'Perhaps it's time you went back to London,' Cathy said, as she pulled a smart black dress from the back of the closet and handed it to Willow. 'If only to get yourself some clothes.'

'Let's get this planning permission out of the way,' Willow said. 'If we're successful tonight I'll try to get back to London for a few days before the festival starts.'

When she had lived in London Willow would get up at 5am to go to the gym where she'd do a yoga or Pilates class or work out with her trainer. Her hair was highlighted every four weeks, her nails manicured weekly and her clothes cost an embarrassing amount of money.

She was still in the habit of waking early but for the last month she'd swapped her gym sessions for walks on the beach. She'd been living out of the small overnight bag she had at the hotel when she had run away and had been wearing her mother's clothes. The roots of her hair were growing out and she'd cut her nails short because it was easier to play the mandolin that way.

When she looked at herself in the mirror wearing her mother's black dress, she liked what she saw. In London

Willow had never quite felt enough. No matter how hard she'd tried she was never polished enough for Charlie. Now when she looked at herself she saw Willow. She was softer than the woman who left London.

And she was happier.

Willow had changed everything about herself to fit in with Charlie and his family. While Charlie had never asked her outright to do so, she had found herself feeling she needed to, found herself needing to close the huge gap between his monied upbringing and hers on the Island. She hadn't been averse to changing herself at first. She'd been eager to let go of the Island once and for all. She'd wanted to start again, to be a different Willow. But over the last eighteen months since she first saw Luc on *American Stars*, she had come to understand that nobody can ever truly let go of the person they used to be.

As Willow had begun to work that out, something had shifted in her relationship with Charlie, something she'd been trying to ignore. He'd started to criticise her more than he used to, point out when she wasn't quite polished enough or ask her if she was sure about an outfit she'd chosen. Willow had told herself that he had her best interests at heart, that he wanted her to get promoted again and live the life they'd always planned. It was the reason Willow had given in so easily to the wedding that his mother wanted instead of the quiet Register Office one she would have preferred.

When she looked at herself in the mirror, she felt more confident than she had in years, as though the quiet energy of the Island was beginning to restore her to the person she used to be. And it gave her the confidence to ask her mother a question she'd been trying to ask since she'd listened to the tape with Luc the week before.

'Mum, do you remember Storm Tyler and King Silver.'

Cathy was standing with her back to Willow so Willow couldn't see her reaction. She didn't reply for a moment.

'That's a name I haven't heard in a while,' Cathy said turning around, her face falsely merry.

'Do you know what happened to him?' Willow asked.

'No idea,' Cathy replied almost too quickly.

'Did the Laurels ever play with him? Or with King Silver?'

Cathy shrugged. 'Oh I think we might have shared festival billing once or twice,' she said. 'Where's this coming from?'

For a moment Willow thought about telling her mother everything, about finding the tape and listening to it with Luc, about the idea she'd had that just might save the festival. But she couldn't, not now – there wasn't time.

'Oh just something Luc and I were talking about,' she said instead.

'Well we'd better get going then,' Cathy said.

The snippet of conversation they'd managed to have about Storm Tyler had been enough though, because Willow knew her mother, knew her reticence to talk about the past and knew she probably wouldn't get much more out of her even if she had told her about the tape. But the look on her mother's face when she tried to shrug off the question, coupled with Cathy's voice on the recording, was all Willow needed to confirm her suspicions and put her plan in place.

The planning committee was made up almost entirely of faces Willow recognised from her childhood – if they weren't people who had been councillors for time eternal, they were people like Roger who she used to go to school with and who had never moved away. With the exception of Roger, everyone smiled warmly at both Willow and Cathy, which had to be a good sign.

It was stifling inside the council chamber and, as the committee discussed the facts of the matter, Willow found herself struggling to stay focused, her mind constantly drifting back to the tape in her bedroom drawer and the look on Luc's face as they'd listened to it. When she heard her name called she knew that it was her turn to stand up and present her case.

'With respect,' Roger said as Willow finished her well-rehearsed speech. 'You haven't set foot on the Island for...' he paused to consult his notes, even though he must know how that sentence finished '...eight years.' He smiled at Willow like a snake. 'How do you know how we operate here these days?'

Willow had tried to be professional and speak without passion or emotion just as she had to do in her job, but she could see it wasn't working. Even some of the councillors who had greeted her so warmly earlier on were nodding in agreement with Roger. She knew she had to do something. Her mother needed this festival and Willow couldn't let her down. As Willow caught Cathy's eye, she saw a look of desperation on her mother's face.

'Why should we continue with this smaller festival?' Roger went on. 'Surely it's had its day. We have a much larger festival on the Island now.' He looked at Willow venomously. Was Luc right? Was this really some sort of revenge because Roger had been in love with her at school and she'd ignored him? Whatever his reasons, she knew she couldn't let him win.

She tried to think about all the things she used to love about the festival, why her mum set it up in the first place, the trade it brought to Seaview.

This festival meant so much to so many people. On Thursday night in the studio, when Luc had called her Lil, everything about who Willow used to be had come flooding back and for the first time in as long as she could remember she didn't hate that person, and she didn't hate the Island or the memories that she and Luc shared.

She regretted walking away, more than ever before.

The festival had to go ahead, not just because it would break her mother's heart if it didn't and not just because Luc was here to headline the final night on the beach. It needed to go ahead because she wanted to be there. Willow wanted to be at the Seaview Folk Festival for the first time in nearly a decade to see what it had to tell her about herself.

'The Seaview Folk Festival is nothing like the Isle of Wight Festival,' she began. 'It's something much more local, more personal, something specifically for the people of Seaview.' She paused to look around. All eyes except Roger's were on her.

'There are lots of reasons why the festival is good for Seaview,' she continued. 'It brings trade to local businesses and brings money into this little bit of the Island that isn't as well known.'

'It also brings riff-raff,' Roger interrupted, but Willow could see that he'd lost the other councillors' attention now. 'And the main festival brings plenty of money into Seaview.'

'Agreed,' Willow replied, trying to stay calm. 'But the

main festival brings people to the Island for a week in June. Our festival makes them stay around.' She thought of Rocco Beezon ordering ukuleles and staying in his expensive apartment and she was sure that The Music Shop wasn't the only store he'd been spending money in.

'The Folk Festival is a major boost to our little part of the Island. But it also has huge significance for Seaview itself. My parents, along with Krystal Kane, were a major part of the folk music revival of the 1990s and their festival has helped so many musicians find their feet, musicians who have gone on to great success and come back to Seaview year after year,' she paused. 'Including, as I'm sure you all know, Luc Harrison.'

A rumble of agreement rolled round the chamber and Willow swallowed, ignoring the butterflies that arrived in her stomach at the thought of Luc. 'The Folk Festival also helped put the Island back on the map after the disaster of the festivals in the 1970s – you might even say it helped pave the way for the main festival to return.' Willow wasn't sure how true that statement was but she was desperate.

'I hear that ticket sales are low this year,' a councillor she didn't recognise said. 'Despite Luc being here.'

'Ticket sales have been low year on year,' Roger interrupted.

'Ticket sales fluctuate from one year to the next it's true,' Willow agreed, grateful that she'd had a good look through her mother's past paperwork after Roger had dropped the hint about poor ticket sales last week. 'But my parents have always tried to keep the festival small and intimate – we never sell huge numbers of tickets and have no desire to do so. However this year is particularly low – that's also true.

I suspect most people don't want to buy tickets to a festival that might not go ahead so they're waiting on the council's decision.'

'There doesn't seem much point going through the process of granting the necessary licences to a festival that might be cancelled because of low ticket sales,' said the councillor Willow didn't recognise. Roger nodded in agreement. 'How can you guarantee that you won't cancel the festival after the council has done all the hard work to approve it?'

Willow looked at Roger who was staring back at her with one eyebrow raised like a pantomime villain. She looked over at her mother who was sitting quietly, wringing her hands in her lap. The festival was the most important thing in her mum's life and Willow didn't know how Cathy would cope without it. The Seaview Folk Festival had to go ahead. It was time to put her crazy plan in motion. Compared to the risks she took in her job in the City on a daily basis, what she was about to do was fairly small fry but she crossed her fingers behind her back for luck anyway.

'How will you guarantee ticket sales?' the councillor repeated.

A voice in Willow's head that sounded a little bit like Charlie, was telling her that she was ridiculous, that this couldn't possibly work. She ignored it and took a deep breath.

'What if I could get a folk legend to play at the festival?' she said. 'That would guarantee your precious ticket sales.'

'A folk legend like who?' asked Roger with a smirk.

'A folk legend like...' Willow paused as though she was pretending to think. 'Storm Tyler.'

A silence descended on the council chamber as Willow looked over to her mum again. Cathy was staring at her in disbelief and suddenly her grand plan didn't seem so grand anymore, it felt more like opening up a Pandora's box.

Roger was still smirking. 'Storm Tyler,' he said. 'The Storm Tyler who disappeared many years ago and has never been heard of since?'

'The very same,' Willow replied with false bravado, quite surprised that Roger seemed to know so much about Storm Tyler.

'And how are you planning to contact the elusive Mr Tyler?' Roger went on. 'How are you planning to tempt him out of retirement?'

Willow resisted the urge to glance over at her mother and forced herself to keep smiling her confident, if fake, smile. Now that her plan had been spoken out loud it seemed more ridiculous than ever.

'Roger,' she said calmly. 'My family were and still are the centre of this folk festival as I've said. We have our contacts. Trust me, I know what to do.'

Willow had absolutely no idea what to do or why on earth she had ever thought this truly ridiculous plan was going to work but she could hardly back down now. She looked around at the other committee members who were regarding her and Roger with interest.

Roger opened his mouth to say something else but the Chair of the Planning Committee stood up, interrupting him. 'Thank you, Ms Cole,' he said. 'Our decision will be available online tomorrow.'

*

'What were you thinking?' Cathy asked in the car on the way back to Seaview. 'Making such a rash promise?'

'I'm trying to save the festival,' Willow replied.

'But why Storm Tyler of all the people? Is that why you were asking me about him earlier? What's going on, Willow? What have you heard?'

Cathy's hands were gripping the steering wheel of the Jeep, her eyes focused on the road ahead. Willow knew she had to come clean.

'Luc and I found a tape in your workshop. It was an old DAT recording and we wondered what it was.'

Cathy didn't say anything.

'When we listened to it Luc recognised it as Storm Tyler and I recognised your voice.'

'You did?' Cathy asked. She didn't deny it being her.

'Of course I did, Mum, I'd recognise your voice anywhere.' She paused but Cathy didn't say anything else. 'Anyway, the tape was dated 1999, which made me think he'd been here at some point and your voice, plus your reaction when I mentioned his name earlier, made me think you must know him and…' She trailed off. She could feel her mother's anger from the passenger seat.

Willow looked over at her mother whose face was pale in the glow of the oncoming headlights.

'You shouldn't have done that,' Cathy said quietly. 'Not without asking me.'

'I was just trying to save the festival,' Willow repeated.

Cathy didn't reply and neither of them spoke for the rest of journey until Cathy pulled the Jeep up in front of her house in Seaview.

'Tell me how you came to be rooting around through

my things,' Cathy said. 'How you ended up listening to the tape.'

Willow told her mother about finding the tape, about how both she and Luc thought it was something important. She told her about booking the studio time so they could listen to it, about realising how special it was.

Cathy was quiet after Willow finished speaking and she sat very still in the driver's seat, still looking straight ahead.

'I'm sorry, Mum,' Willow said.

Neither of them said anything for a moment.

'And what is your grand plan to tempt Storm Tyler out of retirement then?' Cathy asked.

'Oh, Mum, you know full well I don't have a plan. I just said that to try to get the council on side.'

Cathy sighed and pressed her hand to her forehead.

'So what are you intending to do?'

'I have no idea,' Willow said. 'Unless you know where he is?'

'I don't want to talk about it,' Cathy replied. 'I can't talk about it.'

She got out of the car then, slamming the door behind her and leaving Willow with a very strong suspicion that her mother knew exactly what had happened to Storm Tyler.

20

Luc

The morning after the planning committee meeting Luc found Willow sitting on the clifftop staring out to sea. He could tell she'd been crying even though she denied it.

He sat down next to her, close enough so that their bodies were touching. The morning sun was warm despite the sea breeze and he felt a sense of calm as he watched the undulation of the waves beneath him. It was a view he'd known his whole life, one he thought of sometimes when he was at home in landlocked Tennessee. He'd missed the sea more than he realised.

'Are you OK?' he asked.

'I'm fine,' she said. 'Honestly.'

'You're not fine, Willow. Tell me what's wrong.'

'The festival,' she said quietly. 'I've done something so stupid.'

'I take it the planning committee meeting didn't go well.'

'It was awful. I completely choked in front of them all. I deal with billionaires and venture capitalists every day at

164

work but put me in front of a small council committee and I completely fold.'

'I thought they'd be on your side,' Luc said. He felt sad at the thought there wouldn't be a festival, but also a sense of relief that he wouldn't have to play. 'I thought Roger Beck would be a lone protestor.'

'So did I and at first it did feel like that but then Roger started talking about ticket sales and how they'd been down year on year. I've no idea how he knew tickets sales were poor this year but he did and he asked what was the point in approving the licences and permissions if we ended up cancelling anyway.' She paused, turning to look at him. 'And that's when I made the stupidest promise I've ever made.'

'What did you do?'

'I said that I'd make sure the festival sold out by getting Storm Tyler to play at it.'

Luc didn't say anything as he digested her words and tried to work out the expression on her face.

It looked like fear.

'I'd been thinking about it since we found the tape,' Willow went on. 'It seemed like a good idea until the words came out of my mouth. I tried to talk to Mum about the tape but she wouldn't say anything'. Luc knew how hard it was to get their respective parents to talk about the past.

'How the hell are you going to get Storm Tyler to play at the festival?' he asked.

'I have no idea,' Willow said, turning away from him to look out to sea again.

'You know, Willow,' Luc said slowly. 'This isn't your responsibility. You don't have to do this; it's your parents' job. You have your own life to get on with.'

'I'm taking some time off work,' she said. 'I'm going to stay here for the summer and try to help Mum sort this out.'

Luc was surprised. It was the last thing he'd expected to hear. He'd thought that she would be eager to get back to London, to her job at least, if not her fiancé.

'But now I've just made everything worse,' she went on. He saw her trying to blink back tears again and he wrapped his arm around her waist, pulling her close. She didn't pull away and he relished the feel of her next to him, wishing just for a moment that things could be different, that he could stay here with her forever.

'You haven't,' he said. 'And I'm glad that you're staying for the summer. But why are you so invested in the festival? Why do you want it to happen so much?' Part of him didn't want her to be so invested, part of him didn't want the festival to happen at all because he didn't know if he could face playing.

'I don't know how Mum will cope if the festival doesn't go ahead,' she replied. 'I sometimes think it's the only thing she's got in her life and that's my fault too for not coming to visit anymore.'

'None of this is your fault, Willow.'

'And then there's you,' she said.

'Me?'

'You've come all this way to play Mum's festival, abandoning your life in America, and now it might not go ahead. I can't let that happen.'

Luc felt stab of guilt at the part of him that was relieved that the festival might have to be cancelled.

She turned to look at him again and he didn't want to resist this anymore. By mentioning his life in Nashville she'd reminded him of how precious this time with her was. He knew that she could feel it too – that sense that they could never be together, but they had been given the gift of this summer. Her blue eyes were locked on his and her lips were just a breath away. If he ducked his head just a little, he could kiss her.

The air around them went still and Luc didn't know who initiated it but the moment his lips touched hers it ignited a fire inside him that he thought he'd put out years ago. He tried to hold back, to let her take the lead and for a moment there was a fleeting thought on the outer edges of his mind telling him to stop, that now wasn't the time, that he was going to hurt everyone. But Luc ignored it as he felt her hands on the back of his neck, her fingers running into his hair, as her tongue found his. For the first time in nearly twelve years he was kissing Willow Cole.

He never wanted to let her go.

She broke the kiss first, and Luc knew why. It was too soon – only a few weeks had passed since she walked out of her wedding and, as far as he knew, she still hadn't worked out why or spoken to the man she was supposed to marry since he went on honeymoon with someone else. But when he looked at her she was smiling and he knew that they had both wanted that kiss, however bad the timing might have been.

'Sorry,' she said, her fingers brushing gently against her lips where his had been a moment before.

Luc smiled. 'You definitely don't have to apologise for that.'

'I've been wanting to do that for weeks,' she admitted quietly. 'It's just—'

'Not the right time,' he interrupted. The breeze blew her hair across her face and Luc reached across to tuck it behind her ear. 'I know.'

She took his hand in hers. 'I want you to play at Mum's festival, Luc,' she said.

'I have played before,' he replied, thinking of the open mic night that he won in The Three Doves all those years ago.

'Yes but this time you'll be headlining. I'm going to make sure of it.'

They sat for a moment, holding hands and looking out towards the sea. There was nobody else around and if it wasn't for the distant sounds from the beach below and the gentle chimes of an ice-cream van, he could believe they were the only people in the world.

'So,' he said after a while. 'Storm Tyler.'

She pulled a face. 'I don't even know how to begin finding him.'

'Maybe just the rumour of him coming will be enough,' Luc said hopefully.

'Do you want to deal with the riot when he doesn't show?'

'I don't know how much you know about Storm Tyler, but not turning up would be pretty on-brand. So much so some people might be disappointed if he did show.'

'I was up half the night researching him and King Silver. He's not the most reliable person is he? Even by rock star standards.'

'Alcoholic, mood swings, broke up his band twice, abandoned his own solo tour and then disappeared completely in the late Eighties,' Luc said. 'No, he's not very reliable at all.'

'There's a message board dedicated to him you know,' Willow said. 'And all these people, men obviously, discussing what might have happened to him. There are so many rumours – rumours he died, joined a cult, recorded a solo album that never got released…' She paused. 'But I guess I thought that he'd been on the Island before so he might come back again.'

Luc nodded slowly. 'What did your mum say about it all?' he asked.

'I don't think she's speaking to me,' Willow said. 'She was angry that we'd listened to the tape without telling her.'

'I can understand that.' He'd been feeling guilty about it since last week.

'Me too,' Willow agreed. 'I think she knows where Storm Tyler is but she says she can't talk about it.'

'Can't or won't?' Luc asked.

'I don't know,' Willow replied, leaning her head on Luc's shoulder. 'She told me that I was interfering in her business and that I should never have listened to the tape. She went to bed as soon as we got home and she was gone when I got up this morning.'

They sat quietly together and Luc wished he could bottle this moment for later, for when the summer was over and he had to go home.

'What do you think happened to him?' she asked.

'I think he's just hiding out somewhere in the middle of nowhere, avoiding both music and his crazed fans like the plague.'

'And how do I find him?'

'Start by emailing his old agent and King Silver's management company – you'll find them easily enough online,' Luc replied. 'In the meantime I'll ask my agent. He might have some ideas.'

He felt Willow stiffen in his arms and move away.

'He?' she asked. 'The agent you call "sweetheart" is a guy?'

He knew that she never believed that phone call was from his agent. He knew that now would be the time to tell her about Annelise, just like Don wanted him to, but he couldn't find the words. It was too much.

'Luc I'm not really in the habit of kissing other people's boyfriends.'

'God, Willow, it's not what you think.' He saw her raise her eyebrows and he cringed at the cliché in his words. 'My life is… complicated,' he said. *Tell her*, the voice in his head whispered but he ignored it.

He watched Willow crumple then, her shoulders rounding forward as though she'd fallen in on herself under the weight of everything that had happened.

'Life seems to get that way for us all,' she said.

'There isn't anyone else,' he said quietly. 'Not in Nashville, not anywhere.'

She didn't reply. She didn't look at him.

'I'm sorry, Willow,' he said. He reached out for her and she turned to him brushing his fingers with hers. All Luc could hear was the beating of his own heart and the sound of the sea in the background. He couldn't push her away, he needed her to be there if the festival went ahead. If he knew that she was in the audience, he might just be able to get on stage.

'I should go,' she said. 'I'm late opening The Music Shop.'

Luc sat on the clifftop watching her walk away, feeling as though he'd been hit over the head. That was what kissing Willow Cole did to him.

Luc bumped into Don outside the apartment building they were both staying in.

'Have you spoken to Willow?' Don asked.

Luc nodded, he knew what was coming.

'Storm Tyler?' Don said. 'Really?'

'It wasn't my idea,' Luc replied defensively.

'No, but I bet listening to that damn tape in the first place was your bloody idea. She'd never have got around to it on her own, and even if she had she'd never have worked out who was playing on it.'

'She'd have recognised her own mother's voice,' Luc said.

Don paused for a moment, running a hand over his face. Luc could hear the sound of the callouses on Don's fingers – from years of playing guitar – brushing against the stubble on his chin.

'It's not your fault.' He sighed. 'I had Cathy banging the door down at dawn telling me all about it but you and Willow weren't to know.'

'Know what?' Luc asked.

'I'm going to meet Rocco for breakfast,' Don said, changing the subject. 'Do you fancy coming with us.'

'Rocco's still here?'

'He's writing an album apparently. The sea inspires him.' There was a resignation in the way Don was talking as though Rocco was getting on his nerves, as though everything was getting on his nerves. Luc had never seen Don like this, but he wished the sea was inspiring him. 'So are you coming?' Don asked again.

Luc shook his head. 'No,' he said. 'I need to work.'

'You're writing again?' Don asked.

'I told you I was.'

'And I wasn't sure I believed you.'

'I haven't been,' Luc admitted. 'But I have to try. If Willow pulls this off and the festival goes ahead I need to be able to get on stage without falling apart and I need at least one song that the audience haven't heard before.'

'Luc, have you…?' Don began but Luc held up his hand. He knew what was coming and he knew Don was right – he had to tell Cathy and Willow about Annelise.

'Not yet,' he said quietly. 'One thing at a time.'

Don stepped away, nodding.

'I'm going to shut myself away for a couple of days,' Luc said, thinking that perhaps after that kiss, he should put some space between himself and Willow before he did something stupid, something he shouldn't be doing. 'Crack this writer's block, then I'll tell her OK?'

'OK,' Don said, walking away.

Before he started work he phoned his agent. He told Sam about the tape that he and Willow had found.

'There was always a rumour that he'd recorded "Gamble Gold",' Sam said. 'Years ago, when King Silver were first getting famous Storm used to do a solo spot in the middle of the show, an acoustic set, and he often played "Gamble Gold" then.'

'But he never recorded it?'

'No, people tried to get him to because he played it so differently to everyone else, but he never did. Rumours went around that he'd left a tape somewhere before he disappeared, but this was recorded in 1999 you say?'

'Long after he disappeared.'

'What's it like?' Sam asked.

'Beautiful.' But that was a completely inadequate description for what listening to that tape had made him feel. It had brought up all sorts of emotions, ones Luc had been burying for a long time. But it had also given him the kernel of an idea, one he was too scared to think about just yet.

'I don't know if you remember this or not,' Sam said. 'But your mum's old band used to play a version of "Gamble Gold" back in the day.'

'I remember.'

'Did your mum ever mention why?'

'I don't think so. Mum doesn't talk about the past very much.'

Sam paused for a moment and Luc heard him sigh. 'I'm surprised that you don't know this already to be honest but a long time ago Storm Tyler went on a rather ill-fated solo tour.'

'OK,' Luc said. 'I know that. But what's it got to do with the tape.'

'Storm played "Gamble Gold" every night on that tour up until his support act started playing it instead.'

He paused and Luc was just about to fill the silence with more impatient questions when Sam spoke again.

'His support act was The Laurels,' he said.

Luc didn't say anything for a moment because that little bit of information had knocked him off his feet. Why had Krystal never said anything? Why had Willow's parents never told her?

'There's a connection there if you want to look for it, I guess,' Sam said.

'Do you know what it is?' Luc asked, sick of him talking in riddles.

'No. I'm old, man, but I'm not that old. I never knew Storm – he'd disappeared before I started working in this shitty industry. I'm just warning you that you might want to think twice before digging much deeper. You might not like what you find.'

Luc felt that familiar sense of tightening around his heart. He needed to sit down. He needed to talk to his mother. He needed to talk to Willow.

'And speaking of this shitty industry,' Sam went on. 'Have you got anything for me yet?'

'I'm working on it,' Luc replied. 'Right now.'

21

August 1987

Cathy woke from a deep sleep. With her eyes still closed, the sheets wrapped around her, she tried to remember where she was. Someone was snoring loudly next to her and it reverberated through her sore head. She remembered how much vodka she'd drunk the night before and as if on cue her stomach lurched, a wave of nausea washing over her. What had she been thinking drinking so much? She hardly ever drank and she shouldn't have been drinking at all; she shouldn't have done that to the baby.

She stretched her legs out, brushing against another pair of legs in the bed beside her. Storm had come to bed the night before after all. Usually when he went out with the band he'd roll in drunk and crash out on the sofa. Then the next day he'd be sad and rueful, apologising constantly.

'You're still my muse, Cathy Cole,' he'd say.

But it had been a long time since Storm had created anything worthy of needing a muse.

Carefully, so as not to disturb either Storm or what

promised to be a horrendous headache, Cathy pushed herself out of bed. As she stood up she saw why Storm had come to bed the night before, why he was sleeping so close to her on the king-sized mattress.

There was someone else in the bed with them, someone young and pretty and fast asleep with her head resting on Storm's chest.

Cathy choked back the mix of tears and nausea and turned away, walking quietly into the kitchen. She was under no illusion that Storm had been faithful to her over the years, but this was a new low. She was angry with herself too for passing out and not realising what Storm had done. Not that he would have been capable of doing much – he was barely capable of anything these days. The groupie in her bed must be quite disappointed and that gave Cathy some consolation at least.

She leant against the sink as she poured herself a glass of water, which she sipped slowly. Since that afternoon two and half years ago when Storm had knocked on Krystal's door asking for her, Cathy had been living with him in Green Park in the flat where she had first slept with him a lifetime ago.

Things had been good at first, really good, despite Don and Krystal's reluctance to let Cathy go. Neither of them thought that Storm could possibly have changed in such a short amount of time. Cathy should have listened to them, but when it came to Storm she was incapable of listening to reason.

The first six months had been wonderful, exactly how Cathy had imagined her life would be back when she lived in the bedsit with Pip. Storm was sober and full of creativity.

Together they would write music – bouncing ideas off one another until late into the night. The Laurels were doing well, playing to fully booked venues all over the country and Don had booked them in for their first overseas tour – supporting another folk band through France and Germany in the spring.

King Silver meanwhile were bigger than they'd ever been – their comeback album had outsold all their other records and their upcoming tour had sold out in days.

He wasn't going to drink again, he'd promised. He wasn't going to ruin another tour by being out of his head. He wasn't going to make the same mistakes.

'And I'll be back by Christmas,' he'd said, kissing her gently as he got ready to leave for the tour. 'We'll have plenty of time together before it's your turn to tour.'

He was drunk within a week; it was all over the papers and she'd felt a fool to have believed a word he'd said.

And yet she had stayed. Despite the drink and the drugs, despite never really knowing where he was half the time, despite The Laurels going from strength to strength as King Silver lurched from crisis to crisis, she had stayed. For two years she had stayed loyal to him, only putting The Laurels and her career before Storm.

Don and Krystal had become increasingly worried. Don had begged her to leave Storm, convinced that she was in danger. But Cathy had stayed and the longer she stayed the more isolated she became from everyone else she knew.

It was Don who intervened in the end. Almost two years to the day that Storm had knocked on Krystal's door looking for Cathy, Don arrived to take Cathy out.

'You can't just stay in all the time waiting for him to come home,' he said.

They went for dinner, the first of many dinners and lunches that they ate together as Storm did whatever it was Storm did when he wasn't on tour or in the studio. Cathy never really knew, never really wanted to think about it.

'You have to get on with your own life,' Don said.

'But this life I have, being in The Laurels, knowing you and Krystal, I owe it to him,' Cathy replied.

Don wouldn't have it. He wouldn't allow Cathy to waste her talents, waste her life on a man who didn't appreciate her, a man who was barely sober enough to notice whether she was there or not. As winter became spring, as The Laurels toured in Europe again, as spring became summer and they were starting to get ready for festival season, Don finally started to get through to her. The more time they spent together the more Cathy remembered how life was meant to be. She was twenty-two years old; she should be out there living her life, not spending her nights sitting alone, worrying.

And at some point, between the daffodils coming into bloom and the festival season starting at midsummer, Cathy and Don became more than friends. Storm wasn't the only one who could cheat on their relationship.

Last night was meant to have been the end. Cathy had arranged to meet Storm at his flat and he had promised to be there. She had been going to tell him that she was leaving, tell him about her and Don. She'd had it all planned out.

But Storm hadn't come home. She'd waited and waited and still he hadn't come. And that was when she'd poured herself a drink – one wouldn't hurt, she had told herself. But one had turned into several and in the end she had taken herself to bed, drunk and sad and crippled with the guilt of what the vodka had done to her baby.

The baby Storm didn't know about. The baby she could never tell him about.

22

Willow

As Willow walked to The Music Shop all she could think about was kissing Luc. She hadn't meant to kiss him; it had only been a month since the wedding that never was. But as she unlocked the door to the shop she touched her lips with her fingertips again and remembered Luc's kiss, how good it felt. It had been a long time since Charlie had kissed her like that. When had it gone wrong? When had she and Charlie started taking each other for granted? When had Charlie changed so much?

She was so lost in thought that she didn't notice Roger Beck creep up behind her until she heard his voice.

'You're late opening up,' he said, making Willow jump out of her skin and push the door open too hard, setting that damn bell off again. She really must take it down.

Roger was the last person Willow wanted to see. 'Hello, Roger.'

'The whole Island is buzzing with the rumour.'

'What rumour?'

'That Storm Tyler is on his way.' Roger smirked. 'Any luck finding him yet?'

'I don't need luck, Roger,' she lied. 'I know exactly what I'm doing.'

Roger looked a little taken aback at that, which gave Willow some satisfaction.

'Well I hope you do know what you're doing,' he said. 'Because if he doesn't show, and I understand he's quite famous for that, you're going to have a lot of angry fans on your hands.'

'He'll show,' Willow said as Roger started to walk away, but she had no idea how to make it happen. She'd clearly upset her mother and she hadn't found the courage to ask her father's opinion yet. She'd only ever meant to help and now she was pretty sure she'd started something she couldn't finish. She'd forgotten how quickly rumours spread through Seaview, and that everyone would have heard about her wild promises by now. Why had she got herself involved in this when she should be back in London trying to sort out the mess she'd left behind there? Her life seemed to be a series of messes – Charlie, Storm Tyler, Luc.

As the shop door shut behind her and the bell jangled again she thought she might replace it with a sign that said: *Abandon hope all ye who enter here.* Luc's kiss had reminded her of all the things she used to be but it had also reminded her of all the things they had lost twelve years ago and how they could never get that time back, not now. Because even the lingering memory of Luc's lips didn't change the fact that everything was hopeless, that she had no idea where Storm Tyler might be, that she didn't love

Charlie anymore, that Luc had mysterious commitments on the other side of the Atlantic.

She took her phone out of her pocket and thought about calling Charlie again even though she knew he wouldn't answer. She could call him at work where it would be harder for him to ignore her, but also it would irritate him – he'd be short with her and wouldn't want to talk in the office. Willow knew there was only one thing for it – she was going to have to bite the bullet and go back to London for a few days. She could easily be there and back before the festival started.

'Morning, Willow,' Tom Newell called as he pushed the shop door open, setting the bell off again. 'I've just popped in for some guitar picks.'

Willow hoped that was all he wanted. She noticed that he'd tied his little dog, Monty, up outside the shop so hopefully he wouldn't be here long. She felt as though she needed to be alone.

As Tom looked at the display of guitar picks, Willow wondered how much he knew about the history of the Seaview Folk Festival. He'd always been the sort of person who stored up all kinds of musical knowledge.

'Tom,' she began hesitantly.

'Mmm?' He looked up at her.

'You've heard of Storm Tyler, right?'

'Of course,' he said. 'Who hasn't? Although it's a mystery what happened to him.' It was interesting that he didn't mention her rash promise. Perhaps Roger Beck had been lying about the whole Island buzzing with the rumour, just as she'd been lying when she told him she knew what she was doing.

'So you've no idea?' Willow felt disappointed that he didn't seem to know anything.

'No, I don't think anyone does do they?'

He went back to examining the picks. Tom was unusually quiet this morning.

'Although,' he said slowly after a moment. 'There was rumour of him coming to Seaview one year.'

'Really?'

Tom nodded and leant on the shop counter, the picks forgotten. 'There was a rumour he was going to play the festival or that he was recording on the Island,' he said. 'But he didn't play and there was no new record so I guess they were all just rumours.'

Willow tried to keep her face as neutral as she could. 'Can you remember when this was?'

'Nineteen years ago,' Tom replied authoritatively. 'It was my first summer on the Island, before I started running the studio. It was the summer of the solar eclipse.' He paused. 'Do you remember the eclipse?'

The summer that she and Luc were eleven, the summer before they were sent to school full-time. Willow could remember the eclipse; she could remember looking up at the sun with Luc, both wearing special protective glasses. She could remember being disappointed that it didn't go completely dark like it had done in Cornwall, just a strange sort of twilight that made all the animals at the zoo get ready for bed.

How could she and Luc not have known anything about it? She tried to remember if they were listening to King Silver by then but she thought that might have been the following summer. Luc would know.

'I'm surprised your mother never mentioned it.' Tom said.

'I suppose if the whole thing was nothing but rumours,' she replied, 'then Mum wouldn't have bothered talking about it.'

Tom shrugged and turned back to the guitar picks, but Willow's brain was whirring from all the implications of what Tom had inadvertently told her. She already knew Storm had been on the Island that summer and he'd spent time with her mother. What had happened to stop Storm recording any more songs, or playing at the festival? She needed to talk to her mother and to Luc.

She needed to talk to Luc about so many things.

Her phone vibrated and it was a text from Luc, as though he knew she was thinking about him.

I need to lock myself away and do some work for a couple of days, it said. *But there's something I have to tell you. Will you have dinner with me on Friday?*

She could hear Tom talking to her as she read the text again, but she wasn't listening. She barely paused before replying. She didn't think about the kiss, or about Charlie or Storm Tyler or the tape that was locked in the drawer by her bed. She didn't even think about the mysterious "sweetheart" on the other end of Luc's phone who wasn't his agent.

This was Luc Harrison and they only had a few weeks together. All she could do was text back one word.

Yes.

Now she just had to worry about what to wear.

'It's not Bond Street,' Skye said as she and Willow got off the bus in Ryde the following afternoon. 'But we should be able to find something for you to wear.'

'I don't only shop on Bond Street you know,' Willow replied, but Skye just looked at her, eyebrows raised.

'Let's start in Primark then,' she said. Willow tried not to pull a face.

'Ha!' Skye pointed at her, smiling. 'I knew it! Don't worry, Ryde doesn't have anything as sophisticated as a Primark yet. But I'm sure the boutique shops will be more in your line!'

Willow had told Skye that she would cobble an outfit together for her dinner with Luc.

'Don't be ridiculous,' Skye had replied. 'We need a shopping trip. You need to look your absolute best.'

'You didn't need to do this,' Willow said now as they walked away from the Esplanade. 'You didn't need to close the studio to take me shopping.'

'Of course I did! What are friends for?'

When she heard those words, Willow had to look away, biting her lip. Her heart suddenly felt too big for her chest as she realised that it wasn't just seeing Luc again that had made her slip back into Island life so easily. It was being with Skye too. She'd never had a friend like Skye since she'd left and she was beginning to wonder if she ever would. She'd heard people talk about those friendships where you don't see each other for years but then, when you do, you just pick up where you left off. She'd always assumed she'd never know what that was like but it turned out she'd had it all along, waiting for her on the Island.

'I'd have lent you something of mine if we weren't such different shapes,' Skye went on. 'But I know exactly the place for you.'

She led Willow to a small clothes shop on Melville Street, with a display of beautiful one-off dresses in the window.

'How long has this been here?' Willow asked. It had been a long time since she'd been to Ryde.

'About five years. The woman who owns it uses bespoke designers from all over, not just from the Island. Whatever you buy from here you can guarantee it will be a one-off. We haven't got time for you to order anything in but I'm sure they'll have exactly what you need.'

Skye smiled and Willow's heart swelled again.

'Why are you being so nice to me?' she asked. 'When I was so awful to you?'

'Oh, Willow, I've told you that it wasn't you who was awful to me and it's water under the bridge now anyway. Life's too short to bear grudges – you know that.'

They stepped into the shop and the owner greeted Skye effusively, kissing her on each cheek.

'We've sold nearly all of your paintings,' she said, gesturing towards a wall at the back of the shop where some of Skye's artwork was displayed for sale. 'Do you have any more?'

'Not today, but I will bring some more soon,' Skye said. 'This is my friend Willow and this is Delia who owns the shop.'

Delia extended a hand and Willow took it.

'We need to get Willow a hot dress for a hot date.'

'It's not a hot—' Willow began.

'I've got a few things that might just be perfect,' Delia interrupted, leading them towards the back of the shop. She loaded Willow's arms up with dresses as Skye pointed to all the ones she thought would be suitable and then pointed them both in the direction of the changing rooms. 'Take your time,' Delia said.

Willow tried on each of the dresses that Skye had chosen for her. They were all so beautiful. Most of them were handmade and finished perfectly. They were as good as anything she could have found on Bond Street and much quirkier and more original.

'I love them all,' she said. 'But I think I'm going to go with the black one.'

'Nonsense,' Skye replied. 'You look magnificent in the red one. Buy that.'

Willow held the red dress up in front of her.

'Really?' she asked. 'Do you think so? It's not really a date. I don't think Luc will be expecting much and—'

'Willow, you could turn up in a bin bag and Luc wouldn't be able to keep his eyes off you.'

'He doesn't—'

'He does, and if you haven't noticed then you're more unobservant than I thought. I get that it hasn't been long since you walked out on your wedding and I get that you still want to play safe, but you aren't buying this dress for Luc.'

'I'm not?' Willow was so used to buying dresses that Charlie would approve of that she had automatically thought about Luc in the changing rooms. She hadn't wanted to look obvious or wear something Luc wouldn't like.

But Luc wasn't like that. He wasn't Charlie.

'No you're not,' Skye said. 'You're buying this dress for yourself, to help you work out what you want and who you are. You don't have to buy the red dress if you don't want to, but don't buy the black one just because it's safe – buy it because it makes you feel and look amazing.'

Willow held the red dress up against herself again,

remembering how she'd felt when she first saw herself in it. It had felt amazing; Skye was right. It wasn't the sort of dress that she could wear in front of Charlie.

But she wasn't buying it for Charlie, or Luc for that matter. She was buying it for herself.

'OK,' she said. 'The red one.'

They took the dress to Delia.

'Good choice,' she said. 'That's a Julia Simmonds original. Her dresses are always stunning.' She wrapped the dress in soft pink tissue and put it in a paper carrier bag for her. 'It was lovely to meet you,' she said as she handed the bag over. 'I hope the dress brings you a lot of joy.'

'Oh it will,' Skye said authoritatively.

Willow and Skye bought sandwiches and cans of gin and tonic and walked back to the Esplanade to sit and eat, looking out to sea. The salty wind whipped around Willow's face, blowing her hair loose from her ponytail.

'I've never had a gin and tonic in a can before,' she said as she tied her hair back again and took a sip. 'It's not bad actually.'

'You haven't lived, my friend,' Skye replied. 'No Primark, no gin and tonic in cans. What do you do?'

Willow shrugged. 'Work mostly.'

'Are you going to go back to work at the end of the summer?'

'What else can I do?' Willow replied. 'I've worked so hard to get where I am; it's all I know.'

'And what about Charlie?'

'It's over,' she said. 'I've known that since before the wedding if I'm honest with myself. But now I've got to do the hard part and unravel our lives. I need to go back to London for that though.'

'You could come back to the Island after you've sorted that out.'

Willow turned to look at Skye. 'I don't know,' she said. 'It's been a long time.'

'And what does it feel like to be back?'

'Some days it feels like I never left.'

'Well there you go then.'

'I'd have to leave so much behind,' Willow said quietly turning to look out to sea again.

'But you'd have so much to look forward to.'

As she looked across the beach Willow felt Skye's arm around her shoulders, pulling her in for a hug and she felt her heart expanding again. This feeling of love and warmth was coming from the Island, from the memories of her childhood, her friendship with Skye and the possibilities of what the future might hold.

Staying on the Island after the summer hadn't been something that Willow had allowed herself to think about because everything had been so tied up with Luc, and Luc would be going back to America in September. It made sense that she left again then as well, to salvage what she could of her life in London.

But as she sat on the beach in Ryde, Skye's arm around her, sipping from her can of gin she realised that not every memory of the Island was about Luc and that this feeling of warmth and contentment came from being surrounded by love and happiness and music. All the things she'd shut her heart down to when she met Charlie.

'You'll be all right you know,' Skye said. 'Whatever you decide.'

Willow rested her head on Skye's shoulder, just as she used to when they were kids. Maybe she could live on the Island again.

They met at Seaview's only decent restaurant. Luc had wanted to pick her up but Willow had told him she'd meet him there. She didn't want this to seem like a date, despite the kiss, even though she had thought about Luc almost constantly since the kiss. Willow wasn't ready for anything that might seem like a date.

He was waiting for her when she got there. He stood up as she sat down and something inside her melted as though this was a first date with a handsome stranger and not dinner with the boy she'd known for most of her life. She watched his eyes drop from her face to her chest to her legs, and then back again and she smiled to herself, glad that she had taken Skye's advice in the dress shop in Ryde, glad that she had bought the red dress instead of the black one.

He ducked his head to kiss her cheek and he smelled amazing. Willow wanted to pull him towards her, bury her face in the soft part of his neck, breathe him in.

'Hey,' he said, sitting down again, his fingers finding hers across the table. 'I missed you.'

'I missed you too,' she replied, thinking about how much she'd hoped he would take a break from writing and come through the door of The Music Shop with her morning coffee, or phone her in the evening as she lay on the single bed in her mother's house alone. He never did. She knew how focused he could be when he was writing.

'How's the hunt for Storm going?' he asked.

She shook her head and felt his fingers squeeze hers. 'It's not,' she said. 'I've been in touch with his old agent and King Silver's old management company but nobody knows what happened to him.'

'Nobody knows anything?'

'His agent says that King Silver's bass player might know. I'm waiting to hear from him, refreshing my email every five minutes.' She paused and sighed – the sense of frustration welling up inside her again. 'He's my last hope,' she said.

'Be patient, Willow,' Luc replied. 'It's only been a few days.'

'I know but rumours have been spreading like wildfire and the festival is selling out as we speak.'

Luc sucked air in between his teeth. 'I'd forgotten how quickly news spreads on the Island,' he said. 'But selling tickets is a good thing, right?'

'Not if I can't find Storm it's not,' she said. 'I've tried to talk to Mum again but...'

'No joy?'

'None. She's refusing to speak about it.'

Luc looked as if he was going to say something and Willow remembered that he had something to tell her. She suspected it was about Storm Tyler but she didn't want to talk about him. She was sick to death of Storm bloody Tyler. Even Skye had opinions on what Willow should do to find him – none of them sensible or useful.

Before Luc got a chance to say whatever it was, a waiter appeared with a bottle of wine that Luc must have ordered before Willow had arrived. Instinctively she put her hand over her wine glass as he poured.

'Oh God I'm sorry,' Luc said. 'I didn't even think to ask if you wanted wine. Let me get you something else.'

Willow looked at her hand and realised what she'd done.

'No it's fine,' she said, pulling her hand away. 'Wine is fine.' She let the waiter pour, watching the yellow liquid fill her glass and feeling Luc's eyes on her.

'Are you OK?' he asked when the waiter left.

She felt her cheeks colour. 'Charlie never liked me to drink too much,' she said. She couldn't look up to meet Luc's eyes. How had she allowed her life to be so tightly controlled? How had she convinced herself that the perfect life that Charlie insisted on was possible?

Luc didn't say anything for a moment and Willow picked up her wine glass and took a sip.

'You don't have to drink it,' he said gently.

But she did. As it slipped down her throat it tasted of freedom and potential. It tasted of escape and new beginnings. It tasted of the Island and the possibility here.

'Cheers,' she replied as he caught her eye. She knew he didn't expect an explanation and she had a feeling he understood, even without one.

They chose their food, knees pressing against each other's under the table just as they had been in the pub the week before – Luc's legs too long to fit comfortably under any table. He had never been happy sitting still for long, always rushing on to the next thing, the next dream. The fire in his heart still shone from him even now but something had dampened it – something that he wasn't telling her about.

'When we were in the studio the other day,' he said as the waiter left them again, 'you said you hadn't listened to "Chord of Plenty" in years. Do you listen to any of the music we used to love?'

'No,' she replied. *Charlie doesn't like it* – but she didn't say that out loud. 'I just have a different life now – we go to the opera, the ballet. Charlie loves jazz…' She trailed off realising she'd been talking in the present tense about a life that she was pretty sure was in the past.

'That's not like you, Willow.'

'People change.'

'No they don't,' Luc replied. 'Not really, not deep down. Why did you let him change you?'

The question was harsh and Willow found herself wanting to defend Charlie, wanting to stand up and tell Luc that he didn't understand, that he had no idea what her life was like now. But she couldn't do it. She couldn't defend the man who, for the last eighteen months, had become increasingly irritated with her, increasingly controlling. She couldn't defend the man who told her what to wear, or how much to drink, or who she could be friends with. She couldn't defend the man she refused to marry.

And she wondered if Skye was right when she'd said that she'd never really believed that Willow wanted that life.

'I wanted to be changed,' she said instead. 'I wanted to forget and he offered me the opportunity to step into a whole new life.'

'Because of me?' Luc asked, his voice so quiet she could hardly hear him above the noise of the restaurant.

'No,' she replied. 'Never because of you.' Willow knew that was true now. It wasn't Luc she had been trying to forget. She hadn't run away because Luc hadn't turned up at the beach hut that morning. It had been so much more than that. 'I wanted to forget how everything had fallen apart after my parents split up. I never understood what happened and I couldn't cope with not understanding so I walked away from it all and Charlie was there to fill the hole in my life.' She didn't tell Luc that she had never told Charlie about him, that she had never spoken about him at all. 'The more time I let myself get submerged in Charlie's life the less I wanted to come back here, to the point where we'd pay for Mum to visit us,' she admitted, leaving out how much Charlie had hated visiting the Isle of Wight.

'Has being on the Island made you want to listen to music again?' he asked. 'To play again?'

'I've been practising mandolin every day since Dad came home,' she replied. 'Does that answer your question?'

He beamed at her, his smile lighting him up as though he was glowing from within. Talking about music had always done that to him, even the merest mention. 'Good,' he said. 'That's good.'

'I'd been thinking about music for a while though,' she went on. 'Since before I came back to the Island.' She paused, looked at him. 'Since I saw you on *American Stars*.'

'You watched it?' he asked, surprise in his eyes.

'You were brilliant. You should have won.'

'Thank you.'

'I even bought your record. It was the first CD I'd bought in years.'

'I didn't think people bought CDs anymore,' he said as his hand found hers across the table again as their food was put in front of them. Everyone in Seaview would know about this dinner by the next morning and Willow didn't care. Let them gossip.

'I'm old-fashioned,' she replied.

'Will you go back to London?' he asked.

'I'll have to and I should go soon. I need to sort my stuff out, work out what to do about the flat, but...' She trailed off, shrugged. 'I don't know.'

They changed the subject as they ate the fresh fish that the restaurant served and talked about the Island they grew up on, touring with The Laurels, the early days of the festival.

Willow was so caught up in Luc, in the touch of his leg, the feel of his fingers, so caught up in reminiscing about the past that, for a moment, she forgot about the festival and Storm Tyler and the fact that her mother was still refusing to talk to her about the tape.

'Have you seen Dad?' she asked eventually, after they'd ordered coffee.

Luc nodded.

'I haven't seen him since before the council meeting,' Willow went on. 'I've been kind of avoiding him. Is he mad?'

'He's not angry,' Luc said. 'But I do think we've raked up a past that your parents might not want to remember. Call him tomorrow, play mandolin with him. Everything will be all right, I promise.' But Willow knew he couldn't promise that and it didn't shake the strange, ominous feeling she'd had since she'd made that promise she couldn't keep in the council chamber on Monday night.

'Did you know,' she said, 'that there's a rumour that Storm Tyler was on the Island in the summer of '99 and that he was going to play the Folk Festival but never did?'

Luc's eyes widened. 'Who told you that?'

'Tom Newell.'

'That must have been when he recorded the demo,' Luc said. 'Have you asked your mum about that?'

'I've told you I've tried but she won't talk about it. She just keeps telling me to leave the past where it is.'

'I said I had something to tell you,' Luc began. 'Something my agent told me.'

'Your male agent.'

'Sam,' Luc said with a smile. 'My forty-eight-year-old male agent.'

Willow sipped her coffee and waited for him to continue. She didn't want to know who "sweetheart" was. Not tonight.

'Back in the early Eighties Storm did a solo tour. It didn't go very well – you know he went completely off the rails on that tour.'

Willow nodded.

'Well according to Sam,' Luc went on, 'Storm's support act on that tour was The Laurels.'

Willow gaped at him. She hadn't come across any of that in her internet searching.

'As in our parents?' she asked.

'As in our parents,' Luc confirmed.

'Why did nobody ever tell us?' Willow wondered out loud. 'Why does nobody seem to know? There's nothing online about it – I've been looking.'

'I've no idea,' Luc said. Willow looked at him. Was there something else that he wasn't telling her?

'Luc, what do you think the chances are of finding Storm?'

'I got the impression that Sam thought we should let sleeping dogs lie, and before you ask, he didn't tell me why.'

'This was the stupidest idea I've ever had,' Willow said. 'Trying to find Storm Tyler is proving to be impossible. Nobody knows where he is. Maybe your agent and my mum are right, perhaps we should leave the past in the past.'

'Maybe Storm doesn't want to be found. I think the whole music industry destroyed him in the end. I think he just couldn't handle the pressure and the publicity and the fame. He had a lot of obsessive fans and if you've been looking him up online, you'll know that he was loathed as much as he was loved. People wrote a lot of crap about him.'

'I guess,' Willow replied.

'This industry,' Luc said quietly, fiddling with his teaspoon. 'This industry is so cut-throat. It squeezes every last drop of blood out of you and there's nothing you can do about it, nothing you can do to save yourself.' He paused, took a breath. 'I think that's what happened to Storm.'

But Willow didn't think he was talking about Storm anymore.

'Are you OK?' she asked. He looked suddenly pale and uncomfortable. 'What aren't you telling me?'

'Can we get out of here?'

23

Luc

They walked down the beach together hand in hand, fingers entwined. For a while neither of them spoke, but Luc was very aware that they were walking towards his apartment, away from the side of Seaview where Willow's mum lived. All he could think about was how good it had felt to kiss her on the clifftop the other day and whether she'd let him kiss her again. He was thinking about what her lips felt like on his and he didn't notice, until it was too late, that they were walking along the stretch of beach where Skye's dad's old beach hut had been before they pulled it down to redevelop, the stretch of beach where he and Willow had swum together that last night. He'd been avoiding it since he got back, not wanting to remember how he'd let Willow down.

He felt that familiar sense of panic in his chest, as though somebody was tightening a rope around his heart, and he started to walk more quickly, trying to get away. Willow's grip on his hand tightened and she pulled him back.

'You can't avoid it forever,' she said softly as she stepped away from him.

She must have noticed that he always walked back up into the village at this point and walked to his apartment the long way around. She must have noticed his excuses and the way he avoided this stretch of beach.

Despite his best intentions, Luc still hadn't started writing the record he was contracted to write. Alone in his apartment all he had been able to think about was Willow. Tonight he'd been more determined than ever to tell her the truth and yet he still couldn't do it. Not completely.

He turned to face her, meeting her eyes. 'I'm sorry,' he said.

'What for?'

'That night,' he replied, his eyes briefly flicking towards the sea. 'Well, no, not that night... the next morning. Not turning up I...'

'Luc you've already apologised,' Willow replied. 'It's OK, I understand now.' She paused. 'That summer was so awful and you were the one thing that kept me going. I didn't see how much you were struggling too and I'm sorry for that.'

He should have made more effort to keep in touch with her, to find out how she was, to help her live the life she should be living instead of hiding behind this person she thought she wanted to be in London. He could see that the more time Willow spent on the Island, the more her mask slipped. The hardness that he had seen in her face on that first day in The Music Shop and then later in Skye's studio had all but disappeared and the Willow he used to know was looking back at him.

'I loved you so much,' she said. Luc tried not to focus on

her use of the past tense, trying not to read too much into the implication that she loved him but didn't anymore.

She reached up and touched his face, gently rubbing her thumb over his cheekbone. 'We were so young, and we were dealing with something we didn't understand. I should have known there was more to it, but I was so wrapped up in my own stuff. When you didn't turn up that morning, I should have tried harder to find you.' She paused. 'I'm so glad you're here now, Luc. I'm so glad I've had this chance to see you again.'

She spoke as though this was temporary, that after this summer they would both go back to their separate lives on opposite sides of the Atlantic and never see each other again. And even though Luc knew that was probably true, that having a relationship with Willow was impossible for so many complicated reasons, he didn't want to let her go. He wrapped his arms around her and pulled her towards him. Her arms snaked around his waist and they stood together, leaning into each other, the shadows of the past circling around them.

After a while, as though following some unspoken agreement, they gently pulled apart and started walking again, hand in hand towards the apartment building that Luc was staying in at the other end of the stretch of sand. It was ridiculous that he hadn't walked back this way before – it was much quicker than walking through Seaview.

'You wanted to tell me something,' she said quietly. 'What was it?'

He didn't want to tell her anymore; he didn't want to spoil this moment between them. But he knew he couldn't leave it like this; he knew he had to tell somebody.

'Shall we sit?' he said, taking off his jacket and placing it on the sand for her to sit on. He sat next to her and she took his hand again.

'You were saying that Storm might not want to be found,' she said. 'That the industry destroys some people. Why do I get the feeling that you weren't just talking about Storm?'

Luc knew he wasn't hiding anything from her. She always could read him like a book.

'You know how I told you I had the panic attacks under control?' he began.

Willow nodded.

'Well that's not strictly true. I did have them under control until *American Stars* but after that...'

'They came back?' she asked, her hand tightening in his.

'Yup.' Luc shifted around a little to look at her. 'I was fine the whole way through the competition – I think I was fuelled entirely by adrenaline as I kept winning round after round. The first time I noticed anything was wrong was right before the live final. I was sick before I went on stage.'

'That's not unusual,' Willow said. 'Dad still gets that sometimes you know.' Luc did know and he still remembered what Don had told him the afternoon he'd found him in the fishing boat at the other end of the beach.

'Maybe not,' he replied quietly. 'But after the live final there was a tour, then I went to LA to record the album, then there was another tour and then...' He didn't know what else to say.

'And then what?' she asked.

'And then nothing.'

'Nothing?'

'I'm contracted to write another album, go on another tour, play European festivals next summer.'

'Is that why you're here?' she asked. 'To practise for next summer?'

'No, Willow. I'm here because everything has fallen apart. My panic attacks got worse and worse throughout both tours, throughout recording the album. I tried to hide them from everyone, which was stupid because I couldn't control them, and my behaviour was all over the place. The press got hold of my erratic behaviour and obviously interpreted it as a drink and drug problem – the rock 'n' roll cliché.' He rubbed his eyes, turning away from her.

'I saw some of the stories,' Willow said quietly. 'I just assumed they were rubbish.'

'And now I can't write,' Luc went on. 'My agent is expecting me to come back with an album full of original songs by the end of the summer and I can't do it. I tried to write this week, cut out all distractions and just get lost in it, but nothing. Just thinking about it makes my throat close up and…' He had to stop at the sense of panic rising in his throat like bile. He felt her arms around him.

'It's OK,' she said. 'Everything is going to be OK.'

And for a few moments he almost believed her.

'What made you do it?' Willow asked as his breathing returned to normal and she moved away from him slightly. 'What made you go on such a huge show, knowing you were prone to panic attacks?'

This was his opportunity to tell her everything, about Annelise and the real reason he decided to go on *American Stars*. But he couldn't. If he told her now then this evening would end here and he didn't want it to. He didn't want to let her go.

'I hadn't had any sign of a panic attack for years at that point,' he said instead. 'I'd been playing bars around Nashville for a while and everything had been fine. All I wanted to do by auditioning for *American Stars* was to prove something to myself.' It wasn't quite a lie. 'I never expected to get to the final.'

'Do you regret it?'

There was a loaded question. 'No, but I wish I'd gone about things differently, been a bit more honest with people.'

'Does anyone know about the panic attacks at all?'

'My agent,' Luc replied. 'I had to tell him in the end when all of the drink and drug stories were coming out in the papers. My mum knows of course and your dad.'

'My dad knows?'

'Your dad always knew,' he said, finally telling her. 'It was him who found me that morning after... well when I was supposed to meet you. He found me at the other end of the beach thinking I was having a heart attack. He helped me, because he'd been there himself. I made him swear not to tell anyone.'

He looked at Willow as she stared out to sea and wondered if he'd said too much. She looked so beautiful and he didn't think he could bear it if she went home now.

'I wish a lot of things were different,' she said eventually. 'But you can't change the past.' She moved closer to him then and he felt the warmth of her body against him. 'We can make up for it though.'

His eyes met hers and he could see the desire there, the

need. He could see that she didn't want this evening to end any more than he did. He stood up, offering her his hand, as he told himself he'd done the right thing by putting off the truth.

'Shall we go?' he asked.

They walked to his building in silence and, when they got there, she followed him into the lobby and up the stairs. 'Would you like a coffee?' he asked as he opened the door to his apartment.

She shook her head as she closed the door behind her and leant back against it. 'I'm not here for coffee,' she replied.

He stepped closer to her, tucking her hair behind her ears and she lifted on to tiptoe, letting her lips brush against his. Luc's hands slid around her to pull her closer as she deepened the kiss and he lifted her up so she could wrap her legs around his waist, supporting her against the door. As he kissed her, he remembered the night on the beach, when they stood like this, naked in the sea and he remembered the clifftop and all the times he had thought of her in between. He pressed himself against her, supporting her with one arm as he buried his other hand in her hair. She smelled amazing and he could kiss her all night, lose himself in this kiss and never come up for air.

After a moment he pulled away. He felt as though he could consume her, and he didn't want to push her to do something she wasn't ready for. He let her go and she stood in front of him again.

'Willow I...' he began, but she seemed to already know what he was thinking and she smiled, her eyes sparkling. Her hands found the front of his jeans and he took a breath.

She pulled him towards her by his belt buckle as she nuzzled into his neck.

'I want you, Luc,' she whispered in his ear. 'Right now.'

How could he resist?

She still slept on her stomach, just like she had done when they were children. Luc could remember the tour buses they used to travel on with The Laurels, and how she would sleep on her stomach across two seats with one arm hanging down like a cat.

He'd always thought she would follow her parents into music but she'd never believed that she was a creative person like her mum and dad. She'd thought she was good at maths and that was all, but it wasn't all. Not by a long shot. She was as good, if not better than her mother. If someone had told Luc back when they were teenagers that she'd end up working in finance he'd never have believed them.

He propped himself up on one elbow and watched her sleep. She'd always slept so well, so deeply. He had envied that. His sleep had been patchy and erratic for as long as he could remember and he often found himself awake in the early hours of the morning with only his guitar for company. There always seemed to be too much going on to allow him to sleep. Too much to think about, too much to worry about.

But last night he hadn't wanted to sleep; he hadn't wanted to miss a moment of this time he had with Willow because he knew it would be short-lived. She was so beautiful and last night had been one of the best nights of his life. He felt as though he'd been waiting twelve years for last night – an opportunity to make it up to her, to make it up to himself.

It was early, the sun had risen but it was still low in the sky, its rays shining through the gap in the blind at the bedroom window. He might not want them to go back to their lives on different sides of the Atlantic at the end of the summer but he knew that what he and Willow had right now was temporary. There was so much he should have told her before he'd slept with her, so much more he should have told her on the beach the previous night. It was selfish of him to have taken this as far as he had without telling her the truth and he knew he had to tell her as soon as she woke up. If he left it any longer she was going to find out from somebody else.

She stirred and rolled onto her side, her back against his chest. He wrapped his arms around her waist to spoon her, brushing her hair away from her neck and kissing her behind her ear. She moaned gently and wiggled against him and he knew he should move away, wake her up properly and talk to her. But he couldn't burst this bubble they were in, not yet. He let his hand trail down her belly and over her pubic bone.

Just a few more minutes.

Luc woke up to the sound of somebody knocking on the front door. The sun was much higher in the sky now judging by the light coming in through the blinds. He looked at the clock. It was past 11am. He should have been up hours ago;

he should have taken Willow out to breakfast and told her the truth.

The door banged again.

Shit.

He rolled out of bed, picking up his jeans and shirt off the floor. He pulled them on and ran his hands through his hair before he turned to look at Willow.

'Get rid of whoever it is quickly,' she said. She smiled slowly at him and he could see her lips were slightly swollen from his kisses, her chin red from his stubble. She had no idea how much a part of him wanted to ignore the door, to curl up next to her in bed forever. But the other part of him needed to answer the door because he knew who it was, he'd been expecting them.

And that made it so much worse.

He took one last look at Willow, naked and beautiful in his bed.

'You'd better get dressed,' he said, knowing he should have said so much more as he walked into the hallway to open the front door, the door he'd pressed Willow against last night.

God what had he done?

'Daddy!' she screamed as soon as he opened the door. 'I've missed you!'

'I've missed you too, Annelise,' he replied, because despite everything that had been going on he had missed her, so very much. He squatted down to give her a hug. His little girl.

She started talking ten to the dozen, telling Luc about the plane journey across the Atlantic, the hotel she and Krystal had stayed in the night before, the car ferry across to the

Island. As she talked he looked up at his mum but Krystal wasn't looking at him; she was looking behind him as the bedroom door opened.

'Hello, Willow.'

'Hello, Krystal,' Willow replied from behind him. Luc couldn't see her, but he could tell from the tone of her voice that he'd already lost her.

24

'Come on, Cathy love, push,' the midwife said. 'Not long now, just a couple more big pushes.'

Cathy was exhausted, she didn't know if she had a couple more big pushes in her. She squeezed Krystal's hand so hard that she heard her friend wince beside her.

'You can do it, Cathy love,' Krystal said. 'And in a couple of months I get to break your hand as payback.'

Cathy turned her head to look at Krystal whose other hand was gently resting on her own bump. In eight weeks' time they'd both be mothers – if Cathy managed to survive these last two big pushes. Krystal had told Cathy that she was pregnant on Cathy and Don's wedding day. They'd married at Marylebone Register Office, where Paul and Linda McCartney had married eighteen years before. It had been a small occasion, no fuss at all and Cathy had worn a simple cream shift dress that covered the beginnings of her baby bump. It was the first time anybody had seen Don Warwick in a suit. A few press cameras waited for them on the steps after the ceremony – The Laurels were well known enough by then to have a small picture printed in the *NME* the following week. Nobody had known that Cathy had been pregnant; she'd managed to hide the truth from everyone.

Cathy hadn't asked who the father of Krystal's baby was and Krystal had never told her. Whether this was because she didn't know or didn't want anyone else to know, Cathy didn't care. There was so much she didn't care about now, so much she'd allowed herself to let go of, grateful for the things she had – Don, Krystal and the baby that she would hold in her arms very soon. They were her family now, a replacement for the family she hadn't spoken to for four years. She'd thought about them of course, especially her mother and her baby brother. Connor would be fifteen now. Over the last nine months she'd thought about getting in touch, telling her family about Don and about her baby. But she wanted to move forward, set her own course in life and she knew her family wouldn't let her do that.

'This is the worst thing that has ever happened,' Cathy grunted through gritted teeth. Beside her Krystal laughed softly.

'Don should be here,' Krystal said.

Don was touring in America, doing whatever he could to earn money for his new wife and the baby that was on the way. Don was a good man, so good that Cathy only thought about Storm occasionally these days.

'One more, Cathy,' the midwife said. 'One more big push.'

Cathy gripped Krystal's hand and closed her eyes. Come on, Cathy, she told herself. You get to meet your baby soon.

It had been six months since she'd last seen Storm Tyler. Nobody seemed to know where he was anymore and Cathy had convinced herself that she no longer cared.

The last time she'd seen him he'd been dripping wet, sitting up in bed after she'd poured a glass of water over him and his little groupie to wake them up. She'd kicked the girl out of the flat and, before he'd had a chance to shower or get himself a coffee, she had told him she was leaving, that she was moving in with Don. She hadn't told Storm about the baby.

She hadn't really known what to expect when she told him she was going – anger maybe, followed by his usual begging and pleading for forgiveness. She hadn't been expecting the resigned acceptance; she hadn't expected him to sit quietly in the living room while she packed her case, or for him to offer to carry it for her. And when she refused his help, she hadn't expected the quiet apology as she left.

And then he simply disappeared. A few weeks after the wedding Cathy had seen an announcement in the *NME* that King Silver had split up for the last time, but there was no interview with Storm, no recent pictures. Rumours flew around – that he'd died, that he'd moved to America, that he was in rehab. The rumour Cathy trusted most was that he'd moved to the South of France – he'd always said he wanted to retire to the French Riviera. She silently wished him well and tried to move on with her life.

Cathy had put Storm out of her mind, knowing that it was worth it as she waited for her baby. And when she heard that baby cry for the first time her heart exploded into a thousand stars.

'It's a girl,' the midwife said.

And when her little girl was placed in her arms, Cathy hadn't known it was possible to feel such love, such adoration.

'Hello, Willow,' she said.

25

Willow

'OK, OK I'm coming,' Skye called as Willow banged on the door of "Clouds in the Skye". She heard a key turning in the lock. 'What do you want I...'

Skye stopped as soon as she saw Willow standing in front of her, barefoot and wearing the previous night's clothes, shoes in her hand and tears streaming down her face.

'Willow, what on earth?'

'Can I come in?' Willow asked.

'Sure,' Skye replied, reaching out to Willow, taking her hand and leading her inside. 'I was just setting up for a client but I've got nearly an hour until they're due.'

Willow allowed herself to be led into the little kitchen at the back of the studio where she and Luc and Skye had shared a pot of tea over a month before. She felt as though she was a different person now.

She sat down as Skye put the kettle on and all Willow could think about was Luc standing there making tea that afternoon.

Luc.

'Did you know?' Willow asked. 'Did you know about Luc's daughter?'

Skye turned around slowly.

'What?' she said quietly.

'You didn't know? He didn't tell you either then?'

'Are you sure?' Skye asked.

'Of course I'm sure, Skye. Why else would a little girl with pigtails and green eyes be calling him "daddy"?'

Skye sat down next to Willow. 'Tell me everything,' she said.

Willow told her how dinner with Luc had felt like a date no matter how hard she'd tried to pretend it wasn't. She told her about the walk on the beach and about the night she'd spent at Luc's apartment, the night she'd finally felt alive again after what had felt like years of hibernation.

And she told Skye about Krystal arriving and the little girl with pigtails and freckles and eyes as green as Luc's.

But she didn't tell Skye about Luc's panic attacks. She still felt loyal enough to him not to mention those.

'Whoa,' Skye breathed when Willow finished.

'I know,' Willow replied. 'I guess that's who he was calling "sweetheart" on the phone the other week.'

'Not a groupie then,' Skye said.

'No, not a groupie.'

'But that didn't bother you?' Skye asked. 'That there was someone out there he called "sweetheart" and he wouldn't tell you who it was?'

'I didn't care about his life in Nashville. It's not like my life in London is simple and uncomplicated or that I'm really free to start seeing anyone new. But it was Luc and we were both on the Island and…' She trailed off. Her excuses seemed pathetic, but she could tell by the look on Skye's face that she understood.

'What happens on the Island stays on the Island,' Skye said with a smile.

Willow put her head in her hands and groaned. 'Something like that,' she said.

'What did you think would happen?' Skye asked. 'After you slept with him?'

'I hadn't thought that far ahead. It just felt so right, so perfect and it felt a bit like we were in this bubble, that nothing else mattered except us. I didn't think at all. Maybe that's the problem.'

'I can't believe Luc's a father,' Skye said softly after a while. 'Of everyone I know he would never have been top of my list of people who'd become a parent first.'

'You should have seen him with her though,' Willow replied as she remembered the moment when Luc took his daughter in his arms. It was so tender, so beautiful. It had made her ovaries explode. 'I think he's probably a good dad.'

'I wonder who her mum is?' Skye asked rhetorically.

'It opens up so many questions,' Willow said. 'Not least why he didn't tell anyone.'

'He must have had his reasons,' Skye replied. 'But yeah, I'm surprised he didn't say anything, especially to you. You've been spending so much time together.'

'We talked about so many things; we really opened up to each other about the past, about the last twelve years. But he chose not to tell me this: the most important thing in his life.'

'Would you have slept with him if you'd known?' Skye asked, direct as ever.

'I don't know,' Willow replied. 'Probably not.'

'There you go then, that's why he didn't tell you.'

Willow looked at her friend for a moment. 'Really?' she asked. 'You think so? This is Luc. He's not like that is he?'

'It's Luc,' Skye said with a small smile. 'But he's still a man.'

Willow smiled too, surprised at how Skye could still cheer her up even in the worst moments. She wondered again how she had let their friendship just disappear all those years ago, how she had let Skye walk out of that pub and never stood up for her. Skye had always been on her side after all. She'd been so stupid, walking away from the Island, from her life and allowing herself to be changed by Charlie, moulded into a life she thought she wanted. Why had she thought that was what she wanted? Because it was as far away from her life on the Island as she could imagine? Or was it just because Charlie had been there, the first person to be kind to her, to notice her, to love her when she thought that nobody else did?

'Seriously though, Willow, I know it's shit that he didn't tell you,' Skye went on. 'But this is probably complicated. He told me he wasn't seeing anyone back home and you said that this little girl arrived here with Krystal?'

Willow nodded.

'Don't run away again,' Skye said. 'Hear him out, listen to his side of the story.'

But Willow's mind was still on Charlie, on the reasons she'd stayed with him for so long, the reasons she'd moulded herself into somebody new. She knew now that she never really loved Charlie, not like she used to love Luc.

Not like she suspected she still loved Luc.

But neither Luc nor Charlie were the answer now. Willow needed to find out what she wanted for herself, by herself. Because until she had learned who she really was and what she wanted to do with the rest of her life, until she had learned to love herself again, she couldn't open herself up to anybody else, not completely.

'I will hear him out,' she said quietly. 'But not yet. I need to go back to London first, I've always known that and so has Luc. I need to talk to Charlie. I need to start sorting out my life.' She paused. 'I need some clothes of my own other than this dress.' She looked down at herself still wearing the dress from the night before. She must look a complete mess.

'But you'll come back?' Skye asked.

Willow thought about all the things that had happened since she arrived on the Island, about the festival and the planning committee and the wild promise she'd made to find Storm Tyler. She thought about how angry her mother was with her and how the festival tickets were selling so fast but Storm couldn't be found anywhere.

Everything was such a mess.

'I'll come back,' Willow replied, squeezing her friend's hand. 'I have to. I still have to find Storm Tyler.'

'Still no leads?'

'Nothing, but I have to keep trying and I'm sure Mum knows something so I'll be back in a few days. I promise.'

'OK then,' she said, screwing up her nose. 'But I think the first thing you need is a bath.'

Willow laughed then, properly. A big belly laugh, the kind of laugh she hadn't allowed herself to laugh in years. She looked at Skye and realised that it was good being back on the Island; it felt right.

'Get out of here,' Skye said as Willow wiped her eyes. 'Before my next client sees the state of you or this'll be all around the Island by this afternoon.'

Willow thought about all the people she had passed as she'd run down the High Street earlier on her way to Skye's studio. 'I think it's already too late for that,' she said.

As she got ready to walk back to her mother's house, Skye called her back.

'I spoke to my parents the other night,' she said. 'I meant to tell you. They say Tom Newell's right.'

'He is?'

'There was a rumour that Storm Tyler was coming to the Island the summer of the eclipse but nothing ever came of it. Mum and Dad were big King Silver fans remember?'

Skye's father's record collection had been fantastic and eclectic, and Luc would spend hours sifting through it, looking for something new, something he hadn't heard before.

'It was your dad that introduced us to King Silver wasn't it?'

Willow remembered Skye's dad putting the record on for them in a reverential manner years ago. How old had they been? Twelve? Thirteen? She had a feeling that unravelling the mystery behind the tape that sat in the drawer of her nightstand might help her understand what she wanted and where to go from here.

'Yeah,' Skye replied wistfully. 'He still listens to old King Silver albums sometimes.'

'Do you?' Willow asked.

'Listen to King Silver? Yeah, sometimes.'

Willow nodded, thinking that maybe it was time she started listening to the music from her childhood again.

'Now get out of here,' Skye said. 'I'll see you in a few days.'

It was late by the time Willow got to London. She'd tried to phone Charlie three times on the journey – from the ferry, from Southampton station and again from Waterloo just before she descended into the underground system – but he hadn't answered, and Willow hadn't left a message. The journey had felt strange – crowded and hot and full of people and the underground, which she'd been navigating at rush hour for years, felt alien and unfamiliar. After six weeks on the Island she'd forgotten how crowded and dirty and noisy London could be. She'd forgotten the roar of the tube trains as they came out of the tunnel and the squash of people trying to get on – nobody waiting for passengers to get off first.

By the time she emerged back into the summer night at Regent's Park she had grown to hate the city that she claimed to love. Willow knew then that her life wasn't here anymore, and it certainly wasn't with Charlie.

But if her future wasn't here, then where was it?

It was much hotter in London than it had been on the Island, an oppressive, sticky heat that made Willow feel claustrophobic as she slowly walked along Great Portland Street towards her apartment building. She didn't try to call Charlie again and she didn't ring the buzzer before she went up to the apartment. It was her home as much as it was Charlie's and she had every right to walk into it whenever she wanted.

Even if it was to say goodbye.

The flat was in darkness and at first Willow didn't think anyone was home. It was late, but not so late that Charlie would have gone to bed. It was Saturday night and Willow guessed he'd gone out somewhere. The coward in her was relieved that she didn't have to face him straight away, that she could pack some clothes and sort herself out before she saw him.

She walked into the living room and turned on the light, surprised at the mess that greeted her. There were empty takeaway cartons on the coffee table, an empty bottle of champagne lying on its side and two empty glasses, one with lipstick marks around the edge. Willow swallowed as she noticed the pair of discarded Louboutin's. She leant against the doorframe and closed her eyes.

Charlie was sleeping with someone else – and she could hardly criticise him for that. But it made everything seem so final, as though walking away on her wedding day was somehow meant to happen so they could both move on.

She should leave and come back the next day, but as she was deliberating about whether to see if one of the nearby hotels had a vacancy, Willow heard female laughter from the bedroom. She headed back into the hallway just as the door to the master bedroom at the other end of the passage opened. A woman stepped out, looking back over her shoulder. There was a lump in Willow's throat that was preventing her from speaking, from swallowing, from breathing.

The woman turned around and Willow noticed that she was wearing her silk robe. Then she recognised the woman. When she looked back at this moment Willow would always be slightly confused that she noticed the robe before she noticed Kate.

'Oh my God,' Kate exclaimed. 'What are you doing here?' She did have the decency to look embarrassed at least.

'I live here, Kate,' Willow replied. 'Did you have a nice time on my honeymoon?'

Before either of them got a chance to say anything else, Charlie appeared in the hallway in his bathrobe and turned on the light, filling the hallway with a harsh white glow.

'Willow,' he said, his voice expressionless. 'You should have rung.'

'I did,' Willow replied walking towards the bedroom. 'Three times.' She'd disturbed his evening anyway so she might as well pack a few things while she was here. 'But as usual you didn't answer your phone.'

'You can't just let yourself in—'

'I can,' she interrupted. 'It's my flat too and my name is on the deeds and at some point you and I will need to sit down and talk about what we're going to do with it. You can buy me out if you like or we can put it on the market.' Charlie's eyebrows shot up in surprise. She was surprised herself by how sure she was about this. She hadn't realised that she was going to leave London until she came back.

'You're not coming home,' Charlie said. It didn't sound like a question.

Willow looked at Kate, who was leaning against the

wall as though she wanted to disappear, and then back at Charlie. 'How long have you two been seeing each other?' she asked.

'Since the wedding,' Charlie replied, looking away from Willow. 'Kate has been a tower of strength—'

'Oh for God's sake, Charlie,' Kate interrupted. 'Tell her the truth. You owe her that much.'

'About a year,' Charlie said, still unable to meet Willow's eyes.

'A year,' Willow replied quietly, coldly. 'You talked to me about shame, Charlie, about all the shame I've brought on you and your family by walking away from the wedding and all the time you were making a mockery of my life.'

Charlie didn't say anything, didn't look at her.

'And you,' she said turning to Kate. 'You were meant to be my best friend, my maid of honour.' She paused. 'It's no wonder you didn't encourage me to go through with it.' She remembered the strange mood Kate had been in on the morning of the wedding. Everything made sense now.

Willow stood in the hallway that used to be hers and looked at her fiancé and the woman she had always considered to be her closest friend. This was the thing that had been missing, the thing that had been bugging her for weeks. She should be crying or shouting, but all she felt was a sense of resignation and a twinge of regret at the time she'd wasted.

She had a strange empty feeling where her life used to be, because where would she go now? What would she do?

'Willow, I'm sorry,' Kate said. 'Let me explain.' She reached out for Willow but Willow stepped away.

'I'm just going to get a few things,' she said quietly. 'And then I'll get out of your hair. You can ring me when you're ready to talk about the flat,' she said to Charlie. She turned to Kate. 'You can keep the robe,' she said.

Willow walked into the bedroom, her old bedroom, turning her head away from the rumpled sheets on the bed. She stepped into her closet and quickly sorted through the clothes she'd need – jeans, tops, jumpers, sneakers, a couple of summer dresses, some underwear. She left the designer suits, dresses and shoes where they were; she wouldn't need them wherever it was she ended up. The life that she'd made for herself in London was over. That life was nothing but smoke and mirrors.

Before she left, she walked over to Charlie's nightstand and placed her engagement ring on it.

'Goodbye,' she whispered to nobody in particular.

The hotel in Southampton was basic but it was all Willow needed. A bed, a bathroom, a kettle and a restaurant to feed herself when she remembered.

She couldn't stay in London; she no longer felt that she belonged there now that Kate had taken over her home. She didn't want to go back to London at all – not even to return to the job she thought she loved. Her boss had been right when he'd hinted she wouldn't come back in September.

But what would she do instead?

She knew she would have to go back to the Island, she'd promised Skye that she would but right now she couldn't face the pity and the sympathy. It had been bad enough after the wedding that never happened and Willow knew it would be worse once everyone found out that her ex-fiancé had been cheating on her.

She couldn't face the disappointed people who had bought festival tickets on the promise that Storm Tyler would be making his longed-for return. She couldn't face telling them that Storm was impossible to find, that email after email had come back with nothing. All she had was a tape and a rumour to suggest that Storm Tyler even existed after 1987.

She couldn't face her mother who still wouldn't talk about the tape or about Storm. She hadn't asked her father about Storm either even though it had been the elephant in the room when they'd played mandolin together in the afternoons.

And she definitely couldn't face Luc.

She'd always known that, by the end of the summer, he would be going back to his life in America. But finding out he had a child, a little girl, was physical confirmation of that other life.

Instead of staying in London and fighting for her flat, her fiancé, her life – instead of going back to the Island like she'd promised, to face the man she was sure she was falling in love with all over again, Willow hid away in a cheap chain hotel in Southampton unable to do anything. Frozen like a rabbit in the headlights.

She slept a lot, consumed by an exhaustion that had been settling around her since long before the wedding. The days ran into one another until she had to check with the woman on reception that it was in fact Tuesday.

Her mother called her that Tuesday afternoon. At first Willow didn't answer but Cathy kept calling until she did. As soon as she heard her mother's voice she told Cathy everything. Everything about Luc and Charlie and how she didn't know what to do or where to go. Cathy had already guessed most of it from her sudden disappearance to London and her vague text late on Saturday night saying she'd be gone for a few days.

Neither of them mentioned the tape, or Storm Tyler.

'Come home,' Cathy said.

'I don't know where home is anymore.'

'This is always your home, Willow,' Cathy said. 'No matter who else is on the Island, no matter what else is happening. This will always be your home.'

At those words something unfurled inside Willow, something that had been curled up so tightly for so long that she'd forgotten it existed. Something warm and comforting that reminded her of the sea, of sunshine, of the sound of laughter and music and the sensation of being part of something.

Home.

London had never been her home. She'd been so focused on trying to escape her past, escape the Island, and become what she'd thought was "a success" that she had lost sight of all the things she loved – the sound of the waves against the shore, the sand between her toes, the taste of fermented apples, mandolin strings beneath her fingers.

Luc.

She still didn't know what she was going to do. Everything was still a mess; she still owned a flat with her cheating fiancé, a fiancé she no longer loved, whom she may never have loved. She still officially had a job in London too, a career she'd worked so hard for, fought for.

And Luc had a daughter, a life elsewhere, twelve years that Willow knew nothing about.

But the warmth that unravelled inside her when she thought about the Island made her realise that this chaos wasn't hopeless. She could do something, she could change the course of her life, she had complete control. She just needed to work out if she could face being on the Island, full of its reminders of Luc, when he wasn't there.

She poured herself a glass of wine from the minibar, not caring that it was three times the usual price. She ran herself a bath and, for the first time in weeks, she allowed herself to relax. She slept for eleven hours and woke up too late for the hotel breakfast. She got dressed and walked down the hotel stairs to go out and find some coffee and food.

He was there, waiting for her in the hotel lobby.

26

Luc

Luc didn't try to phone Willow to explain afterwards. He certainly didn't try to beg her forgiveness. He had no idea what he was going to do or how he was going to salvage any of it. He knew he should have told Willow about Annelise weeks ago and he knew he should have listened to Don. But his daughter was finally on the Island and he'd missed her with every ounce of his being, so he concentrated on Annelise instead, spending the weekend with her and trying to forget about the look on Willow's face when she came out of the bedroom on Saturday morning.

On Monday he finally ventured into Seaview again with a vague idea of passing by The Music Shop to see if Willow was there. And that was when he discovered that she'd left the Island and he'd missed her.

Skye called out to him from her studio as he passed. He turned and saw her in the doorway of her shop, her arms folded. He knew he had to talk to her, to tell her everything.

But he turned his head away for a moment, looking towards The Music Shop.

'She's not there,' Skye said. 'She's gone back to London.'

He felt his stomach drop as he slowly turned back towards Skye, walked towards her.

'She's gone back to him?' he asked.

Skye shrugged. 'I doubt it,' she said, ushering Luc into the studio. 'Let's not have this conversation on the street,' she said.

'Have you seen her?' he asked as they sat down in Skye's little kitchen.

'She came here on Saturday morning, she told me everything.'

Luc felt as though the room was spinning.

'Start by telling me about your daughter,' Skye said putting a cup of tea down in front of him, as though she knew he had no idea where to begin.

'She's called Annelise,' he said. 'She's seven but I didn't know she existed until two years ago. She's the reason I did *American Stars*. I wanted to do something worthwhile, something to make her proud.'

He told Skye everything. He told her about meeting Annelise for the first time in a Chuck E. Cheese in Antioch, ten miles outside of Nashville, about how shy she had been – so different to the girl she'd grown into. Her mother had finally got in touch after five years to tell him about his daughter because she needed help, needed money, needed someone to look after Annelise in the school vacations. When the initial shock had subsided Luc had been more than happy to help, more than happy to finally have a purpose to his life.

'I'd never been able to settle when we moved to Nashville,' he said. 'Mum got the record deal of her dreams and I got a job as a short-order cook in a diner.'

'How American,' Skye said with a smile. 'But did you not play too?'

'I got a few gigs at some of the smaller bars off the back of being Krystal Kane's son, but I was a very small fish in a huge pond. I don't know what I'd have done if I hadn't found out about Annelise.'

'Why had Annelise's mum never told you before?' Skye asked.

'I think she'd thought she could cope on her own, thought I was just another flaky musician who wouldn't care. But then her mother died and she was desperate. I'm not sure she would ever have told me otherwise. But I did care, from the moment I set eyes on Annelise I cared so much.'

Krystal had been less accepting, cynical even, and had insisted on a DNA test. It had come back confirming that Luc was the father, but he hadn't needed a test. He'd known that Annelise was his from the moment her green eyes met his across a plate of cheap pizza.

'I should have told Willow,' Luc said. 'I should have told her weeks ago.'

'Why didn't you?'

He told Skye about the panic attacks and the way he'd fallen apart on tour. He told her about the record he was meant to be writing and the fact that he didn't seem to be able to. He told her about the tape, although Skye already knew about that, and the idea it had given him.

'I thought,' he said, voicing his idea for the first time. 'That instead of writing new stuff I could work on some Ballad

Book songs – rearrange them for the twenty-first century or something.' The idea didn't sound quite so brilliant when he said it out loud.

'None of that explains why you didn't tell Willow about Annelise,' Skye said.

'I thought that if I told her she'd walk away and I needed her.' He paused. 'When she's there I feel like I can do all the stuff I'm meant to be doing – I can play the festival and record the album and even find Storm Tyler for her. But if she's not there…' He trailed off. 'She's playing again you know,' he said, trying to change the subject.

'Mandolin?' Skye asked.

'Yeah.'

Skye nodded and Luc couldn't work out if she already knew this.

'I was intending to tell her about Annelise on Saturday morning,' Luc said. 'I was going to take her out for breakfast and tell her then but—'

'Oh, Luc,' Skye interrupted. 'You really do know how to screw things up don't you?'

'What am I going to do, Skye?'

'I think you're going to have to wait for her to come back. She promised she would – she'll be back for the festival.'

'If the festival even happens.'

But Luc knew it was the right thing to do. This wasn't something they could sort out over the phone or by WhatsApp.

'Don't give up on her though,' Skye said, reaching over to squeeze his hand. 'She hasn't run away this time, I'm sure of it.' She paused, looking at Luc. 'And in the meantime have you got any leads on Storm Tyler? I know Willow has come to a dead end.'

'Nothing,' Luc said. 'It's like he's disappeared off the face of the earth. Nobody knows where he is. Cathy must know – she was on that tape too, but she's not talking. At this rate there's either going to be no festival at all or a lot of very angry folk fans.'

'You never know,' Skye replied, smiling. 'Miracles can happen.'

Cathy called Luc the next day, asking him to come and see her. He left Annelise with Krystal and went round as soon as he could. He had to face the music sometime. He knew it was time to start being honest, and Cathy was a good place to begin. She and Don would be worried about Willow and Luc knew it was time to tell the truth.

But when he arrived Cathy wasn't angry with him for what happened with Willow or for not telling her about Annelise. Cathy was worried. She and Don sat at opposite ends of the sofa as Cathy told Luc that Willow wasn't in London and that she was holed up in some hotel in Southampton licking her wounds after finding out the truth about her almost husband.

'He's been cheating on her,' Cathy said.

'I knew it,' Luc said quietly and Luc was suddenly aware of a tension between her and Don, as though they'd been arguing about something.

'I know Willow,' Cathy went on. 'She pretends she's all right but I know she isn't. How could she be?'

Luc nodded, not trusting himself to speak. He was so angry with Charlie for hurting Willow. But he knew he'd hurt her badly too – he and Charlie were as bad as each other.

Cathy stood up and walked over to Luc.

'Bring her home,' she said, pressing the keys of her Jeep into his hand. 'Tell her you're sorry, explain everything as best you can and bring her home. Go first thing tomorrow and if your mum can't look after Annelise then bring her here and I'll take care of her. We need Willow to come home.'

'Luc,' Willow said softly as she walked across the hotel lobby towards him. He stood and smiled at her. He felt a wave of relief when she smiled back. 'What are you doing here?'

'Everyone was worried,' he said. 'They want you to come home.'

'Everyone?' she asked.

'Your mum and dad. Skye.' He paused. 'Me.'

She held his gaze for a second longer than she needed to.

'Your mum told me what happened in London, Willow,' he went on. 'I'm so sorry.'

'I was going to get some breakfast,' she replied. 'Do you want to come? I think we probably need to talk.'

They walked side by side and he had to dig his fingernails into his palms to stop himself from touching her, just as he had done when they'd walked to Tom's recording studio a couple of weeks before.

She stopped outside a café. 'Shall we sit outside?' she asked. 'It's a beautiful morning.' She sounded tired and sad.

Luc sat down as the waitress came over to them, chatting

to Willow like they'd known each other for months. He wondered how many times she'd walked down to this café on her own and how long she would have kept doing that if Cathy hadn't intervened. She ordered her breakfast and he asked for a coffee for himself.

'What are you doing here, Luc?' she asked as the waitress moved away, echoing the words she had said to him in The Music Shop the first time he'd seen her again.

'Your mum wanted me to come,' he replied. 'She wants you to come home.'

'And what do you want?'

'I want you to come back to the Island,' he said. 'And I want us to talk properly. But mostly I want you to do whatever you want to do. Whatever makes you happy. Because I have a feeling you haven't been happy for a long time.'

She crumpled in front of him at those words, leaning her elbows on the table, her head in her hands. 'Talk to me,' she said. 'I don't want to talk about Charlie so tell me about your daughter.'

Luc smiled. 'She's called Annelise,' he said. 'And I first met her just over two years ago.'

'You didn't know about her?'

'No,' he replied. 'I had no idea until I got a phone call from my agent about it. Annelise's mother had got in touch with him. I was really small-time back then, just playing in bars and small venues, but I had got myself an agent and I'd recorded a few tracks for a compilation album. That's how Annelise's mum got in touch.'

'How did you not know?' Willow asked.

'How do you think I didn't know?' Luc replied, looking away from her and towards the street. He could feel himself blushing, embarrassed at the memory of who he used to be, how badly he had behaved. He'd been so unhappy in Nashville, so lost. He'd tried to bury his feelings in music and drinking and women but none of it had worked. He'd still found himself thinking about the Island, about Willow, whenever he was alone.

He looked over at her and an expression of understanding passed briefly over her face as their eyes met. He didn't need to tell her everything. He didn't need to tell her the details – they'd both had their own methods of forgetting the Island, of forgetting each other. That much was clear to him now.

'She never told you she was pregnant,' Willow said quietly.

'I don't think she would ever have told me if she hadn't been desperate,' he replied.

Willow's food arrived then, and he waited for the waitress to move away before he continued. He'd noticed the way people looked at him as though they recognised him but couldn't quite place him. He didn't want to be overheard.

As Willow ate he told her everything that he'd told Skye two days before. He told her about meeting Annelise for the first time, about how he knew from the first moment – long before the DNA test – that she was his.

'Her eyes,' Willow interrupted.

Luc was surprised that she'd looked at his daughter for long enough to notice before running away from him.

He told her about the early days of getting to know Annelise and about why he auditioned for *American Stars*.

Willow didn't say anything at first, she just sat back in her chair, wiping her mouth with her napkin. She didn't look at him.

'What was it like?' she said. 'At first. What was being a parent like?'

'The hardest thing I've ever done. She didn't want to spend time with me really. She had no idea who I was and I knew less than nothing about five-year-old girls. The last five-year-old girl I ever came across was you.'

Willow smiled but she still didn't look at him.

'It was Mum who saved the day really. She just knew how to cope, how to handle Annelise. How to handle both of us really. She took some time off from touring and helped us settle in Nashville over the summer. Then, in the fall when Annelise had gone back to her mum to start school I auditioned for *American Stars*.'

'Why didn't you tell me any of this, Luc?' Willow asked. 'Why didn't you tell me weeks ago? Before we...' She trailed off and Luc reached across the table, resting his fingers gently on top of hers. She didn't move her hand away.

'I didn't know how,' he said. 'When I was with you everything felt like it used to; everything felt right. I wasn't getting panic attacks. I thought that maybe I could get on the stage for the festival. I'd even had an idea about this record I'm supposed to be writing. I thought that if I told you about Annelise that I'd chase you away when I needed you. I was wrong and selfish and...'

She pulled her hand away from his then and crossed her arms across her chest.

'You were,' she said.

'I'd been going to tell you the morning after you stayed with me,' he said, knowing how unlikely it all sounded now. 'I'd been intending to take you out for breakfast and tell you before they arrived. But I overslept.' He paused. 'I've been a complete idiot and I understand why you're angry, why you might not want to talk to me.'

'I'm not going to pretend that I'm not pissed off with you,' she replied. 'But I've got bigger things to be pissed off about right now.' She stopped, uncrossing her arms and resting her hands on the table. 'You're Luc,' she went on, her tone softening. 'You're my friend and you're struggling. We're both struggling. There are a lot of reasons why we shouldn't have slept together and some of those reasons are mine. But I don't hate you for this, Luc. I'm not angry and I'm not running away from you again – I just don't really know where to go.' She ran her hand through her hair.

Luc knew how that felt, knew how all his hopes and dreams – the ones he used to share with Willow late at night when nobody else was around – had never come to anything. He knew that the front that he put on for the world bore no relation to the emotional turmoil going on inside and he was fairly sure that Willow felt the same. Nothing had turned out how either of them expected. Maybe nothing ever turned out how anyone expected.

'Who else knew?' Willow asked. 'I mean I'm sure half the Island knows now, but who else knew about Annelise before this summer?'

'Rocco,' Luc said. 'And your dad. We kept it quiet to protect her once things started taking off with *American Stars*. I didn't want anyone to bother her or take photos of her.'

Willow didn't respond, she just sat looking down at the table.

'What are you thinking?' he asked.

'Do you ever wonder who your father is?'

He hadn't expected that. 'I never used to,' he said. 'But since Annelise came into my life it's all I can think about. But Mum still won't say anything and your dad says he doesn't know so what can I do?'

'You and Dad are really close, aren't you?'

Luc made a noise in the back of his throat that he hoped sounded non-committal. He was close to Don Warwick. He had been since the day on the beach when Don found him curled up in the fishing boat but he didn't want to talk about it. He knew Willow wasn't as close to her father as she used to be and he didn't want to hurt her any further or make her jealous.

Willow picked up her empty coffee cup and put it down again.

'Will you come back to the Island with me?' Luc asked. 'Just for the rest of the summer?'

'Can I meet your daughter?'

'Of course you can, Willow. Nothing would make me happier.'

'And what happens when the summer is over?' she asked. 'Are you going back to America?'

'I have to,' he said. 'I have to put Annelise first.'

He watched her try to hide the disappointment she clearly felt. He wished he could think of a way he could be with Willow and be the father Annelise deserved. But he didn't have an answer so all he could do was make the most of the next few weeks with her.

'Shall I get the bill?' he asked.

But she didn't reply; she just reached over, placing her hand on Luc's arm, sending a shiver through his body that he tried, unsuccessfully, to hide.

27

Cathy sat on the beach with Willow asleep in her arms. She couldn't remember the last time she'd felt this happy, this loved, this needed. Having Willow had changed everything for the better and Cathy felt as though she could start to forget the past and build a future for herself and her daughter.

Next to her Krystal's baby started to cry again. She'd had a boy two months after Cathy had given birth to Willow. She'd called him Lucien but already everybody just called him Luc. He was the exact opposite to Willow – where she was calm and placid and slept remarkably well, Luc cried a lot, screaming in the night and refusing to sleep as though he was afraid of missing out on something. Krystal looked shattered and Cathy knew how lucky she was to have a baby like Willow. Her Willow, her saviour.

Cathy had been there for Krystal as she gave birth just as Krystal had been there for her and the two of them had become inseparable, bringing up their children together, helping each other get by. Neither woman had any family to rely on or anyone to help and so they became each other's family.

A few weeks after Luc had been born Don had taken them all to the Isle of Wight to show them the place where he had grown up.

'What do you think about getting out of London for a while?' he'd asked Cathy when they were alone. 'About maybe moving to the Island to bring up Willow?'

'I'd love to,' Cathy had replied. 'But we can't leave Krystal behind. It wouldn't be fair.'

Cathy still hadn't asked Krystal who Luc's father was, and Krystal had never told her. But there had been one thing Cathy had needed to know.

'It isn't you is it?' she'd asked Don late one night, just after Willow had been born. 'The father of Krystal's baby?' They were both punch-drunk from lack of sleep and adoration of the new baby and the question had come from nowhere, throwing Don off kilter.

'Of course it's not me,' he'd replied. 'What makes you think it is?'

'Nothing,' Cathy had said. 'I just needed to be sure, to know where I stood.'

Don had touched her chin then, turned her face towards him. 'I'm not Storm,' he said. 'And I never will be.'

'Do you know who the father is?' Cathy had asked, looking away from Don at the mention of her ex-lover.

'No, and it's not my business,' Don had replied. 'She'll tell us if she wants to.'

But she never had.

'Krystal could come too,' Don had said as he and Cathy

lay curled around each other in the little bed and breakfast in Seaview, Willow asleep in the cot at the end of the bed. 'If she wanted to.'

The next day Don had shown Cathy and Krystal the house that he'd grown up in, the house that he had inherited a couple of years earlier but had been too busy with The Laurels to do anything about.

'It needs a bit of work,' he said. 'But it's structurally sound. We could live here,' he paused, looking over at Krystal. 'All of us could live here,' he went on. 'At least while the kids are babies.'

They left London with a speed and organisation that Cathy hadn't thought any of them capable of, lured by the sea air and the peace and quiet. They had hoped it would help Luc, help him calm down. But the only thing that ever seemed to help Luc settle was music.

The Laurels went on hiatus. 'We'll be back,' Krystal had told a music journalist. 'Just as soon as the kids are a bit older.' But in the meantime, Krystal and Cathy were alone a lot while Don took as much work as he could, mostly in London but sometimes further afield, sometimes touring for weeks at a time. Cathy missed him when he was gone, but she also loved being at home with Krystal and the babies. She had never thought a life so simple could bring her such pleasure.

'Do you trust him?' Krystal asked as the two women sat on the beach staring out to sea, as Krystal tried to settle Luc again. 'Do you trust Don when he's touring?'

'Of course I do,' Cathy replied.

'I just wondered, after Storm—'

'Don isn't Storm,' Cathy interrupted. *Nobody will ever*

be Storm, she thought to herself but pushed the thought away. She couldn't allow herself to think about him, not now she had been given a second chance at happiness.

It was Don who came up with the idea of the folk festival when he came back to the Island that autumn.

'We'll just keep it small,' he said. 'Just playing in the pubs in Seaview and see how it takes off. It could commemorate the festivals of the Seventies.'

'It would be better than those festivals,' Cathy said. 'We'd show everyone how it can be done without trashing the Island, without putting all the locals offside. We'd have to make sure there was something in it for them, trade for the pubs obviously, but also for the shops and hotels.'

It started as something small, a celebration of folk music and a way of enabling Cathy and Krystal to play again and allow Don to spend a bit more of each summer at home. It had begun as a gathering of friends and like-minded people and an opportunity for new bands. Nobody had any idea how important it would become in all their lives and the lives of their children.

Cathy and Krystal sat on the beach watching their children playing in the sand nearby. Nearly two years had passed since Don first came up with the idea for the festival and behind them they could hear the music, laughter and applause from one of the pub gardens – one of many gigs at the inaugural Seaview Folk Festival. Neither woman spoke; they just sat and absorbed the atmosphere, absorbed their own happiness, the sensation of achievement at what they had managed to organise.

Eventually Don came to join them. He opened a bottle of cheap fizzy wine and poured it into plastic cups.

'Cheers,' he said, holding his cup aloft. 'We did it.'

They all took a drink as Willow came over to sit on Don's knee. She had been a daddy's girl since she was a baby, always settling quicker for Don, always missing him when he was away. Cathy had never minded; Willow was such an easy child to be around – happy and content no matter where she was or who she was with. It had been a godsend for Cathy that Willow was happy to be looked after by their neighbour over the last few months while she'd been planning the festival. It had been immensely hard work and had involved calling in a lot of favours, not just from the other residents of Seaview but from all their old musician friends in London. She'd been surprised how many Don had convinced to play – some even just for the price of a pint and a sofa to sleep on. So it had been good that Willow had been happy with whoever was looking after her.

Krystal hadn't been so lucky. Luc was still as difficult as he had been when he was a baby and still found it hard to settle.

'Would you like to come sit with us?' Krystal called to him. He hadn't followed Willow over, which was a surprise as he usually followed Willow everywhere.

He shook his head and pointed to his ears and turned his back on his mother.

'Music,' Krystal said. 'He's always happy when he's listening to music.'

Cathy knew that feeling, knew that she too was happiest when music was playing. But nothing made her as happy as playing the music herself. That high that she got from playing live had never left her, not since that very first gig in the pub in Green Park, the gig where she played a duet of "Gamble Gold" with Storm at the end. During the early planning stages of the festival Cathy and Krystal had tossed around the idea of getting The Laurels back together for the last night. They'd gone back and forth for a couple of weeks until Don came back off tour and convinced them it was a brilliant idea.

'What about Luc?' Krystal had asked. 'Who can I leave him with when I play?'

But Don had thought about that too. Out of all of them Don seemed to be the one who Luc got on with the most, the one who Luc would settle with. Cathy would often come home to find Don lying on the sofa with both children asleep on top of him. She had never worked out if it was because Don wasn't there all the time or just his general laid-back energy that made both kids so fond of him.

Don had noticed how music affected Luc too.

'If we're playing,' he'd said, 'then maybe Luc will settle with someone else while he listens.'

They'd tried out Don's theory in rehearsals. They'd practised in a room at the back of The Three Doves, the pub that was putting on most of the gigs during the festival. They'd kept everything as quiet and acoustic as possible to protect the children's ears, buying them ear defenders for the festival itself.

And Don had been right, Luc had settled as he'd listened to them. Staring at his mother, his face a mask of amazement and joy. Willow had been less interested but Willow, even at two, could entertain herself while they played, with her picture books and her building blocks.

Krystal drained her fizzy wine and stood up. 'I'm going to take him back to the pub garden for a bit,' she said. 'Let him watch the musicians.'

Don nodded.

'See you later for the gig,' Cathy said excitedly. She'd been looking forward to this for weeks; she couldn't wait to start playing again.

As Krystal picked Luc up and took him back towards the pub, Don pulled Willow into a hug and draped his other arm around Cathy's shoulders.

'If tonight goes well,' he said, 'we could start talking about touring again.'

'Do you think?' Cathy asked. She missed touring more than anything. When they'd first come to the Island she had been glad of the peace and quiet, of staying in one place for longer than a couple of nights, but two years on and she was itching to get back on a tour bus, to play night after night to a different audience. 'What about the kids?' she asked.

'They'd come too.'

Cathy gave him a dubious look.

'It worked for Paul and Linda McCartney,' Don said. 'Why not us?'

Why not us indeed, Cathy mused.

'I know you miss it,' Don went on. 'And all I want is for you to be happy, to give you everything you want.'

Cathy looked at him then, her handsome husband who she had first set eyes on when she was eighteen, supporting King Silver at the Astoria in London. And she looked at their beautiful daughter and thought about the gig they were going to play later.

She had everything that she could ever want right here. Except…

Cathy looked away again, towards the sea, a worm of guilt eating into her stomach. Planning the festival and rehearsing for the gig tonight had brought it all back. She had started to remember those early days of touring, being on the road with The Laurels, being on the road with Storm.

She'd thought about Storm a lot over the last few months and about how brilliant it would be if he could have played at the festival. And she had realised that, despite everything, she missed him.

That, despite everything, she was still in love with him.

28

Willow

As they drove across the Island, back towards Seaview, Willow was glad Luc had come for her, glad that she was returning with him. One of the reasons she'd been avoiding going back to the Island was not knowing how she would react when she saw Luc. Her emotions were all over the place after everything that had happened, and she could still remember the gentle warning in Luc's voice when she'd told him about Charlie taking Kate to the Maldives. She'd been a fool to think it was innocent. She'd thought she would be angry with Luc for being right, for charming her again, for stealing her heart, for not telling her about his daughter.

But when she'd seen him sitting in the hotel foyer waiting for her, she hadn't felt anger at all. She'd felt relief. Somebody cared enough to come and find her, to see if she was all right. Seeing him had made her feel anchored and reminded her that she had a home, a family, people who loved her.

Even if Luc wasn't going to be part of that after the festival.

Willow could make sense of a few things now at least – why everything had felt so off between her and Charlie, why she suddenly hadn't seemed good enough for him. It hadn't all been to do with seeing Luc on *American Stars*.

If it wasn't for the fact that Storm Tyler still couldn't be found, Willow could almost pretend that everything was going to be fine. She knew she had to concentrate on the festival, and she had to get one of her parents to talk because she was convinced they both knew more than they were letting on and one of them at least could tell her where Storm was these days.

Luc pulled the Jeep up outside Cathy's house and Don came to the door to greet them. Willow ran towards him, straight into his arms and she felt like a little girl again. She didn't see Don enough; she didn't see any of her family enough anymore. Over the years she'd put them to one side so she could create her dream life with Charlie. Don Warwick and Cathy Cole hadn't fitted into any of Charlie's five-year plans, so Willow had cut them out, pretending she was fine with that, swallowing down her real feelings for the sake of presenting a united front with Charlie.

Was that the reason why they were keeping things from her now? Because she'd tried to live a life without them?

'Thanks for bringing her home,' Don said to Luc as he returned the car keys.

'No problem,' Luc replied. 'I'll see you soon.'

'Luc, wait,' Willow said as Luc turned to go. He stopped on the path and walked back towards her as Don went inside, giving them some space.

As Luc approached her, Willow reached up to touch his face, just for a moment. 'Thank you,' she said. 'Thank you for coming to get me, for showing me that people care about me.'

'Anytime you need me,' Luc said, his voice a whisper.

'You're my best friend, Luc. Whatever happens at the end of this summer I want us to stay in touch this time.'

Luc smiled. 'Can I see you tomorrow?' he asked.

'Yes,' she said. 'I'll be in The Music Shop.'

Luc nodded once and disappeared into the gloom as he walked back towards the beach, towards his apartment.

Willow didn't know what she was going to do when he went back to America.

Luc arrived at The Music Shop early the next morning with two coffees and two pastries. It was exactly as it had been all summer, except today he brought his daughter as well.

'Hey,' he said as the door closed behind him, the bell jangling. That slow lazy smile spread across his face and her heart skipped a beat. She looked away from him, turning her attention towards his daughter.

'Hi, I'm Annelise,' the little girl said with a lot more confidence than Willow had ever had at seven. 'And you must be Willow.' She was Luc's daughter through and through – the eyes, the smile, even the dimple. She could see the little boy he used to be in Annelise.

'That's right,' Willow replied, catching Luc's eye as she bent down to shake Annelise's hand. Luc winked at her, his face full of pride.

'Willow is a pretty name,' Annelise mused. 'Please may I

look at some guitars?' Willow glanced at Luc to check that it was OK and he nodded.

'Do you play guitar?' Willow asked, turning to the racks of guitars on the wall and picking out a couple of half-size ones that might be suitable.

'Daddy's teaching me,' Annelise said. 'I've only been learning for a year though so I'm not as good as him yet.'

'Give it another year,' Luc said. 'And she'll be better than me.'

Annelise turned to her father and beamed. The look of love that passed between them melted Willow's heart and reminded her of how things used to be with her own father, how far she'd let everything slip.

And it reminded her of the life that Luc had across the Atlantic, far away from her and the Island.

Luc helped Annelise with the two guitars that Willow had selected for her.

'Why don't you try them both out?' he said. 'While I talk to Willow for a bit.'

Annelise nodded, a look of intense concentration on her face as she started to play one of the guitars, her tongue poking out the corner of her mouth. Luc stood next to Willow, leaning on the shop counter.

'She's very confident,' Willow said.

'She wasn't always like that,' Luc replied. 'She was so shy when she first came to stay with me, scared of everything. Mum worked hard to get her to trust us. I can't take any of the credit really. I had no idea what I was doing.' Willow could feel the tension in his body as he spoke. It was no wonder his anxiety had been so bad, the amount of pressure he seemed to put on himself.

'But you taught her to play like that,' Willow said, looking over at Annelise. 'She's really good.'

Luc smiled. 'The music seems to have really helped her confidence,' he said. 'She's obsessed with learning guitar.'

'Just like her dad. You were only ever really interested in music too.'

Luc caught Willow's eye, holding her gaze for a moment. 'Not just music,' he said.

They stood and drank their coffees, watching Annelise.

'Something weird happened last night,' Luc said, his voice barely more than a whisper, clearly not wanting his daughter to hear or ask questions.

'What?' Willow asked, looking towards Annelise. She didn't know much about young children but she did know that they heard a lot more than adults thought they did.

'Your dad called me, not long after I dropped you home. He's worried about you.'

'He doesn't need to be.'

'Doesn't he?' Luc asked.

'No, I'm OK, really. Is that all Dad wanted, to tell you he was worried?'

'No, he wants us to meet him here this afternoon. Just the two of us. He has something important to tell us.'

'Something so important that he couldn't tell me about it?' Willow said, raising her voice slightly above a whisper and noticing Annelise turn around to look at them.

'This afternoon,' Luc whispered. 'One-thirty.'

He turned back to his daughter. 'Which guitar would you like?' he asked her.

'This one,' she said holding the one with the blue spiral

patterns around the sound hole. Willow knew she'd pick that one; it was so pretty.

'Well why don't you bring it over so Willow can find you a case for it?' Luc said. 'Did you know that Willow's mum made that?'

Annelise looked at Willow, her mouth an "o" of surprise. 'Really?' she asked.

'Yup,' Willow replied. 'She's been making guitars since I was as little as you.'

'I'm not that little,' Annelise announced. 'I'm seven years and seven months old.' Willow found herself doing the maths in her head. Luc would only have been twenty-two when she was born, the same year that Willow was doing her internship at the bank. She shook the thought away.

'How much do I owe you?' Luc asked, taking his credit card out of his wallet.

Before Willow got a chance to tell him Annelise ran to the door of the shop.

'Daddy, look,' she said. 'Monty is here!'

Tom Newell was walking past with his strange-looking black and white dog.

'Can I go out and say hello?' Annelise asked.

'Sure,' Luc replied. 'But don't go where I can't see you.'

Willow wasn't used to this version of Luc. It was bad enough that she thought she was falling in love with him all over again, without seeing him like this. It was disarming her, and it hurt her heart to know that nothing could happen between them now, that Luc's priorities were elsewhere. It reminded her of her own priorities too.

'She's only been on the Island a few days and she knows

more people than I do,' Luc said as he punched his PIN into the credit card machine. He caught Willow's eye and for a moment everything stopped mattering…

'I'd better go,' Luc said, stepping away from her.

'Save Annelise from Tom's endless conversation.' Willow smiled.

'I'll see you at one-thirty,' he said as he left.

'Your mum has emailed Storm Tyler,' Don said as he turned the sign on the door of The Music Shop to "Closed". 'I didn't want her to but she has. She wants him there for the festival.'

'You've known how to get in touch with him all this time and you never told me?' Willow asked in disbelief.

'Is he coming?' Luc asked at the same time. He was standing next to her, his hand on the small of her back.

'He hasn't replied,' Don said.

'You've known where he is all this time and you never said anything?' Willow repeated. 'I know you knew him years ago, that you toured with him and I know Mum was there when he recorded that tape, but you never said a word. All those afternoons we sat here and played together, and you never mentioned it. You knew how worried I was about the festival. Why didn't you tell me how to get in touch with him weeks ago?'

She stopped and stared at her father. Don rubbed a calloused hand over his stubble, as he closed his eyes.

'You never asked,' he said. 'Not outright. And I didn't want him here on the Island. I never wanted to have to see him again.'

Willow didn't reply straight away, she didn't know what to say and was grateful when Luc broke the silence.

'I think you'd better tell us,' he said. 'Tell us what's going on.'

'It was while you were in Southampton,' Don said. 'Your mum was so worried about you – we both were – and that's when she told me she was going to email Storm and beg him to come and play the festival. I tried to stop her; I tried to tell her not to meddle but she insisted. She wanted to save the festival for you. I know you and she aren't as close as you used to be, Willow, but she did it for you, because she loves you.'

'I don't understand what you're talking about,' Willow said.

'I just want you to know how much your mum loves you, how much we both love you before I tell you everything.'

Willow felt herself tense, as though her body was getting itself ready for something she'd known was coming since the day she and Luc had listened to the tape in the studio, the day he accidentally called her Lil.

Don began to tell her how he and Cathy really met and about how The Laurels came into being on Storm Tyler's ill-fated solo tour. He told her about her mother's affair with Storm Tyler and how that ended before Storm disappeared.

When he finished Willow turned to Luc who was staring at Don, his brow furrowed.

'You and Cathy have known where he was all this time,' Luc said. 'You've known even as you've watched Willow worry about what to do, worry about the festival.'

Willow felt as though everything around her was spinning

out of control, as though all the things she had believed about herself were coming undone.

'Cathy wanted to get in touch with Storm Tyler from the start,' Don said. 'Well, once she'd got over the shock of you promising the council that you'd find him. Even though she knew she'd have to tell you everything about the past, Willow, she still wanted to help you. It was me who tried to stop her. Blame me not your mother.'

Willow pushed herself away from Luc's hand and towards her father. She felt rage roiling inside her, rage she had been bottling up since Krystal and Annelise knocked on Luc's door, since she'd found out about Charlie and Kate.

'I don't think I can talk about this anymore,' she said, her voice thin with anger. 'I think I need some time to think.'

'I'll go,' Don said.

'I think that's a good idea,' Willow replied.

'Willow.' She heard Luc's voice, gentle and soothing from behind her.

Don's eyes darted towards Luc's before he turned to leave. For some reason that made Willow even more angry, as though there was something else that her father wasn't telling her.

'Why?' she asked her father's back as he stood in the doorway. 'Why did you never say anything?'

'Your mother never wanted—'

'You're my dad,' Willow interrupted. 'You should have told me everything years ago. You certainly should have told me as soon as you knew I was looking for Storm.' She stopped, turning her head to look at Luc. 'I wish I'd never listened to that bloody tape,' she said.

When she turned back towards her father he was facing

her again, but he wasn't looking at her, he was looking at Luc as though there was something else.

'You all love keeping secrets though, don't you?' she said. 'You've kept Luc's little secret from me for the last two years as well.'

'Willow, come on,' Luc said, a warning in his voice. 'That was my fault. I asked him not to tell anyone.'

'What else are you hiding?' Willow asked her father. And for a moment he looked as though he might say something before he turned and left.

As her father walked away Willow knew there was more to the story, and she knew that she'd been right all those weeks ago when she felt she'd been opening a Pandora's box.

'My mother had an affair with Storm Tyler when she was a teenager,' Willow said, unable to believe it. Her heart was still pounding in her chest from the argument with her father as Luc handed her a cup of herbal tea.

'So it would seem,' he replied, his voice neutral. 'Are you OK?'

Willow shrugged. 'No. Not really.'

He leant in towards her, draping his arm around her shoulders, but she moved away, pacing the shop floor. She was angry with her father, angry with her mother and she hadn't made up her mind as to whether she was angry with Luc or not. But she was glad he was there all the same. He looked as shell-shocked as she was.

'Why has Mum never spoken about any of this?' Willow said. 'I had no idea that she got into the Royal Academy let alone that she left to go on tour with Storm and that was where she met Dad and Krystal.'

'Where did she tell you they all met?' Luc asked.

'She always said she met them in a pub in London, that Don and Krystal had been playing there and asked her to join them.'

'That's what Mum told me too.'

'Well at least they got their stories straight,' Willow said, standing still for a moment to look out of the window towards the sea.

'Did you ask questions? Did you wonder about your mum and dad and The Laurels before we were born?'

'All the time,' Willow replied. 'I was always asking questions, wanting to see photographs but whenever I talked about it I either got the brush-off or Mum would look so sad that I kept quiet.' She paused. 'Did you? Did you ask Krystal?'

He nodded. 'Yeah, but she never told me much. She was always too busy making me focus on my own music. I stopped asking in the end.'

Willow could feel the anger rising inside her again and took a few deep breaths, trying to calm herself. She heard Luc walk over to her. He stood behind her, one hand on her shoulder. She didn't move away this time, instead letting herself lean into him, into his warmth and strength.

'We should have kept asking,' she said.

'They should have told us.'

As Luc said those words, something in Willow broke apart. She turned around to look at him.

'And you should have told me about your daughter,' she snapped at him. 'Krystal's taught you all about keeping secrets, hasn't she? You know all about not telling people things, about lying to your friends, about hurting the people who love you the most...' She stared at him for a moment before turning away, walking towards the back of the shop, towards her mum's workshop, away from him.

He caught up with her before she got to the door, a light touch on her arm. She stopped and turned around.

'You love me?' he asked.

She hadn't meant to say that to him. She hadn't meant to say any of it. She was taking her confusion out on him, her anger at her mother. Whatever secrets Luc had kept from her, none of this was his fault.

'I didn't...' She paused.

Luc looked away. 'I'm sorry,' he said. 'I never meant to hurt you, not then and not now. I should have told you about Annelise. I...'

'It's OK,' Willow said. 'I know you're sorry. So much has happened over the last few weeks and this feels like the final straw.' She felt tears burning the backs of her eyes again. She didn't want to cry in front of him but it was too late. 'Every time I think I know what I want, every time I try to move forward, something falls apart all over again,' she said.

He took her hand and led her into her mother's workshop. They sat there together surrounded by the smell of wood shavings, memories falling around them like autumn leaves. She leant her head against his shoulder and let herself cry. She felt his lips brush the top of her head.

'It's going to be all right,' he said. 'I promise.'

She didn't know how long they sat there like that or how many customers had tried the locked door of The Music Shop in that time, but she didn't want to move or let this moment end. She didn't want to have to face the reality that waited for her.

Eventually, she sat up and rubbed her eyes, that feeling she'd had earlier when her father looked over at Luc had returned. That feeling that her father was keeping something else from her, something significant.

'When did King Silver split up?' she asked. 'When did Storm Tyler disappear?'

'Towards the end of 1987,' Luc replied.

'A few months before I was born.'

Luc nodded slowly at the statement as though he knew exactly what she was thinking.

'Luc, do you think Storm Tyler is my father? Do you think that's why Mum and Dad haven't told me any of this? Do you think that's why Dad left in the end?'

He sighed and leant back in his chair. 'I don't know,' he replied. Willow's heart sank. She'd been hoping he'd laugh at her, tell her she was being ridiculous. 'But does it matter? It was Don who brought you up, Don who taught you to play mandolin, Don who loves you.' He looked away from her. 'Anyone can father a child, not everyone can be a dad.'

She exhaled deeply trying to let go of the tension she'd been holding on to.

'Are you still playing?' Luc asked.

Willow nodded. She'd picked up her father's mandolin as soon as she'd opened the shop that morning. Playing had calmed her down after everything that had happened in London and Southampton and she knew she'd missed playing more than anything – she regretted the years she'd spent ignoring music. If one good thing had come out of this disaster of a summer, it was picking up the mandolin again.

'What do you want to do?' Luc asked.

'I just need some time if that's OK,' she replied. 'Time to process everything that's happened. I know I need to talk to Mum but it will have to wait.'

'Do you want me to be there when you do talk to Cathy?' he said as he stood to leave.

'Is that OK?'

'Of course it is. Anything you need me to do, I'm here. All you have to do is ask.' He smiled and Willow's stomach flipped. 'You never know,' he said. 'Some good might come out of all of this. Storm Tyler might play the festival after all.'

Over the next week Willow saw Luc every morning when he and Annelise brought her coffee and pastries.

'I've eaten my own body weight in carbs this summer.' Willow laughed. 'I've finally got my clothes back and I won't be able to fit in them.'

'You look amazing,' Luc replied. 'Much better than when you first got here, so shut up and eat your croissant.'

Luc and Annelise never stayed for long. Annelise got bored easily, just as Luc had done at that age, and wanted to play on the beach or have another guitar lesson, but they came every day. Each morning Willow watched the bond between father and daughter grow and knew that she could never come between them, that she and Luc could never be more than friends. Even if there was a chance for her and Luc one day in the future, both he and Annelise had a life in America that they were going back to. This summer was nothing more than a hiatus for all of them.

Each morning she told Luc that she'd talk to her mother the next day, but she never found the courage to do it. Cathy must know that Don had told them everything, but she seemed as reluctant as Willow to actually talk about it and the two women danced around each other if they found themselves in the house at the same time. Willow wanted to know how the festival was going, whether her mother had heard back from Storm Tyler but something always stopped her from asking.

She thought about her mum's past all the time though. She couldn't imagine having parents who would stand in the way of what you wanted to do the way Brian seemed to have done with Cathy.

Willow had never known her grandfather, but she'd heard about him from various musicians over the years. If she had a pound for everyone who told her they knew Brian Cole she'd be a very rich woman. Either Brian Cole knew a lot of people or a lot of people wished they knew him.

She'd always wondered why Cathy fell out with him and now she knew. But she also knew that there were two sides to every story and she couldn't believe that Cathy and Brian hadn't spoken to each other in nearly thirty-five years because of a crazy affair Cathy had with a rock star.

Unless there was more to it than that, unless it was more than just an affair.

The more she thought about it, the more convinced she was that her mother must have kept in touch with Storm regularly over the years to just be able to email him about the festival like this. Storm and Cathy recorded the demo together in 1999. Had Cathy kept in touch with him after that? Did they still have feelings for each other? Was Storm Tyler the reason Willow's father left seven years later?

And Willow couldn't stop thinking about the possibility that Storm was her father or connected to her somehow. She couldn't imagine any other reason for the strange feeling she'd had when she found the tape, the way she'd known right from the beginning how important it was.

She needed to talk to her mother but she could only do it when her father wasn't there.

One morning Luc arrived at The Music Shop without his daughter.

'Annelise is with Mum,' he said. 'And your dad's gone to Newport with Rocco so today we're going to Cathy's and the two of you are going to talk. You can't avoid this anymore, Willow.'

If Cathy was surprised to see them both together on a Friday afternoon she didn't show it. Willow felt Luc's hand on her shoulder, squeezing gently just for a moment, encouraging her.

'Can I get you anything?' Cathy said. Her voice sounded strained, as though she knew what was about to happen.

'Mum, can you sit down?' Willow asked.

Cathy did as she was told, sitting opposite Willow and Luc, her eyes flicking from one to the other.

'You want to talk about Storm Tyler I suppose,' she said, giving Luc a look that Willow couldn't quite interpret.

'Dad told me about how The Laurels met,' Willow said.

'About you and Storm. He told me that you emailed him. Have you heard anything back?'

Cathy shook her head.

'You should have told me when I found the tape,' Willow said. Her mother sat still and straight, her mouth a thin line, her face pale, just as she had in the car after the planning meeting. She didn't say anything.

'I tried to talk to you after the planning meeting,' Willow went on. 'I tried to get you to tell me what you knew then but you wouldn't. You've known where Storm was all along and you didn't say anything.'

'I've been in touch with Storm for years,' Cathy replied. 'And as I'm sure you've worked out, he was here on the Island in 1999 when we recorded the demo. He wanted to start again, make a comeback but it didn't work out that way.' She paused but didn't look at Willow. 'He was here again the summer before you went to university.'

Don hadn't told her that and Willow felt a wave of nausea wash over her. She felt as though all her mother's most well-kept secrets, her hopes and dreams had been spilled on to the floor and she didn't want to know any more. She wished that she'd never listened to the tape, never made her rash promise at the council meeting in her hope to save the festival.

'Do you think he'll come again this summer?' she asked. 'Do you think he'll play?'

'I have no idea,' Cathy replied. 'I thought he would have replied to me by now. Maybe he's away.' Willow saw a sadness pass across her mother's features and she cringed inside as she realised how stupid she'd been promising the council that she'd find Storm without talking to her mother first.

Cathy turned to look at Luc. 'You should have known better,' she said. 'You shouldn't have helped her in this mad endeavour.'

Luc held his hands up and looked as though he was about to say something.

'Luc told me Storm probably didn't want to be found,' Willow interrupted. 'But I insisted we try and find him. This isn't Luc's fault, Mum; this is entirely on me.'

'How much do you know about Storm Tyler?' Cathy asked, still looking at Luc.

'Not much,' he replied. 'I just figured that as he's been gone so long that he disappeared for a reason and probably liked it that way.'

'Storm Tyler was the reason your father left in the end,' Cathy said quietly. 'The reason The Laurels split up.'

Willow had suspected as much and she closed her eyes for a moment as though that would somehow turn back time and stop this horrible moment from happening. She should never have listened to the tape without her mother; she should never have gone behind her back.

'Cathy...' Luc began. He sounded as though he was about to apologise, but Willow thought it was too late when she saw the look of pale resignation on her mother's face change to anger.

'Luc,' Cathy said, turning to look at him. 'Well you're very good at keeping secrets too aren't you? Very good at going behind people's backs and pretending that you're somebody you aren't.'

'Mum,' Willow said in shock. She'd never seen her mother like this.

'Yes, Willow, you should have told me about the tape when you first found it,' Cathy went on. 'We could have avoided all of this. But you, Luc Harrison, you should have told Willow about your daughter before you broke her heart for the second time. She had come home to heal, to find herself, not to be broken by you all over again.'

'It wasn't like that, Mum,' Willow said. 'It isn't like that.' She started to stand up but she felt Luc's hand on her thigh, warm and solid, and she sat back down again.

'It's OK, Willow,' he said. 'Your mum's right. I do keep hurting you. I never meant to but I should have done everything differently.' He paused. 'Everything,' he repeated.

He looked so sad and Willow thought her heart would break all over again. She wanted to reach out and hold him, draw him into her arms and tell him that it was OK, that everything was going to be all right. But she didn't know if that was true. Luc had hurt her and now, between them, they had hurt Cathy. She was furious with her mother for keeping this from her for all these years, furious with her father and Krystal too, but at the same time she was angry with herself for causing her mother pain.

'Isn't it better that we all know the truth?' Willow asked, trying to swallow down her anger, trying to swallow down the question that had plagued her since her father had told them everything.

Cathy didn't speak and Willow could see the hurt in her eyes. She had come back to the Island to try to heal, to try to find a new path, a new way of life but now she knew that she wasn't the only one who had been broken.

Cathy reached across to Willow and took her hand. Luc's hand was still on Willow's thigh, soft and gentle. The three of them sat like that for a moment, lost in their own thoughts. There was so much still to say, so much to unravel, so many questions to ask but Willow knew that now wasn't the right time. It was something that she and her mother would have to work out together, alone.

But there was one question that Willow had to ask, the one she hadn't been able to stop thinking about. She had to now.

'Mum,' she said quietly. 'Is Storm Tyler my father?'

Cathy looked up at her and smiled. 'No, sweetheart,' she said. 'Don is your father – you can be sure of that.' She paused for a moment as though considering something, her eyes flicking to Luc for a moment.

It was then that it hit her, a flash of realisation. All those nights Willow had spent trawling the internet looking at old pictures of Storm Tyler and it was only now that she worked it out and knew what her father had almost told them in The Music Shop earlier in the week.

But before she could think about it any further, somebody started banging on the front door.

29

Luc

'I'll get it,' Luc said, standing up. He needed to get away, to get out of this room. His chest had been tightening as Cathy and Willow had spoken. He didn't want them to argue, he didn't want to cause either of them any pain and yet he knew he'd hurt them both. He wanted to tell Willow that he was still there for her. He wanted to ask her if she'd go for a walk with him. He didn't want to know any more about their parents and Storm Tyler, because he had a feeling that Cathy and Don were keeping something from them. He just wanted to sit somewhere quietly and listen to the sea, and whoever was at the door was the interruption he needed.

He left Cathy and Willow sitting together and walked out of the room and into the hall. Everything seemed to slow down and the sunlight shining through the hall window seemed very bright. He took some deep breaths before opening the door.

'Oh, Mum, it's you,' he said.

'Luc, thank God,' Krystal said. 'I've been looking everywhere for you.'

'Is everything OK?' he asked, putting out a hand to steady his mother who seemed very worked up about something, her usually immaculate appearance in disarray. He didn't know if he could stand any more parental dramas.

'Annelise has run off,' she said. 'I can't find her anywhere.'

Luc's heart, which had been holding together by a thread for weeks now, shattered into a million pieces.

An hour later and most of Seaview were out looking for Annelise. Tom Newell was asking questions of holidaymakers and Skye was going from shop to shop to see if anyone had seen her. Don and Cathy were looking inland while Luc and Willow focused on the beach. An hour had passed and nobody had found her, nobody had even seen her.

'It's like she's disappeared into thin air,' Luc said, his hands raking his hair as he squatted down on the beach. 'Where is she? What am I going to do?' He was trying to keep the anxiety at bay, but Annelise's disappearance was tearing into him, his emotions a mix of anger, sadness and panic. 'I'm going to have to tell her mother,' he went on, but Willow placed her hand on his arm.

'Not yet,' she said. 'It's only been a couple of hours.'

'You don't understand,' Luc replied. 'Her mother can be really difficult. I had to fight for months for her to give permission for Annelise to come to the Island this summer. I'm only supposed to see her in Nashville – that was the agreement.' He paused and looked at Willow and the unsaid words that were hidden in that statement passed silently between them. The unsaid words that they had both been ignoring.

We can never be together because our lives are in different places. This summer is all we have.

'We'll find her, I promise.'

Luc knew that Willow couldn't promise that, but just hearing the words was enough to give him a little bit of hope. Willow had always given him hope.

'We should go down to the far end of the beach,' Willow said, taking Luc's hand and drawing him up to standing. 'I know you don't think she knows where that is, but you remember what being seven is like surely? How far we used to explore?'

'But we had each other,' Luc said. 'She's all alone.'

'Your daughter is clever and sensible and seems very happy in her own company. She'll just have wandered off playing some game or other and lost track of time. She'll be fine.'

'The tide will be coming in soon,' he said quietly.

'I know,' Willow replied calmly. 'Which is why we should get down to the other end of the beach now.'

'She doesn't know about the tides. Not like we did.' Luc and Willow had grown up on the Island with an ingrained respect for the power of the sea and the fickleness of the tides. They had learned to love it but known they could never truly know it or its capabilities. Annelise had none of that knowledge and that thought scared Luc more than anything else he had heard today.

They walked together along the sand. Luc didn't let go of Willow's hand. He felt as though he would float away if he did, like a forgotten balloon after a birthday party. He felt as though Willow was his only tether right now.

What am I going to do without her? he thought.

He wasn't sure if he meant Annelise or Willow. Probably both. He needed them both. But he knew he could never have that.

As they approached the far end of the beach, the place where he'd had his first panic attack, where Don found him and helped him, Luc felt his breathing shorten again, the tightness around his heart return. He slowed down.

'Willow I can't...'

'You can,' she said gently.

He pulled away from her, turning his back to the beach in front of them. All he could think about was that morning, lying in the fishing boat thinking he was dying. He needed to pull himself together, to find Annelise. He looked over at Willow but she wasn't looking at him; she was looking down the beach at something else, her face a mask of shock.

'Luc, look,' she said, pointing to the beach behind him. He hardly dared to turn around.

When he did, he saw them at the end of the beach, walking towards him. Annelise was holding hands with an old man. What the hell was she doing? Who the hell was he?

'Annelise,' he shouted down the beach. Adrenaline took over as he started to run towards her. 'Annelise come here,' he shouted. He watched as his daughter let go of the man's hand and started running towards him.

'Hey, Daddy,' she called.

He caught up with her, pulling her into his arms, picking her up.

'Where have you been?' he asked. 'I didn't know where you were, you must never do that...'

He trailed off as the old man walked towards him and realisation dawned. He understood the shocked look on Willow's face now; it had nothing to do with Annelise holding hands with a stranger and everything to do with who that stranger was. He didn't seem so old now that Luc was closer to him and Luc noticed his green eyes.

'Daddy, this is Neil,' Annelise said. 'He's my new friend.'

Luc stared at the man in front of him.

The man who used to be Storm Tyler.

And a strange feeling washed over him.

30

August 1999

' "Gamble Gold" Take One,' Storm Tyler said into
the microphone in the recording studio at The
Music Shop. Cathy sat in the corner smiling to herself. This
was the moment she'd been waiting for, the moment all of
Storm's fans had been waiting for. He had finally decided to
record "Gamble Gold" and he'd chosen to record it in her
tiny studio on the Isle of Wight.

Nobody but Cathy knew about it so far. Don and Krystal
knew that Storm was here on the Island and knew that he
was going to be headlining the festival, but neither of them
had been enthusiastic about it.

'Let's see if he's sober enough to turn up,' Krystal had
said. Don hadn't said anything at all. The two of them
had been drifting apart for several years; Don spending
more and more time working as a session musician in
London or touring with other bands. He only seemed to
be home for the festival and for Christmas these days and

Cathy wondered if he would have come home at all if it hadn't been for Willow.

Cathy had spent a lot of time alone, which was when she'd started making mandolins and guitars. It had been something to do while Don was away but had turned into a small business that took up so much of her time. She was happy, mostly.

She'd got back in touch with Storm after the second Seaview Music Festival. She knew she shouldn't, but she hadn't been able to stop thinking about him. Being involved in the festival, involved in music again, had made her thoughts turn to Storm Tyler. When the Laurels had started touring again she knew she wouldn't be able to resist.

She'd written to his old manager who she'd known from when The Laurels toured with Storm and given him her address. She hadn't really expected Storm to write to her. She had been over the moon when he did.

Their correspondence was tentative at first – just two or three letters a year. But gradually, over time and as they both got email addresses, they wrote more often.

I'd love to see my muse again, Storm had written and that was when Cathy had decided to ask him to play the festival.

The threads that her marriage was hanging on by were severed the night she told Don about it. When he walked out of the house slamming the door behind him, she hadn't thought he'd come back. She suspected he only did because of Willow. Cathy and Don had kept up the show of their marriage for years to keep Willow happy. Cathy knew that if it hadn't been for Willow there would have been no marriage anyway.

'He can come,' Don relented in the end. 'He can play the bloody festival and then he can go. It will bring in money and get us publicity. But if he gets drunk, or does anything to upset anyone, especially Willow, I swear to God...'

'I promise,' Cathy had said. 'He'll be on his best behaviour.' Although Cathy had no idea how she could control him. She'd never been able to before.

Recording "Gamble Gold" had been her idea but Storm had loved it.

'Perfect,' he said. 'This is the right time, the right place, with the right backing singer.' He snaked his arm around Cathy's waist.

'Me?' she asked.

'Of course you,' Storm replied. 'Always my muse.'

They recorded it in one take with no mistakes, Storm's voice as clear as it had been at the Astoria seventeen years before, his mandolin playing as precise and unique.

'This is it,' Cathy said. 'Your big comeback.'

'I'll have to start thinking about what other Ballad Book songs to record,' Storm replied.

Afterwards Cathy had to pick Willow up from Krystal's house and Storm said he'd see Cathy the next day. He was staying in a hotel, keeping himself to himself so that nobody would see him and ask questions, especially Willow.

'I'll stop for a celebratory lemonade,' he said.

Cathy had been a fool to think that Storm Tyler could set foot in The Three Doves on his own and buy a soft drink.

He'd turned up at Cathy and Don's front door hours later, singing loudly and barely able to stand. Don hadn't wanted to let him in at all, but Storm pushed past him.

'Where's Cathy Cole?' he slurred. 'Where's my muse?'

Then he threw up in the living room and passed out on the sofa.

'I thought he was meant to be clean,' Don said through gritted teeth.

'He told me he was,' Cathy replied.

'Jesus, Cathy,' Don fumed. 'How could you let this happen with our daughter in the house? He's not supposed to come here. Thank God Willow's asleep.'

Don had taken Willow back to Krystal's for the night. Cathy hadn't known what story he'd spun her when he'd woken her up and told her they were going on an adventure. He must have stayed at Krystal's too because neither of them had come back until the next day.

Cathy had cleaned up by then and Storm was awake, showered and caffeinated. He had reverted to the apologetic version of himself, begging for Cathy's forgiveness just as he had when they'd lived together.

'You need to go to rehab,' Cathy said. 'You need to stop thinking you can get clean on your own.'

Storm was still there when Don came back with Krystal.

'Where are the kids?' Cathy whispered, meeting them in the hallway.

'At the beach,' Don replied. 'We thought they should stay away until he'd gone.'

Cathy nodded. 'I'm going with him,' she said.

'What?' Krystal and Don stared at her.

'He needs to go to rehab,' Cathy replied calmly. 'He's not going to do that on his own so I'm taking him back to France and checking him in.'

'Nothing's changed has it?' Krystal said. 'Neil Flannigan

says "jump" and you say "how high?"' Her cheeks were flushed with anger.

'It's not like that—' Cathy began.

'And what are you going to tell Willow?' Don interrupted. 'Sorry I can't be here for the festival, love, but I'm off to France with your real father?' His voice had grown louder and Cathy turned towards the living room door behind which she knew Storm was listening.

'Don't say that, Don,' she said. Cathy had known for years that Don had harboured doubts about Willow's paternity and nothing she said could ever really convince him that he was her father.

'How do I know he's not her father?' Don went on. 'I've only got your word for it and now he's back in our lives and damn it, Cathy, he's not taking her away from me.'

'You do only have my word for it,' Cathy said quietly. 'And you've never been able to bring yourself to believe me. Storm and I hadn't slept together for months before I found out I was pregnant. I've told you that more times than I care to remember.'

'Prove it,' Don said, his voice ice cold.

'Shut up, Don, right now,' Krystal said sharply. 'Don't start this again after all these years. Willow is your daughter. Do you really think that I'd have let her and Luc get so close if I thought for a second that Neil was Willow's father too...' She stopped abruptly, clapping her hand over her mouth as she realised what she'd said.

In the silence that followed Cathy looked at her husband, quietly searching his face to see if he knew – he'd always been close to Luc, maybe he'd guessed? Because now that

Cathy had found out, it seemed obvious. Of course Luc was Neil's child – those eyes should have given it away. Even at eleven years old Luc looked like his father. How had she never figured it out before now?

And there was something else as well, that strange question that Krystal had asked when the children were still small, when they first started to become inseparable.

Willow isn't Storm's daughter is she? You would tell me wouldn't you?

Cathy hadn't understood why it was so important at the time.

She could tell by the look on Don's face that he hadn't known either, that this was all new information to him too.

'He's Luc's father?' Don asked incredulously.

Behind him the living room door opened. 'I'm what?' Storm asked.

'You're Luc's father,' Krystal repeated, rubbing her eyes with her palms.

'Why did you never tell me?'

Cathy felt as though she was watching a play or a television programme or something else that she wasn't directly involved in. She found it hard to believe that these were her friends, her bandmates, her family. How had she not known? Why had Krystal never told her?

'I never told you, Neil, because you are an utter mess,' Krystal said. 'Because who wants a drunk and a drug addict as the father of their child?'

Cathy tried to find something to say to articulate the whirlwind of emotions that were slamming into her. She had always assumed Krystal hadn't really known who Luc's father was – life had been crazy back then and Krystal had been enjoying it to the full.

Krystal turned to look at Cathy. 'I'm sorry I never told you,' she said. 'I was embarrassed to admit it. I broke all the rules and slept with your ex and I'm sorry for that.' She stood up a little bit straighter. 'But I'll never regret it,' she went on. 'Luc is the best thing that ever happened to me.'

'You slept with Neil,' Cathy said quietly to herself. 'You slept with Storm.' She looked over at Don who was just standing there in stunned silence.

'Luc has his eyes,' Don said, but nobody replied.

'Can I meet him?' Neil asked.

'No, absolutely not.' Krystal was resolute. 'This conversation stays in this room. Nobody tells Luc. Do you all swear?'

Don nodded and looked at Cathy. She didn't want to swear anything, she was still reeling from the fact that Krystal, her best friend, had slept with the love of her life, had a child with him but had never told her.

'Cathy?' Don asked.

'I have a right to see my son,' Neil interrupted.

Nobody spoke for a moment. Nobody moved.

'Please,' Krystal said, her tone softening. 'I'm begging you. Luc is sensitive, fragile and you're...' She paused, waving a hand at Storm Tyler. 'You're too much for him in this state. I'm asking you, for Luc's sake, to keep this amongst ourselves.'

And Cathy understood that, understood the power of a mother's love. She would lie down and die for Willow. She would do anything to make her happy, to make sure she had a good life.

'I promise it won't go any further,' Cathy said, turning to look at Neil and Don. Both men nodded, promising to keep quiet as well.

Don and Krystal had played the headline slot at the Seaview Folk Festival that summer, thankful that they hadn't told anyone Storm was on the Island. Thankful they could dismiss the whole thing as a rumour that had got out of hand.

Cathy hadn't joined them on stage because she had taken Storm Tyler back to France, making sure that he booked himself into a rehab clinic this time, telling Willow that she had to go and see a friend who was unwell. Willow hadn't seemed to mind – it was the summer and she had Luc and her dad. What else did she need?

The recording of Storm and Cathy singing "Gamble Gold" sat gathering dust in a drawer in Cathy's workshop for the next nineteen years. She had never been able to bring herself to listen to it again.

31

Willow

Willow knew Luc's focus was on his daughter, so it was no surprise that he didn't notice who the stranger was until he was sure Annelise was safe. But Willow recognised him straight away, even from a distance. He was taller than she'd imagined and he moved with a languid grace that she recognised.

She wondered what he was doing here and how he'd come to bump into Annelise.

And she knew, as soon as she saw them together, that the suspicions she'd had in her mother's living room earlier were right.

Willow ran down the beach after Luc. She caught up with him the moment he looked at Storm Tyler and realised who he was. The expression on Luc's face was unreadable and Willow looked at the three pairs of green eyes – Storm, Luc, Annelise.

'I met Neil at the rock pools,' Annelise explained. 'I

wanted to be on my own for a while – I was writing a song in my head.'

Willow's heart leapt as she heard this. Luc used to do the same thing when he was Annelise's age.

'Just give me a minute, Lil,' he'd say. 'I'm writing a song in my head.' Willow would mock him relentlessly but deep down she had always been in awe of his innate talent. It made her heart break to think that he couldn't write at the moment. She wondered if that talent was something hardwired into Luc's DNA, something he'd passed down to his daughter.

Willow stepped forward, holding out her hand to Storm Tyler.

'Hi, I'm Willow Cole, Cathy's daughter,' she said. 'I'm the one who's been looking for you.'

Storm took her hand in both of his and held her gaze for a moment too long. Willow wasn't sure whether it made her feel uncomfortable or not.

'Indeed you have,' Storm repeated softly. 'You look just like your mum.' He paused, letting go of her hand. 'I'm Neil by the way.'

Willow involuntarily raised an eyebrow.

'I prefer Neil these days,' he said with a smile.

Annelise babbled into the silence that followed about a crab that she'd found and about how Neil or Storm or whoever the hell he was had been telling her about the different sorts of crabs she should be looking for.

Willow looked at Storm again – she couldn't think of him as Neil. She was standing in front of one of the biggest rock legends of the twentieth century and they were chatting about crabs. It felt like a dream. She almost laughed until she caught sight of Luc's face. He was staring at Storm as though he wanted to say something but didn't know where to start. Did Luc know? Did Storm? Willow felt as though everything was spinning out of control. Was she just making things up? Seeing things that weren't there? She needed to stay calm for Luc.

'I need to go,' Luc said suddenly, turning away.

He started walking quickly down the beach, away from Willow, away from Storm, with Annelise still in his arms. Willow could hear Annelise complaining about being dragged away from her new friend. She could hear Luc scolding her for talking to strangers.

Except, if Willow's suspicions were correct, Storm Tyler wasn't a stranger. He was Annelise's grandfather.

'Luc,' Willow called, turning to follow them.

'Leave me alone, Willow,' Luc shouted back. 'Just leave us both alone.'

Willow turned back to Storm Tyler, ignoring the pain that Luc's words had caused, and Storm looked at her, holding her gaze again in that disarming way of his. *It's no wonder he had such a cult following*, Willow thought.

'Does he know?' Storm asked.

'Know what?' Willow replied, feigning ignorance.

Storm held her gaze for a moment longer, sending a shiver down her spine.

'That I'm his father.' He said looking away. He said the words so calmly it felt as though he assumed everyone must know. Perhaps they did. Everyone except her.

But then she remembered something that Luc had said when they were in Southampton.

But Mum still won't say anything and your dad says he doesn't know so what can I do?

Luc didn't know.

Willow was trying to think of something to say when she heard someone calling her name. She turned to see Krystal running towards them from the direction of the cliff path.

'Where's Luc?' she called as she approached. 'Have you found...?' She stopped when she saw who Willow was talking to.

'We found Annelise,' she said. 'Luc's taken her home.'

She watched Krystal visibly relax for a moment before she turned to Storm.

'Neil,' she said. 'What the hell are you doing here?'

'To play the festival like Cathy and Willow asked,' he replied, still so calm as though he was completely unaware of the bizarre nature of the entire situation.

'You haven't said anything to Luc have you?' Krystal asked, her voice betraying panic.

Storm Tyler smiled his disarming smile and shook his head. 'I didn't say a word,' he said. 'I'm assuming this means he doesn't know?'

'No, he doesn't know,' Krystal said.

'Still?' Storm asked. 'You still haven't told him?'

'For God's sake, Neil,' Krystal said. 'Why did you come?'

'I've already said because Cathy and Willow asked me,' he replied simply. 'Because they needed me to save the festival.' He paused. 'And to see Luc,' he added.

Krystal looked at Willow with a wary expression and Willow shrugged.

'I already know,' she said. 'Storm... I mean Neil told me. But I'd worked it out.' She paused. 'Luc doesn't know,' she went on. 'But he might have worked it out for himself too.'

Krystal didn't say anything for a moment.

'You know I'm going to have to tell him don't you?' Willow said quietly. 'It's Luc. I've never kept anything from him. We've never had secrets from each other.' But even as she said it she knew it wasn't true. Luc hadn't told her about Annelise or about his panic attacks. But she had never been completely honest with him either had she? She'd never replied to his letters, never given him a chance to explain. How had they let this happen? How had she been so stupid as to just let him go twelve years ago?

The expression on Krystal's face was a mix of concern and sadness. 'I should have told him,' she said. 'I should have told him years ago.'

'Why didn't you?' Storm asked, but Krystal threw an ice cold look at him.

'Has he really taken Annelise home?' Krystal asked Willow.

'I'm not sure. He just walked off. I don't think he really knew what he was doing.'

'Will you try to find him?' Krystal asked, her expression softening.

'I'll try,' Willow said. 'I'm not sure he wants to see anybody though.'

'He'll want to see you,' Krystal replied.

Willow started to walk away but Krystal called her back.

'Willow, I know we need to tell him the truth but will you let me do it?' She paused for a moment. 'Please?'

Willow nodded, not trusting her voice. How could they have kept this from Luc for all these years?

'You come with me, Neil,' Krystal said, the hardness coming back into her voice. 'We need to talk, and we need to find Cathy.'

*

She found them half an hour later a little bit further along the beach. Luc was sitting on the sand watching Annelise paddle on the very edge of the shore.

'Don't go any further than that,' he called as Willow sat next to him.

'She's looking for crabs,' Luc said wearily.

'Is she OK?' Willow asked.

'She's fine. A bit pissed with me for shouting at her. She doesn't really see what she's done wrong.'

'You were exactly the same at that age,' Willow said, nudging him gently. 'You used to wander off to write songs in your head. Do you remember?'

He turned to look at her. For a moment it seemed as though he didn't know what she was talking about. But then he smiled.

'I remember,' he said. But Willow could see the sadness in his eyes. 'I'm sorry.'

'For what?'

'For shouting at you, for walking away,' he paused. 'For everything.'

Willow reached towards him, taking his hand in hers. He squeezed her fingers gently.

'How are you, Luc?' she asked. 'Are you OK?'

He didn't say anything at first; he just looked out towards the sea. He sat so still for so long that Willow thought he hadn't heard her.

'No,' he said eventually. 'No, I'm not OK. But at least the festival can go ahead now.'

Willow shifted closer, wrapping her arm around his waist

and leaning her head on his shoulder. After a moment he shifted closer too and leant against her. She could hear his breathing, but he didn't say anything else. She didn't know what to do, how to make this right again.

'I should never have listened to that tape,' she said quietly. 'I should never have made that crazy bargain.'

'None of this is your fault, Willow,' he replied. 'You have to stop blaming yourself for everything.' He paused and she wanted to say something, to tell him who his father was, to confess that the can of worms they'd opened on that day they listened to the tape was bigger than either of them could have imagined.

It had all started to fall into place as she walked along the beach looking for Luc and Annelise. She remembered that faraway look in her mother's eyes when she spoke about somebody else still having a piece of Willow's heart. It was weeks ago now, right after the she'd walked out on her wedding but how right Cathy had been. Luc did still have a piece of Willow's heart, perhaps all of her heart in fact.

But it wasn't just Willow Cathy had been talking about. She'd been talking about herself too and Willow wondered if her mother knew that Storm Tyler was Luc's father. She must do surely? And how would it have felt to find out that her best friend had slept with her ex-boyfriend – if Storm had been her ex at the time? And yet Cathy had kept in touch with Storm all these years. Willow had always suspected that there was a third person responsible for the breakdown of her parents' marriage. She'd always thought it was Krystal. But what if it was actually the man she'd been hoping would save the festival?

'I guess I'll be sharing a stage with Storm Tyler,' Luc said after a while.

'You're still going to play?' Willow asked.

'I'm going to try,' he replied, looking towards Annelise again.

Willow wanted to tell him everything. He deserved to know but she'd promised Krystal she wouldn't. Krystal had to tell him as soon as possible.

'I'm a terrible father,' Luc said quietly, interrupting her thoughts.

'No, Luc, don't say that. You're doing your best.'

'It's not good enough though is it? She should know not to run off like that.'

'She's a dreamer, Luc,' Willow said. 'Just like you. She's always going to wander off with her head in the clouds.'

'Then I need to be keeping a better eye on her,' Luc said. 'And not palming her off on Mum just like she's an inconvenience.'

'I've seen you with her, Luc – you're a good father. Nobody's perfect. Kids run off all the time. You do remember when we were kids right?'

'I don't even know what I'm meant to be doing,' he went on as though he hadn't heard her. 'I never had a dad. I've got no idea what that's like. I've got no idea who my father is.'

Really? Willow thought to herself. How could he not have seen it too? How could he have looked at Storm Tyler and not felt as though it was like looking at an older reflection?

She sat on the beach, holding on to Luc like her life depended on it and thought about the strands of DNA spiralling around each other and implanted deep within everyone, making them unique, but also somehow hardwired to repeat the mistakes of the generations that came before. She thought about her mother's long feud with Brian and the way Willow had mirrored that by leaving the Island and insisting her life was somewhere else and involved other people. She wondered if her mother had made herself as miserable with her choices as Willow had with hers.

'Willow,' Luc said softly. 'I don't know what to do.'

She turned to look at him, her eyes dropping to his lips. He was so close she could breathe him in. She knew they couldn't do this, that they had no future together, but she didn't know if she could stop herself.

'Urgh,' shrieked a voice in her ear. 'Are you two about to kiss? That's so gross.'

Luc started to laugh, his eyes flicking away towards his daughter and the moment disappeared. Willow couldn't decide if she was relieved or disappointed.

'Come on, you,' Luc said. 'Put your sandals on – we're going home.'

'Can we get ice cream?' Annelise asked.

'No, Annelise, we can't. I'm still cross with you for running off.' As he turned away from her, Willow saw her stick her tongue out at him behind his back and she bit her lip to stop herself from laughing.

'I have to go,' Luc said. 'But can we talk soon? Tomorrow maybe?'

Willow nodded, and her phone started to ring. She took it out of her pocket and looked at the screen.

'It's Mum,' she said, remembering that Krystal had been going to look for Cathy. 'I'd better take it.' As she turned around she heard Annelise say something.

'No I wasn't going to kiss her,' Luc replied. 'Please put your sandals on.'

Willow smiled to herself as she took the call. She was very aware of Luc and Annelise behind her as she listened to what her mother was asking of her.

'I'll see what I can do,' she said and ended the call, not knowing if she would be able to convince Luc or not.

'Everything OK?' Luc asked.

'Your mum wants to see you,' Willow said.

'Now? I can't. I have to take Annelise home.'

'It's important, Luc,' Willow said, already knowing what it would be about. 'My mum is going to come and pick Annelise up.'

'Good,' said Annelise. 'Auntie Cathy will buy me an ice cream.'

Willow looked at Luc. 'Auntie Cathy?' she asked.

Luc shrugged, smiling. 'She seems to have made herself at home,' he said.

32

Luc

Krystal and Storm were sitting together on the sofa in Cathy's living room when Luc and Willow arrived.

'What's this about, Mum?' Luc asked as he looked from one to the other.

'I'll leave you to it,' Willow said, turning to walk away.

'No,' Luc said softly, grabbing her hand. He had a feeling he needed her to be there. 'Stay... please?'

Willow sat down opposite Krystal.

'What's going on?' Luc asked again.

'Why don't you sit down?' Krystal said.

'Oh for God's sake,' Willow sighed. 'Just tell him.'

'Tell me what?' What did they all know that he didn't?

'This is Neil Flannigan,' Krystal said.

'Otherwise known as Storm Tyler,' Luc replied, digging his hands into the pockets of his jeans. 'Yeah, I know.' He turned to Storm. 'I'm sorry about earlier, I was just worried about my daughter. It's a real honour to meet you, I've—'

'Luc,' Krystal interrupted. 'I need to tell you something.'

'I already know that you know Storm Tyler,' Luc said. 'How you toured with him back in the Eighties and how… well… Don told us everything didn't he, Willow?'

Willow looked over at Luc but she didn't say anything.

'He didn't tell you everything, Luc,' Krystal said. 'He didn't tell you that Neil is your father.'

Luc remembered the strange feeling he'd had when he first saw Storm on the beach with Annelise. The feeling of looking into a mirror. And then he felt his chest tightening again, the pain in his arms and ribcage.

'What did you say?' he asked quietly, running his hand through his hair, making it stand on end. He looked over at Willow. He wanted her to come over to him, to hold him, to tell him that none of this was true. He'd always wanted to be the one who looked after her – but now, for the first time, he wanted to admit that he couldn't cope, that he needed her.

As if reading his mind Willow stood up. She looked as though she was moving in slow motion. She walked over to him and slipped her hand into his.

'Luc,' she said quietly. 'Why don't you sit down?'

He could feel the tightness around his heart, the pain in his ribs and arms. He could feel his breath shortening. He sat down, still holding Willow's hand tightly.

'Take some deep breaths if you can,' Willow said. She placed her other hand on the centre of his chest. It felt warm and soothing and his breath began to steady, the pain in his chest started to fade.

'Are you all right?' Storm asked. 'I know this must be a shock—'

'He's fine,' Krystal interrupted.

'I'm not fine,' Luc said quietly. 'None of this is fine. I thought Willow's mum dated Storm Tyler.' He spoke about the erstwhile rock star as though he wasn't sitting in the room. He couldn't quite bring himself to look over at him. 'That's what Don told us anyway.'

'I've done a lot of things I regret in my life, Luc,' Krystal said. 'But you really were the best thing that ever happened to me. I'm sorry I never told you who your father was, and I hope you can understand that I was just trying to protect you.'

Luc looked up then, his eyes flicking between his mother and Storm Tyler. 'Protect me from what?' he asked.

'From me I think,' Storm replied.

'How long have you known?' Luc asked. 'When did you find out you were my father?'

Storm looked over at Krystal who nodded once as though giving him permission to say something. 'I found out the summer that I recorded the demo that you and Willow found.'

'You've known I was your son since I was eleven years old,' Luc said. 'And you were never curious about me, never wanted to find out how I was?' He felt Willow's hand give his a little squeeze as though trying to stop him from getting too upset, reminding him to breathe. 'What were you doing with my daughter?' he asked, trying to keep his voice calm.

'My granddaughter,' Storm replied.

Luc hadn't even thought of that. How the hell was he going to explain any of this to Annelise, or to her mother? Finding out that your daughter's grandfather is a notorious womaniser and alcoholic is hardly any mother's dream.

'I met her on the beach,' Storm went on when Luc didn't

say anything. 'She was on her own and I was trying to find out where her parents were or to take her back to Seaview. I had no idea who she was until she started talking about you.' He paused. 'She's a clever independent little girl, isn't she?'

Luc still didn't say anything.

'We were coming back to Seaview when Willow spotted us. There was no hidden agenda, just one of life's coincidences. I didn't tell her who I was if that's what you're worried about.'

'What are you doing here?' Luc asked. 'Why now after all this time?'

'Cathy asked me to come,' Storm said. 'She told me that Willow was looking for me, that the festival was in trouble. She told me she needed to tell Willow everything and at first I was angry. I felt that if we started talking about the past again it would be like opening up the door to my house and telling the world where I lived – all those crazy fans on the internet, all the people who've been waiting for me to come back and screw up all over again.' He stopped, a wistful look on his face. He was nothing like Luc had expected him to be, he was gentler somehow and kinder than the media would have had you believe.

'If you're expecting sympathy,' Luc said. 'You've come to the wrong place.' He tried not to think about how much he and Storm Tyler had in common.

'I'm not expecting anything,' Storm replied.

'Then what are you here for?'

'Willow wanted me to save the festival,' Storm said quietly. 'And she mentioned you were playing too. I wanted to see my son.'

Luc dropped his head into his free hand. He felt suddenly exhausted. Nobody spoke and he felt Willow shift in the seat beside him. He should tell her that she could go. He shouldn't have dragged her into this mess.

'Perhaps you can just tell us what happened after you got Mum's email?' Willow said, breaking the silence. 'What made you come to the Island after all this time?'

'Are you two together?' Storm asked.

'No,' Willow said.

'None of your business,' Luc said at the same time. He looked at Willow. She was right to say "no". They weren't together, however much he might want them to be. There were too many reasons for them not to be together. They were doomed, star-crossed. That was just how life turned out sometimes.

'Shall we just stick to the one subject?' Willow said. Luc didn't know how she could stay so neutral, so diplomatic.

'A couple of days after your mum's email I realised I wasn't angry at all, that anger had been a knee-jerk reaction – it's the way I react if anyone tries to interrupt my routine, my solitary life. And I owed it to Cathy to save her festival after all these years.' He paused for a moment, looking at Willow. 'And I wanted to see my son,' he repeated.

Still Luc didn't say anything, didn't even look up.

'When I first found out about you Luc,' Storm continued, 'you were still so young. Krystal had never told you who your father was and she begged me not to tell you either. I agreed, nobody wants someone like me as their father. I didn't come here with the intention of telling you this time. I just wanted to see you.'

He stopped talking and a silence as heavy as lead sat over

the room. Luc had so many questions but he couldn't bring himself to ask any of them. He needed to get out of this room. He stood up, pulling his hand away from Willow's and walked to the door. When he got there, his hand on the doorknob, he turned back into the room.

'Why?' he asked. 'Why did nobody tell me about you?'

'Because I'm an addict,' Storm said quietly. 'And my life has been a chaotic mess since I had my first pint of beer when I was fifteen. I've never known when to stop. Nothing has ever felt as though it's enough – drink, drugs, women. I hurt everybody when I broke up King Silver and I went to live in France. Krystal didn't want me anywhere near you, which is why she never told me about you.'

'But you found out,' Luc said. His voice was cold but the anger that had been streaming through his veins like poison a few minutes ago had gone. He felt resigned and exhausted. He glanced over at Willow, but she was looking at Storm not at him. He wanted to wrap himself around her, lose himself in her. He wanted to allow the feelings he had for her, the ones he'd been denying since the night they slept together, to consume him.

But she had made it very clear where she stood with that one word she'd spoken to Storm.

No, she'd said. *No we're not together.*

'You found out,' Luc repeated. 'Nineteen years ago you found out that I was your son. Why did you never get in touch?'

'I wanted to,' Storm replied. 'But I wasn't worthy of you. I hadn't been living a chaste and sober life in France. All I'd done was disappear from the public eye. I'd fallen off the wagon more times than I could count and Krystal knew it.'

'How did she know?' Luc heard Willow ask. He briefly wondered why Willow was so interested before remembering that Storm had a history with her mother. That until earlier today Willow had been worried that Storm might be her father.

'Because I'd kept in touch with Cathy,' Storm admitted. 'And because as you both must know seeing as you've listened to the tape, I came to the Island nineteen years ago to play at the festival and Krystal saw me fall off the wagon spectacularly.'

It seemed as though Don had skipped quite a lot of the story and in the aftermath of the initial shock neither of them had thought to ask questions.

'Don sent me back to France,' Storm said. 'He told me to never darken his door again.'

What the hell had Storm done? How bad it had been? But still Luc didn't ask any questions. He felt numb.

'You did though, didn't you?' Willow asked. 'You came back again.'

'I came back twelve years ago.'

'The summer we—' Luc began, looking over at Willow.

'The summer we left the Island,' she interrupted.

'I'd been clean for a couple of years at that point,' Storm went on. 'I'm just coming up for fourteen years clean for what it's worth. Anyway, Cathy and I had stayed in touch after my disastrous trip to the Island nineteen years ago. Around 2006 she told me her marriage was over and that she wanted to see me – we'd written regularly but we hadn't seen each other for nearly seven years. She wanted to meet in France but I came to the Island to surprise her. I hadn't realised Don would still be here. I hadn't realised he'd been serious about me never coming back.' He stopped and shook his head slowly.

Willow's face was pale but blank and Luc couldn't work out what she was thinking. All her life she'd wondered why her parents split up, why her dad went to America and now she was finding out. Luc didn't understand how she could sit there so quietly, so calmly. If he was in her position he'd be raging at Storm right now for splitting up his family.

But then he remembered that Storm did split up his family. What had happened that summer had driven Krystal to America, which in turn had made him leave the Island and leave behind the only woman he'd ever loved.

Luc and Willow turned to each other at the same time, their eyes locked. He didn't know what to do, he didn't have the capacity to cope with anything else. He wanted to go home, to sit on the sofa and watch cartoons with Annelise and eat junk food and forget, forget, forget.

'I have to go,' he said. 'My daughter needs me.'

'I watched *American Stars*,' Storm said as Luc turned to go. 'I thought you were excellent.'

Luc didn't reply.

As he was leaving he wondered what he was going to do now, what he was going to say to his mother, to Cathy, to Don. And he wondered how the hell he would ever be able to get on that stage for the festival or how he would ever record another album.

'Luc,' Willow said softly behind him as he opened the garden gate at the end of the path. He turned around. She seemed small and broken, even more so than she had when he first saw her, a few days after she'd walked out on her wedding.

'How does it feel?' she asked. 'To know who your father is?'

'I honestly don't know,' Luc replied. 'I thought I wanted to know when I found out about Annelise but now I'm not sure I needed to. I kind of wish I'd never got curious. It was better before, when I didn't care.'

'I think it's probably normal,' she said. 'When you find out you've got a child, I'd have thought it was natural to think about your own parents.'

'Isn't it weird how he didn't know about me, just like I didn't know about Annelise?'

Willow looked at him. 'Are you all right?' she asked.

He shook his head.

She didn't come up to him and put her arms around him like he wanted her to and he suddenly felt completely alone.

'I have to go,' he said again. 'Thank you for being there today.'

'That's what friends are for,' Willow replied.

But Luc knew now that he couldn't just be friends with her. He needed so much more, or nothing at all.

33

August 2006

'Why?' Don demanded. 'Why the hell are you here again, Neil? Isn't it enough that you've finally won, you've finally got Cathy? Do you have to come here and rub my face in it too?'

Cathy cringed at her husband's words. She wasn't a prize in a raffle that could be won, and Don knew as well as she did that their marriage was over and that Neil, as she'd known him for years now, was no more than a catalyst. But she hadn't known Neil was coming – she was meant to be meeting him in Paris.

'It wasn't like that,' Neil began.

'Don't speak to me,' Don raged. 'I can't do any of this anymore. This man...' He pointed at the man who used to go by the name Storm Tyler. 'This man has hurt us all over the years. Why is he still here in our lives? He nearly destroyed our band along with his own and now he's broken up my marriage.' He turned to Krystal. 'It's no wonder you don't want Luc to know. I'd never tell him if I were you.'

'I have no intention of telling Luc,' Krystal said. 'He's eighteen and right on the cusp of his life. He has got on perfectly well without a father all these years. He doesn't need to know.'

'Good,' Don said.

'And nobody else is going to tell him, are they?' Krystal asked.

'Not me,' Don replied.

'Nor me,' said Neil. 'You're both right. I don't deserve him.'

'This isn't a Storm Tyler pity party,' Don said.

'Luc is my whole world,' Krystal went on. 'I've always tried to do what's best for him and I'm sure this is the right thing.' She paused, looking across at Cathy. 'You understand, don't you?' she asked.

Cathy nodded. She understood about loving your child and worrying about them and the choices they were making. She understood about protecting them as much as a mother could. She knew that Willow was struggling with all the changes that were going on just as much as Luc was. Cathy could smell the alcohol on Willow's breath every evening when she came in, could see the fear in her eyes. Finding out who Luc's father was would hurt Willow too and Cathy didn't want that.

'I understand,' Cathy said. 'But I have a condition. We all need to leave each other alone for a while. After Sunday night, after The Laurels close the festival, that's it. We draw a line under this part of our lives, under The Laurels.'

'What are you saying?' Krystal asked.

'I'm saying that we all get on with our lives. You and Don and Luc go to America and you,' she said turning to Neil. 'You go back to France.'

'And what about you?' Neil asked, a look of sad resignation washing over his face.

'I'm staying here,' Cathy said. 'I'm not saying we'll never see each other again, or that we shouldn't stay in touch because I know we will. The Island is your home, Don, and I know you'll be back.' She turned to her soon-to-be ex-husband and smiled sadly. 'But for now,' she went on. 'I'm staying here. I'll run The Music Shop and make sure the festival continues and I'll look after Willow. Because in a few weeks' time I'm the only person she's going to have.'

34

Willow

Days passed and Willow didn't see Luc again. He didn't come to The Music Shop in the mornings and she didn't see him in The Three Doves in the evenings. She texted him a few times to see if he was all right, but when he did reply it was just two words.

I'm fine.

'He's still on the Island,' Cathy said to Willow one afternoon in the shop when she came in to start work on a custom-made mandolin order. 'He hasn't gone home.'

Home.

Willow didn't want to think about Luc having a home anywhere but on the Island. She had always known that this summer would have to end, that they would all have to go back to their lives, but she hadn't expected it to end like this.

'Is he still playing the festival?' Willow asked.

'As far as I know,' her mother replied. 'But I haven't checked. I don't want to push him right now.'

'Have you heard from him?'

'No, but I've spoken to Krystal a few times. Luc's spending time with her, talking things through. I guess he's just trying to get his head around everything.'

There wasn't anything Willow could do to help. She just needed to keep herself busy and wait for the right time to talk to him again. She should be using this time to work out what she was going to do with her own life, but all she could think about was Luc and the fact that after the festival he'd be going back home.

Home to Nashville, to where his family was.

Where was Willow's home? The more she thought about that the more often she found her thoughts settling on the Island, on Seaview.

'I know you're avoiding me,' Cathy said, interrupting Willow's thoughts. 'Let's not do this, Willow. Let's talk.'

'A bit hypocritical,' Willow replied. 'Considering it was you who refused to talk in the first place.'

It was true that Willow had been avoiding her mother – both her parents in fact. Since everything had come out, Willow hadn't known what to say. She kept thinking about these huge secrets that her parents had kept from her and Luc all these years, secrets that could have changed the course of Luc's life, of both their lives. She was angry that nobody had told Luc who his father was and believed that he had a right to know and to make the decision about meeting Storm for himself.

He hadn't deserved to have Storm Tyler thrust upon him like that.

Willow was angry because she'd never been told the truth about her parents' seemingly sudden break-up and she was furious with her mother for keeping in touch with Storm for all those years when she was married to Don.

For the last few days, instead of going home after closing The Music Shop, Willow had taken to walking down the road to Skye's. They'd eat dinner together, taking it in turns to cook, before going to The Three Doves or watching TV. Skye joked that they were like an old married couple. Bob was away and Willow knew that Skye was missing him. After their initial conversation when Willow had told Skye everything, neither of them mentioned Luc again and neither of them had seen him.

'Your dad and I wondered if you'd spend an evening with us,' Cathy said.

'Both of you?' Willow asked, surprised at their show of solidarity now all the secrets were out in the open.

'What happened was a long time ago,' Cathy said. 'Don and I have moved past it.'

'Unfortunately I haven't had time to move past anything,' Willow replied. 'What with only finding everything out last week.'

'Please, Willow.'

'OK,' Willow sighed. 'I'll spend the evening with you as long as the two of you aren't fighting or anything.'

'Is that why you've been avoiding us?'

'One of the reasons,' Willow replied. Willow hadn't been able to stop herself thinking what a mess her parents and Krystal and Storm Tyler had got themselves into and she hadn't really known what to say to them.

'Your father thought we could go into Ryde tonight,' Cathy went on. 'Have dinner somewhere and talk.'

Nobody had mentioned Storm Tyler for days. Willow was going to have to be the one who did.

'Where's Neil?' she asked.

Cathy looked out of the shop window towards the sea. 'He's staying with Rocco,' she said. Willow had forgotten that Rocco was staying in the apartment building with Luc. 'They don't know each other but Rocco offered his spare room when Luc asked him. All the hotels in Seaview are full.'

'I thought Dad was in Rocco's spare room,' Willow said.

'Your father's staying with Tom.'

'God, poor Dad.' Had Storm really turned up in Seaview with nowhere to stay? Typical musician, assuming someone would put him up. 'Have you seen Neil?' she asked.

'Not properly. He's spending time with Luc and Krystal. The three of them have a lot to talk about. They don't need me interrupting that.'

Willow noticed the wistful look in her mother's eye and thought again about what she'd said all those weeks ago, right at the beginning of the summer when Willow had first arrived back on the Island.

Perhaps someone else still has a piece of your heart.

'I meant…' Willow paused. 'I meant have you seen him over the last twelve years?'

Cathy sat down in the workshop and gestured for Willow to join her.

'Yes,' she said quietly. 'For the last few years Neil and I have met up for a few weeks at the end of every summer, after the festival. I go down to his house in France. He lives in a little village just outside of Nimes in Provence. It's an old ramshackle farmhouse with temperamental hot water but it's so peaceful and the views are beautiful.'

A look of pure happiness flashed across Cathy's face as she talked about Storm and his home in France.

'He makes you happy, doesn't he?' Willow asked.

Cathy nodded and looked away, as though she was embarrassed.

'Why didn't you tell me any of this? Why did you keep it all a secret?'

'There have been so many reasons not to tell you over the years,' Cathy said. 'At first I was embarrassed and ashamed of what I'd done, of my past. And I felt I had to let go of the whole Storm Tyler episode, cut it out of my memory for your father's sake. I didn't want the ghost of my ex to be shadowing our marriage.'

Willow didn't say anything, but she thought of Luc and how she had cut him out of her life so that his shadow didn't follow her and Charlie around. Were we all destined to repeat the mistakes of our parents, of our grandparents, for all eternity?

'I couldn't do it though,' Cathy continued. 'I'd find myself thinking about Neil every now and then. He behaved appallingly towards the end, completely at the mercy of his addictions and he refused to get proper help, but I still loved him no matter how hard I tried not to. After we set up the festival, I used to think of him every summer. I used to think how much he would have enjoyed playing on the beach.'

'But he never did?' Willow asked.

'No, he never did,' Cathy replied. 'He was supposed to play in 1999. It was meant to be a big celebration to commemorate the eclipse but...' She hesitated, as though she didn't want to remember everything.

'What happened, Mum?'

'Oh it was all my fault,' Cathy said. 'I should never have let him go to the pub on his own. We'd just recorded that demo you found. He had this idea for a comeback, an album of rearrangements of Ballad Book songs but he only got as far as that one. He got so drunk after he recorded it that your father threw him out and told him to never set foot on the Island again.'

'And he stayed away until the summer that Dad left?' Willow asked, trying to piece everything together in her head and trying to work out where she was the summer that Storm was on the Island. She'd spent a lot of time at Luc's that summer and it was perfectly possible that her path and Storm's never crossed. It was perfectly possible that her parents made sure they didn't.

'And we all knew he was Luc's father by then,' Cathy said. 'Which was yet another reason not to tell you about him.' Cathy sighed. 'I wanted to keep you away from him when you were a child and he kept falling off the wagon. I didn't think you needed to know. The longer I left it, the harder it was to tell you anything at all.'

'But you went to France every year after Dad left,' Willow said, shocked that her mother had been going away every year, having a secret relationship with someone who used to be ridiculously famous, and she'd never known about it.

'You had your life, Willow,' Cathy said. 'And I had mine. You compartmentalised your life – you don't think I noticed but I did. You shut away the Island and your family and everything that happened and you didn't think about it.'

She paused. 'Well maybe I did something similar. As long as Neil was in France, he didn't have any bearing on my life here, or my relationship with you.'

'Until he turned up,' Willow said, understanding the need to compartmentalise, to separate out the different parts of your life. She understood where she got it from now as well, but she wasn't sure it was a particularly healthy thing to do.

'Until he turned up,' Cathy repeated. 'Again.'

Willow saw her mother in a whole new light. She had a life that Willow had known nothing about, just as she'd had a life in London that she'd never really talked about to Cathy.

'I think perhaps we both need to stop shutting each other out,' Cathy said slowly. 'And be a bit more honest with each other.'

'Charlie and I are over,' Willow said.

'I'd figured that out, Willow, and after what he did I'm glad.'

'And I was thinking I might move back to the Island if that's OK? Back home.' The words spilled out of her mouth before she knew she'd said them but as soon as they were spoken she knew they were true.

The Island had always been home, so naturally she was going to move back.

'Of course it's OK,' Cathy replied. 'And what about Luc?'

'I have no idea,' Willow replied. But she knew that after the festival Luc would go back to Nashville and she would get on with her life in the only way she knew how.

★

She sat with her parents at the restaurant table later that evening making small talk.

'We haven't seen you for days, Willow,' Don said. 'Where have you been hiding?'

'I've been at Skye's,' Willow replied. 'I just needed some space. I'm sorry.'

'You have nothing to be sorry about,' Don said as the waiter brought their main courses. 'It's us who should be sorry. We should have told you everything a long time ago.'

Cathy began by telling Willow about the first time she'd seen Don, when he opened for King Silver all those years ago.

'He had the bluest eyes I'd ever seen,' Cathy said.

'I was hailed as the new Nick Drake you know.'

'My friend said you looked more like Kris Kristofferson.' Cathy laughed.

The story took all evening to tell as her parents broke off on tangents like this. The main course was finished, and dessert had been and gone. Coffee cups sat empty in front of them before the tale was over. Willow knew everything, from Cathy meeting Storm when she was sixteen to her going on tour with him. She knew about his addictions, his behaviour, his inability to stay faithful or sober and she knew, for the first time really, how famous and talented The Laurels had been before she and Luc were born. She could put her own childhood into the context of the story – the summer of the first Seaview Folk Festival and the year that The Laurels started touring again, what she was doing when Storm recorded the tape and where she and Luc were when he found out he was Luc's father.

'It was my fault that it came out when it did,' Don said. 'I

was so angry with Neil for falling off the wagon again. He'd
screwed up so badly time and again and he was supposed
to play the festival, which he couldn't do of course. I'd
bent over backwards to accommodate him, and he let us
all down.' Don paused, wiping his brow with his napkin.
'But he had hurt us all over again and I couldn't stand him
being there. It was when we were arguing about it all that
Krystal told us. She didn't mean to; it just slipped out and
Neil was there of course. He overheard.'

'And yet, despite all that, you and Mum managed to stay
friends,' Willow said.

'Yes. The break-up itself was amicable enough. Despite
how angry I was with Neil, he wasn't the reason we split up.
Our marriage was over and we both knew that. It had been
for years. I'd really only stayed around for you, Willow, and
you were off to Cambridge.'

But I needed you, Willow thought to herself. But that
was something to talk to her father about some other time,
when they were alone.

'And all of this is why you don't speak to your father?'
Willow asked her mother instead.

'He gave me an ultimatum and I chose Storm Tyler.'

'Do you regret it?'

'I've never regretted a moment of it,' her mother said.
'Because at the end of the day I got to have you.' Willow
met her mother's gaze then and she knew how much her
parents loved her, how they'd kept things from her to
protect her. She wished they'd told her why they'd broken
up though. She wished she'd been able to understand that at
least before she'd gone to Cambridge. It might have helped
her make sense of her life instead of running away from it.

'But you never told me anything,' Willow said quietly.

'No,' Cathy replied. 'And perhaps we should have done. Perhaps we should have told both you and Luc. Perhaps that would have made the whole thing easier, but at the time we thought we were doing the right thing.'

Nobody spoke for a moment.

'And now Luc is headlining the festival his father never turned up for,' Willow said.

'And his father's going to bloody well turn up for it this time too,' Don said.

'He is?' Willow asked.

'He is,' Don replied. 'If I have to drag him on to the stage myself.'

Willow smiled. 'I can't believe I pulled it off.' She paused thinking of Luc. 'We pulled it off.'

'Your mum says you're thinking of moving back to the Island,' Don said.

Willow took a deep breath. 'Yes,' she said. 'I'm coming home.'

Willow had always known she would stay for the festival, but after that her life had felt like an unknown in which anything could happen. She'd spent the summer assuming that, as soon as the festival was over, she would just go back to London, go back to work and get on with her life. But she knew now that she couldn't do that.

She knew she had to build herself a new life.

Two months ago, when Willow had walked away from her own wedding and left Charlie at the altar, she hadn't really known why she'd done it. But she did now. It wasn't because things had changed between her and Charlie – although they had of course and now Willow had found out about her ex-fiancé and her ex-best friend she knew why – it wasn't even because she didn't love him. It was because things had changed in her and they had started changing when she'd watched the musician who called himself Lucien Hawke pick up his guitar on the very first audition episode of *American Stars* and she'd realised who he was. She had started to understand that she needed to learn to love herself again.

She hadn't realised what had been happening at the time but watching Luc play had reminded her of everything she had left behind, everything she truly was. She had thought that she had needed to change everything about herself to have the life she thought she wanted, to have Charlie.

But nobody could hide their true self forever.

Despite her parents' marriage falling apart, Willow believed that there was no going back from a wedding. That it was forever. And she'd known, as she had stood with her father in the doorway of the church on her wedding day, that she couldn't keep it up forever. She couldn't keep up this act of being somebody she wasn't.

She'd come back to the Island because she'd had nowhere else to go, but while she had been here, she'd finally remembered who she really was – someone who loved playing the mandolin, someone who never much liked wearing make-up or having to brush her hair. She had spent years blaming everybody else for her inability to quite grasp on to happiness – her parents for breaking up, Luc for leaving her, Charlie's family for never really liking her, Charlie himself for always wanting her to be somebody she wasn't.

But the only person Willow had to blame for her own

unhappiness was herself. She had chosen to leave the Island; she had chosen to stop playing mandolin and stop listening to the music she had loved to listen to with Luc. She had chosen not to reply to Luc's letters, or to try to apologise to Skye and she had chosen to change herself to make Charlie happy.

Ultimately none of it had made Charlie happy, and none of it had made her happy.

The only person in charge of Willow's happiness was Willow. She had made a lot of mistakes over the last twelve years, but she knew now that she could fix them and she could find the person she used to be again.

She loved the Island and she loved being back, with or without Luc Harrison.

A few days before the Seaview Folk Festival began Annelise barrelled into The Music Shop, the bell on the door that Willow had never gotten around to taking down, jangling behind her.

'Hello,' Willow said as Annelise came up to her and gave her an awkward hug. 'What are you doing here?'

'I haven't seen you for ages,' Annelise replied. 'And I wanted to say hello.'

'Well it's lovely to see you, Annelise, but are you here on your own?' Willow asked, worried that she'd wandered off again and that Luc was somewhere frantically looking for her.

'No,' she replied. 'Daddy's on his way too. I just ran on ahead.'

Willow's breath caught in her throat. She hadn't seen him

for nearly two weeks and she hadn't realised how much she'd missed him.

'He misses you,' Annelise went on. 'I heard him telling Gramma Krystal how much he wants to see you.'

'You did?'

But before Annelise had a chance to reply the shop door opened again and Luc walked in. He leant against the doorframe and hooked his thumbs into the pockets of his jeans just as he had at Skye's studio all those weeks ago.

He smiled his lazy crooked smile.

35

Luc

'Hey,' he said quietly as Willow turned to look at him. 'I've missed you.'

'That's what I was telling her,' Annelise said as she sat down on the shop floor, making herself at home. Luc looked away from Willow, feeling himself blush.

'I've missed you too,' Willow said.

'I just needed some time, you know?' he said.

'I know,' Willow replied. 'Me too.'

Her expression was unreadable and he didn't really know what he expected – for her to throw herself into his arms and declare her undying love? He'd missed her for most of the last twelve years after all; there was nothing new about that. Willow had told him she didn't want to lose touch with him this time when he went back to America. But he didn't want to go back to America at all, not without her.

He'd have to though, for a while at least. He had a lot of changes to make.

'Is it true you play the mandolin?' Annelise asked Willow.

'I used to,' Willow replied. 'But I haven't played for a long time.'

'That's not true,' Luc interrupted. 'You've been playing all summer. You must have picked it up again by now?' He winked at her and remembered that first day all those weeks ago, watching her as she sat on the counter with her back to him.

'Will you play for me, Willow?' Annelise asked.

Willow hesitated for a moment. 'OK,' she said warily. Luc knew she didn't really want to. She had always been private about her music and had never wanted to play on stage no matter how much Luc had pestered her. 'Would you like to play with me?' Willow asked.

Annelise's eyes lit up. 'Oh yes please,' she said.

'I'll go and get you a guitar from the back,' Willow said, turning away.

'Hey, Willow,' Luc called after her. 'Bring me a guitar too. We'll all play.' If they all played together she wouldn't feel the pressure of him watching her. She turned around and smiled at him and he saw relief there.

'What would you like to play?' Willow asked as she came back with two guitars.

'I've been learning a new song,' Annelise replied. 'It's one Daddy's been playing a lot. It's about Robin Hood.'

'"Gamble Gold"?' Willow asked, looking at Luc. He shrugged and smiled.

'Why not?' he said.

'Do you know it, Willow?' Annelise asked.

'Yeah.' Willow smiled. 'I know it.'

Playing "Gamble Gold" with Willow and Annelise in the shop he had spent so much time in when he was growing up, made Luc feel as though everything had come full circle. As they played faster and faster until Willow got in a muddle and collapsed into giggles, he knew that the Island was his home whether he lived there or not.

The shop door opened, the bell jangling, and Luc looked around.

'Tom,' he said as Willow and Annelise carried on giggling behind him.

'Sorry to interrupt,' Tom Newell said.

'Come in, Tom.' Willow stood up, wiping her eyes. 'We were just messing around.'

'I've got Monty with me so I won't come in,' Tom said. 'But I saw you as I was passing, Luc, and just wanted to confirm I've cleared the next two days at the studio for you.'

Luc felt Willow trying to catch his eye. 'Thanks, Tom,' he said.

'Daddy, can I go play with Monty?' Annelise asked.

Luc looked over at Tom. 'Is that all right?' he asked. 'I'll be out in a minute.'

'Sure,' Tom said as Annelise followed him out of the shop.

'You're recording?' Willow asked as the door shut behind them. 'That's fantastic.'

'I'm practising for the festival really,' Luc said. 'But I've been playing around with this idea so I might see what it sounds like while I'm there.'

'What idea?'

'I still haven't been able to write anything,' Luc said, leaning on the shop counter. 'But I've been teaching Annelise some old Ballad Book songs and I thought I might do an album of them – rearrange the ballads for a modern audience.'

Willow grinned at him. 'That sounds like a brilliant idea!'

'Starting with "Gamble Gold" of course,' he said.

'Of course!' Willow replied. 'Are you recording it here on the Island?'

Luc paused. 'I can't,' he said. 'After the festival Mum is taking Annelise back to Nashville – she needs to go back to her mum before school starts.'

'And what about you?'

'I'm flying out to LA with Rocco to record this album. I'm not sure how long it will take.'

Willow's eyes flicked away from him but not before he saw the flash of disappointment on her face.

'Willow,' he said, reaching out for her. But she stepped away before he could touch her.

'It's fine,' she replied, still not looking at him. 'Your life is in America. I always knew that.'

'What about you?' he asked. 'What are you going to do?'

'Talk to Charlie,' she said. 'Put our flat on the market, sort out all our things and learn to move on with my life I guess.'

His heart broke for her, for everything she'd been through this summer, for everything he suspected she'd been through these past twelve years. He wanted to tell her how beautiful she was, how unique, and how happy he was that she'd finally started to find herself again.

'What will you do after that?' he asked instead.

She didn't reply. She folded her arms across her chest as though stopping him coming any closer.

He felt as though he was losing her all over again.

'I'll come back, Willow,' he said. 'I promise.'

He could feel the weight of the words unsaid between

them. He wanted to talk to her about Storm Tyler, or Neil Flannigan as he preferred now, about his mum, about what happened all those years ago. He wanted to compare stories – compare what his mother and Neil had told him to what her parents had told her. He wondered if they'd ever get the chance to do that before he had to leave again, before she went back to London.

He took a step closer to her, but there was a knock on the window behind him. Annelise beckoned him to come out.

'You'd better go,' Willow said, smiling a smile that didn't quite reach her eyes.

'You're coming to the festival, aren't you?'

'I'll be there,' she said. 'Cheering you on. Just try and keep me away.'

36

Willow

The closer the festival got, the more disconnected from it Willow felt. She watched the preparations from the safety of The Music Shop. She saw the signs going up for the car park on the clifftop – the clifftop where she'd kissed Luc – she watched as bunting appeared above the doorways of the local pubs and she passed endless posters that listed which bands were playing where. She tried not to notice Luc's name on the posters for the final day; she tried not to think that when she saw him play it might be the last time she ever saw him. And when she heard the soundchecks drifting towards her on the breeze she tried not to wonder if one of them was Luc.

The weekend of the festival was glorious, warm and sunny with cloudless blue skies. Willow spent most of it basking in the sun outside The Music Shop so somebody was there for the few stragglers who wanted to buy guitar strings, or have their mandolins restrung, but she wasn't busy. She wandered around the food stalls at the festival in her lunch break and she went to The Three Doves in the evening with Skye to watch the open mic competition.

Skye's partner, Bob, was on the Island for the weekend. The two of them were making plans for when Bob finally moved here in the autumn. Willow tried to be happy for them, tried not to think about Luc leaving in a few days, about Charlie and Kate in London.

Skye had been over the moon when Willow told her she'd decided to stay on the Island. Once she'd been back to London and spoken to Charlie, once she'd sorted out the flat to be put on the market and reclaimed her things, she'd move back for good. She was hoping that once the money from the flat came through she'd be able to buy a small house of her own in Seaview. She'd remembered the words her mother spoke to her right at the beginning of the summer about how every musician needs a good accountant and had decided to set herself up as just that. Tom Newell had already booked her services. He had presented her with a plastic bag full of receipts to sort through the day before the festival began. It was a far cry from the tall glass building of the investment bank, but she knew it was the right move.

'It'll be just like old times,' Skye said, hugging her.

'Not old times,' Willow replied. 'New beginnings.'

On the Saturday afternoon she closed her mother's shop for the final time. Cathy would take over the running of it again from Monday and Willow felt a sense of sadness at that. She'd enjoyed these strange halcyon days of the summer. They'd been like an unplanned break from life – a chance to recalibrate, to find a new way. Sad as she was to be shutting the shop for the last time, she was also excited for her new venture, her new business.

'You are coming tomorrow aren't you?' Skye asked her in the pub that evening. 'You'll be there for Luc?'

'Of course I will.'

On the last day of the festival she went to the beach with Skye and Bob and together they shared a picnic and a bottle of cold white wine. They listened to the bands that played during the afternoon and chatted to whoever happened to be passing. The atmosphere was a heady mix of laid-back and electrifying. There were fairground rides for the children, a candyfloss stall and people on stilts tiptoeing through the crowds, standing ten feet tall. A man on a unicycle passed by.

'It hasn't changed has it?' Skye said with a smile.

'I hope it never does,' Willow replied and they both laughed at the look of incredulity on Bob's face.

'It's worse than Covent Garden in tourist season,' he said.

'Get used to it.' Skye laughed, nudging him. 'This is Island life!'

Island life, Willow thought. *It's good to be back.*

They didn't see Luc or Annelise or Krystal, and Willow wondered where they were and what they were doing. She hoped Luc was all right, that he wasn't too nervous, that he had managed to keep his panic attacks at bay.

Roger Beck wandered by, looking remarkably at ease for a man who supposedly hated the festival. Willow hadn't seen or heard from him for weeks and she called him over and poured him a glass of wine. If she was going to be staying on the Island she wanted to start again with a fresh slate, with no hard feelings.

'Hello, Willow,' Roger said as he sat down. 'Skye.'

Skye introduced Bob and the two men shook hands.

'You pulled it off then,' Roger said. 'You sold all the tickets.'

'As if there was any doubt,' Willow replied, knowing full well there had been a lot of doubt.

'And what about Storm Tyler?' Roger asked. 'Rumour has it that you found him too.'

'You'll have to wait and see.'

He nodded slowly. 'Well for what it's worth I'm impressed.'

Willow saw the expression on Skye's face and tried not to laugh. She opened her mouth to ask Roger why he'd tried block the festival but Roger changed the subject before she had the chance.

'I hear you're moving back to the Island,' Roger said. 'Setting up as a bookkeeper.'

'Word travels fast.' Willow smiled. The Island grapevine was one of the fastest on earth. It would take her a while to get used to that again.

Roger didn't say anything for a moment and she braced herself for a scornful remark.

'I might have some work to put your way,' he said eventually.

Willow thanked him, astonished. 'As long as it's legit,' she joked.

Just for the briefest of moments she thought she saw Roger smile. The Seaview Folk Festival had always weaved magic in the air.

He drank his wine as he watched the band on stage.

'If you can't beat them join them,' he said, tapping his foot.

After he left Skye was incredulous.

'Why didn't you ask him what he was playing at trying to stop the festival in the first place?' she asked.

Willow shrugged. 'I didn't want to break the spell. Festival days were always the best days. I can't believe I missed so many of them.'

Skye didn't reply, she just pulled Willow into a hug. Perhaps Willow would never know why Roger had wanted to stop the festival. Perhaps Luc and Skye had been right when they said they thought it was a sort of revenge for the way she'd treated him at school when he'd clearly had a huge crush on her. Perhaps it didn't matter. Nobody could change the past after all.

As the sun sat low in the sky and the temperature dropped enough for Willow to need to put a jumper on, Luc took to the stage and the crowd erupted into cheers. He'd been advertised all over the Island as "*American Stars* finalist Lucien Hawke" but as Willow looked at him, his guitar slung around his neck, his hair standing up on end from where she knew he'd been running his hands through it, all she could see was Luc Harrison – the boy she'd been in love with since she was eleven years old.

He was magnificent, blowing all the other acts out of the water. He didn't show any signs of panic or anxiety; he just played song after song from his first album – including the one he played at the live final of *American Stars*, the one Willow had listened to in secret so many times that she knew all the words, the one she now realised he'd written for Annelise. She hoped he knew that she was here, just as she'd promised. She hoped he knew that she was cheering him on, just like she used to at The Three Doves when they were teenagers.

The crowd demanded two encores and, as he came on to the stage for the final time, he started to speak to the crowd.

'There's been a few rumours around the Island over the years about the return of Storm Tyler,' Luc said. There was a roar of cheering at the mention of the music legend's name and Willow felt a strange prickle of excitement running up her spine.

'Well this year it's not a rumour,' Luc continued as he turned towards the wings of the stage.

Storm Tyler, or Neil Flannigan, walked slowly on to the stage with a mandolin tucked under his arm. Willow stared as the crowd around her went out of their minds – cheering and shouting, screaming and stamping their feet.

Nothing happened.

Luc just stood in front of the microphone with Storm at his side, waiting. Eventually the crowd started to quieten a little, intrigued by what would happen next.

'You probably all know this one,' Luc said, fiddling with the tuning pegs of his guitar. 'But this song is for you, Willow.' Luc paused again as the crowd rumbled and cheered. Willow felt Skye's hand on the small of her back.

'Willow, I know you're out there,' Luc went on. 'And in case you hadn't worked it out yet, I love you.'

The crowd erupted as Luc and Storm launched into the opening bars of "Gamble Gold".

What other song could it be? Willow thought.

'Did he just say he loved me?' Willow asked, turning to Skye. She felt as though the whole beach was spinning, as though everyone was staring at her.

Had Luc Harrison just told her that he loved her in front of everyone?

'He did.' Skye grinned. 'I knew he would.'

'You knew?' Willow asked.

Skye shrugged. 'He might have mentioned it,' Skye said grabbing Willow's hand as she began to pull her through the crowd. 'I bumped into him the other day. Gave him a piece of my mind.'

'I need to see him,' Willow said. 'I can't let him go back to America until I've spoken to him. I don't want it to be like last time.'

'We need to get you backstage before they finish this set,' Skye replied.

Bob trailed in their wake carrying handbags and blankets and other picnic detritus.

Don met them backstage. 'Luc will be pleased to see you.' Don grinned. 'Thanks for bringing her,' he said to Skye. Bob was standing next to Skye, his arms full, looking thoroughly confused and, from behind her father, Tom Newell and Rocco Beezon grinned at her.

'Were you all in on this?' Willow asked, her heart pounding.

'I didn't know anything about it,' Bob replied with a shrug.

Don led Willow away to the wings of the stage and she stood with Annelise and Krystal as she watched Luc and Storm finish the song. She could remember standing with Luc watching The Laurels from this very spot year after year as teenagers. She felt Annelise take her hand.

'My friend Neil is quite a good mandolin player, isn't he?' Annelise said.

'He really is,' Willow replied.

'But not as good as you.'

Willow couldn't take her eyes off Luc and Storm Tyler. His father. She wanted this moment to last forever while at the same time was impatient for the song to end so she could see Luc, talk to him, touch him.

And then, suddenly, Luc was there in front of her, his hands sliding down her arms.

'You came,' he said.

'I love you too,' she replied.

She barely got the words out before his lips found hers.

37

Luc

It had been Skye who had given him the idea when he'd bumped into her on the High Street after he had left The Music Shop.

'She's staying on the Island,' Skye had said as Annelise went off to Cartwright's sweet shop to load up on sugar. 'She's not going back to London.'

'But she said…' Luc had begun before pausing. Willow hadn't actually said anything; he hadn't given her the chance because he'd been too scared to hear the answer.

'Don't leave the Island without telling her how you feel,' Skye had said. 'Even if you have to do something drastic.'

The weeks leading up to the festival had been stressful as he'd tried to unravel the stories of the past while trying to keep it all from Annelise. She still didn't know that her "good friend Neil" was actually her grandfather and Luc knew he'd have to tell her at some point, but not until after the festival. He'd deal with all of that later.

The thought of getting on that stage still filled him with fear, and he still didn't know if he could go through with it. But after he'd spoken to Skye, after he'd worked out what he was going to do, he knew he had to do it. Knowing Willow was out there in the audience, knowing what he had to say to her would get him through.

It had been Krystal's idea for Storm to play "Gamble Gold" with Luc to close the festival. She'd felt it would be a way of bringing everything to a natural conclusion and to satisfy the rumours about Storm that had been haunting the festival for years, as well as placating all the festival goers who had only bought tickets on the promise that Storm Tyler would be there. Cathy had agreed and Luc had noticed a look pass between her and Neil that he recognised, one of a love that had been lost and may finally get the second chance it deserved.

But he hadn't had much time to think about it. All he had been able to focus on was the gig and the woman in the audience watching him.

He'd played as though he was playing only for her and now she was in his arms, kissing him and he didn't care that half of Seaview were witnessing it.

'Oh that is so gross,' squealed a little voice and Luc felt Willow's laughter against his mouth.

He pulled away from Willow and ruffled his daughter's hair, noticing that she was still holding tight on to Willow's hand. It gave him so much hope for the future, their future, that Willow and Annelise got on so well.

Even if that future was a long way off. The obstacle of Annelise's mother still hovered in the back of his mind like a small cloud. But he knew he couldn't leave the Island without Willow knowing how he felt.

'We should find somewhere more private,' Willow whispered.

'Get your dad to take you to the dressing room,' Luc replied quietly. 'I'll be there in a minute.' He prised Annelise's hand out of Willow's and took her to his mother who was talking with Cathy and Storm.

'Can you look after her for a few minutes?' he asked.

Krystal smiled at him. 'I'll take her home,' she said. 'We'll see you when we see you.'

The "dressing room" at the Seaview Folk Festival was just a backstage portacabin, but Willow was waiting there for him when he got there. He locked the door behind him and walked up to her.

'Where were we?' he asked, kissing her forehead, her nose, her lips.

She pressed herself against him.

'Skye says you're not going back to London,' he said. 'She says you're going to stay here and set up a business and buy a house.'

Willow laughed. 'Skye never could keep a secret. But I do have to go back to London to talk to Charlie and to put the flat on the market.' She looked sad for moment.

'Are you OK?' he asked.

'Yes, it's what I want to do but it's just hard to think about. I'm going to be packing up twelve years of my life and starting over.'

'I'm going to be making some big changes too,' Luc said quietly.

'What do you mean?'

'I meant what I said last week in the shop,' he said. 'I want to come back. I don't want to move away from you again… but—'

'Your record contract,' Willow interrupted.

He nodded, resting his forehead against hers. 'I have to record this album in LA, and…' He stopped, hesitating over what to say next.

'Annelise,' Willow said. 'I know she always has to come first.'

'I wish things could be different Willow, but Tennessee is Annelise's home. It's where she goes to school, where her friends and family are and I have to be there for her.' He paused. 'At least some of the time, because I also want her to spend time here on the Island too, to get to know the places where I grew up.' His hand cupped Willow's cheek. 'Where we grew up. And I want to be here with you,' he said. 'I will always come back. I want to make music Willow, but not like this. Not with this pressure. I'll go back and record this album, but then I need to make some big changes.'

He stopped talking but she didn't say anything. She stepped away from him, leaning against the table in the corner that was covered in empty beer bottles and half-eaten plates of sandwiches. He felt his stomach clench at the thought that she might not want this as much as he did, that he'd taken a risk that might not pay off.

'Are we mad?' he asked.

She tilted her head to one side, looking at him.

'No,' she replied at last. 'We were mad to ever walk away from each other in the first place. This is our second chance and I'm willing to do whatever it takes to make it work. Besides—' she smiled '—I'm my own boss now; I can do what I like. I can always come to America to see you, if you want me to.'

He hadn't wanted to ask, to presume or put pressure on her but when she said those words he grinned, relief washing through him.

'I'd love that,' he said simply. 'I love you.'

She walked back to him, back into his arms.

'We'll figure it out, Luc,' she said. 'As long as we have each other.'

He looked at her, the woman he had loved for his whole life, and he knew she understood. He knew that she'd wait for him and Annelise, that she'd be there for them both and he knew he and his daughter were safe.

'I can't believe you told me you loved me in front of everyone like that.'

When she smiled it lit up the whole room. He loved that smile.

'We've spent too many years running away,' he said. 'I don't want to run from this anymore.'

He felt her hands on his hips. 'Me neither,' she said. 'I stayed away because of my parents, but what they've done with their lives doesn't matter anymore. The Island is my home.' She looked up at him. 'You're my home,' she said quietly and he knew that what she said was true: Willow was his home and wherever he was, however far apart they were, he carried her with him.

He bent to kiss her but she stopped him, ducking her head. 'How long will you be away?' she asked.

'I'll be back before Christmas,' he replied and she stood on tiptoe, her lips brushing his. He pulled her towards him, deepening the kiss, losing himself in her.

How could he resist?

Epilogue

June 2019

Willow smoothed down the front of her cream silk dress and scrunched her bare feet into the sand.

'Are you ready?' she whispered to Annelise.

Annelise looked up at Willow and nodded.

'Off you go then,' Willow said.

Luc's daughter had taken her job as flower girl extremely seriously and had been practising for days. Willow watched her now walking up the makeshift aisle in the gazebo on the beach as she scattered red and cream rose petals on the sand, a look of intense concentration on her face. Willow felt a giggle bubble up in her throat as she watched and had to swallow it down.

It was her turn.

She followed Annelise, feeling the sand underneath her toes as she walked. Luc turned around to look at her, and when he grinned her heart flipped over.

But she had a job to do and so she carried on walking

past Luc towards the celebrant who stood at the front of the gazebo smiling beatifically.

When Willow got to the front she stood next to Annelise, who slipped her little hand into hers and gave it an excited squeeze.

'You did really well,' Willow whispered and Annelise nodded solemnly.

And then it was Skye's turn. She walked into the gazebo on the arm of her father to the opening notes of an acoustic version of Bowie's "The Man Who Sold the World", Skye's favourite song. She looked magnificent, her cream silk dress clinging to every curve, her hair falling down her back in waves. They'd bought their dresses together at the shop in Ryde where they'd bought Willow's red dress the summer before.

'Should we both be wearing cream?' Willow had asked.

'Of course we should,' Skye had replied as they'd stood in front of the mirror while Delia pinned the dresses to fit them both. 'That way we'll match in the photos!'

Willow snuck a glance at Bob now as he stared at his future wife walking towards him and she was sure she saw tears in his eyes.

As Skye approached the celebrant, her father kissing her on the cheek as he took his seat, she handed Willow her bouquet of cream roses and stepped towards Bob. And as the celebrant began the wedding ceremony Willow looked around at all the people here today to celebrate Skye and Bob – Tom Newell and old Mrs Cartwright from the sweet shop, her father and Krystal, her mum and the man who she'd finally got used to calling Neil, Rocco Beezon standing at the back in dark glasses trying and failing to look inconspicuous next to, of all people, Roger Beck. Rocco hadn't been officially invited but when he'd turned up with Don to celebrate the wedding of 'the best tattoo artist I've ever known' nobody was going to turn him away.

And Luc.

Luc, who'd only been back on the Island for a week, but it already felt like he'd never been gone. Luc, looking so beautiful in his white shirt and linen suit. Luc, who couldn't stop looking at her any more than she could stop looking at him, even though they were both meant to be looking at Skye and Bob.

Everybody she loved, right here on this beach, on this Island.

Willow thought her heart might burst.

Later as Willow stood on the beach waiting to be called by the photographer, she felt an arm around her waist, a kiss on the side of her neck.

'Hello, you,' she said.

'You look so beautiful,' Luc said. 'I can't stop looking at you.'

'I don't think I'm meant to be the centre of attention today,' she laughed.

They stood together quietly watching the photographer try to persuade Bob's dad to take off his tie and shoes like everyone else. Bob's parents weren't quite accustomed to Island life yet and everybody cheered when his dad finally capitulated. Willow leant into Luc's warmth, his strength as his arm tightened around her. It was so good to have him back.

And this time he was back for good.

He'd come back before Christmas just as he'd promised he would, his album recorded, but he'd had to go back to Nashville after a couple of weeks to spend Christmas with Annelise. Willow felt like she had spent most of the spring flying back and forth across the Atlantic as Luc tried to balance promoting his new record with seeing his daughter. Then, the week after the record was finally released he surprised her by turning up on the doorstep of the house she'd just bought near the cliff where he'd first kissed her the summer before.

'I'm free,' he'd said. 'I'm out of contract and I can do what I want.'

'And what do you want, Luc?' she'd asked.

'To come home,' he'd replied.

In those few days of April when he was back, and Seaview was enjoying an early heatwave, Luc explained that he'd come to an arrangement with Annelise's mum. He'd had to tell her everything that had happened over the previous summer of course, had to tell her that Storm Tyler was Annelise's grandfather. She'd taken it better than he'd expected and agreed to be more flexible so that Annelise could get to know her families on both sides of the Atlantic. He'd still have to spend time in Nashville but he wanted to be based on the Island, with Willow. And Annelise would be spending the summer with them.

'If that's OK with you?' Luc had asked.

'Of course it is,' she'd replied, wrapping her arms around him. 'Nothing would make me happier.' And she showed him the small back bedroom of the house that could be Annelise's.

'What will you do once you're back?' Willow had asked.

Luc had thought of that too and he and Cathy had already been plotting.

Willow's mum had been wanting to move to France with Neil but had no idea what to do about The Music Shop or the studio.

'I'll have to sell them,' she'd said. 'But whoever buys them will be taking on Tom Newell as well. I haven't got the heart to get rid of him.'

'I'll buy them,' Luc had said. 'I can cope with Tom, but I do have a condition.'

'What condition?' Cathy had asked.

'You keep making your mandolins. We'll work out the logistics later, but The Music Shop is nothing without your bespoke instruments.'

Cathy had smiled, nodding. 'I have a condition of my own though,' she'd said. 'I want you and Willow to keep the festival going, and I want you to keep playing at it.'

Luc had held out his hand. 'Deal,' he'd said.

And just like that everything had fallen into place.

'Serendipity,' Skye had said when she found out.

Willow stood now on the beach amongst all the people she loved and thought back to the last wedding she'd been at just a year earlier. So much had changed.

'We should do this,' Luc said, interrupting her thoughts.

'Do what?'

'Get married.'

Willow turned around to look at him. 'Lucien Harrison, are you asking me to marry you?'

Luc shrugged and grinned. 'Yeah,' he said.

'OK then,' Willow replied, laughing.

'OK,' Luc said, kissing the top of her head.

'What are you two laughing at?' Annelise asked, appearing from nowhere.

'Oh nothing much,' Luc replied. 'But how would you like to be a flower girl again sometime soon?'

Annelise frowned as she thought about it. 'No I don't think so,' she replied. 'It was quite hard work. Anyway I have to go now, I promised Grandpa Neil I'd play guitar with him.'

'Grandpa Neil?' Willow asked as Annelise ran off again. 'She's definitely taken all of this in her stride. Do you think she'll be OK about us?'

'About me asking you to marry me?' Luc said.

'Yeah, I don't want her to feel uncomfortable about anything.'

'Oh she'll be fine,' Luc said. 'It was her idea anyway. She told me to ask you.'

'Oh well if Annelise says we should get married then we definitely should.'

Luc laughed, kissing Willow again. 'I love you,' he said.

Luc and Willow's Playlist

1. Castle Kelly's – Damien O'Kane
2. Ticket to Ride – The Beatles
3. Somewhere in My Heart – Aztec Camera
4. Gamble Gold – Steeleye Span
5. The Original – Incubus
6. Pompeii – Bastille
7. Flowers in Your Hair – The Lumineers
8. Iris – Goo Goo Dolls
9. Howl – Florence and the Machine
10. Nearly Forgot my Broken Heart – Chris Cornell
11. Last Goodbye – Jeff Buckley
12. Metal & Dust – London Grammar
13. America – Simon & Garfunkel
14. With You – Dan Gautreau/Wolfgang Black
15. Yours – Russell Dickerson
16. Time Has Told Me – Nick Drake
17. The Man Who Sold the World – Nirvana (from MTV Unplugged)

Acknowledgements

I grew up in a house full of books and records so I suppose it was inevitable that one day I would write a book about music! One of my earliest memories is listening to Steeleye Span's "All Around My Hat" with my dad and hearing "Gamble Gold" for the first time. I loved that song and made Dad play it over and over again until I learned how to work the record player myself. I suspect my parents ended up hating that song!

I'm indebted to several people for the expert knowledge of niche subjects that helped me write this book. Firstly, I owe the entire contents of Chapter Three to Bex Ackland and her dad Peter Beckett. Peter was part of the crew that set up The Reading Festival in the early days and I had one of the most interesting telephone conversations of my life with him back in the autumn of 2018. Being Peter's daughter Bex got to be backstage at Reading when she was sixteen (to see Nirvana no less) and I've been hearing about it since we were at university! It's good to put those stories to use at last. Thank you both so much!

Thank you to Jacki Badger and her dad Chris Evans for answering a lot of weird questions about mandolins, to Islander Rebecca Evans for answering another bunch of weird questions about living on the Isle of Wight, to my brother for knowing an awful lot about Digital Audio Tapes and my husband for knowing how guitars and ukuleles are actually made (including all the correct terms, rather than 'you know that hole in the middle').

Thank you to my beta readers Katey Lovell and Lauren North for reading a very early draft of this book and encouraging me to keep going despite a bunch of setbacks way beyond my control. Thank you to my agent, Lina Langlee, my editor Hannah Smith and the whole team at Aria Fiction for seeing the potential in my little book about an obscure song I used to love as a child. Particular thanks to Lisa Brewster and the design team at Aria for the best cover I've ever had. I've waited years to having bunting on a cover! And thank you to Helena Newton for another brilliant copy edit – I'm sorry that I use the word 'suddenly' so much.

Thank you to my usual team of cheerleaders – Max, Sarah, Natalie, Lisa, Rachel and Rachael. One day we will be in post-Covid times and meet again!

Thank you to everyone on Twitter and Instagram who cheers me on and thank you to the book bloggers and reviewers.

And big, huge thanks to you the reader – whether this is your first Rachel Burton book or your fifth I am indebted to you for buying it so that I get to make up weird stories for a living!